The sound of t merlon, but she could not reach pressed against her, shielding her from the cold. Though the touch of his lips was gentle, he kissed her like a man savoring a feast. Tasting first her lips, then the line along her jaw, and the skin at the curve of her neck. She shivered as his breath tickled the sensitive place behind her ear.

"You are cold, my sweet." He took her hand and started toward the stairs. "Come, let us—"

"No!" Sela yanked her hand from his and backed away. "I cannot, Jamie." She had not called him Jamie since that day on the rooftop. Since the day she had dammed away her love for him.

"Why, Sela? We used to share something special. Do you no longer like me?"

No. She did not *like* him—she *loved* him. Tears breached the rims of her eyes and rolled down her cheeks. No longer able to stand the pain, she sobbed, pushed past him, and ran down the stairs.

Jamie looked down the dark staircase until he could no longer hear her footsteps.

She was crying. The tears on her cheeks sparkled in the moonlight, and her sobs still rang in his ears.

He cursed and pounded his fist against the stone wall. She must despise him now. Yet, he had felt the passion in their kiss.

What stood between them? His thoughts turned back to the past that no one would speak of. He had to find out what had happened to her. He would not need to worry about convincing his mother or the King if he could not break through her wall and claim her as his own.

Praise for *WIDOW'S PEAK*

"*WIDOW'S PEAK* is good reading from the very first to the very last word."
~Long and Short Reviews (4 Books)

"I loved this book. The love story is heart-wrenching and poignant, from its hopeless beginning to the beautiful conclusion."
~The Romance Studio (5 Stars)

"*WIDOW'S PEAK* is an enchanting way to spend the evening and will sweep you into a medieval world full of intrigue, danger, chivalry, love and great sex."
~Delilah Marvelle, International Bestselling Author

"Entertains with an accurate rendering of the time period and a beautiful love story."
~RT Book Reviews

"Richly rewarding."
~Coffee Time Romance and More (4 Cups)

A Knight's Kiss

Scorpion Moon, Book Two

by

Hanna Rhys-Barnes

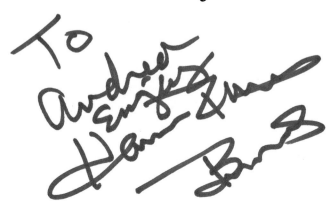

This is a work of fiction. Names, characters, places, and incidents either are the product of the author's imagination or are used fictitiously, and any resemblance to actual persons living or dead, business establishments, events, or locales, is entirely coincidental.

A Knight's Kiss: Scorpion Moon, Book Two

Cover Art by *Nicola Martinez*

The Wild Rose Press
PO Box 708
Adams Basin, NY 14410-0706
Visit us at www.thewildrosepress.com

Publishing History
First English Tea Rose Edition, 2011
Print ISBN 1-60154-908-3

Published in the United States of America

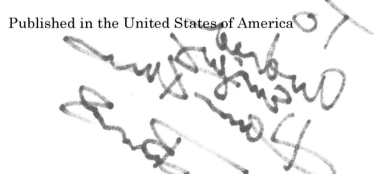

Dedication

To my ever-patient editor, Amanda Barnett,
who kept me going when I needed it most.

Chapter One

Ceredigionshire, Wales
In the Reign of Henry II

Castle Cilgerran loomed beneath the dull gray of an overcast morning sky. Sir James Barnard reined his horse to a stop. The thick growth of tall trees cut off his view of everything except the square tower jutting from the top of the hill. At last, he neared his mother's new home. A realization took hold like a knife drawn across his chest.

At the moment, *he* had no home.

Anger overpowered his exhaustion. The muscles tightened at the back of his neck as memories of the bitter battle with his brother, John, flooded his thoughts. Perhaps it had been a bit much to call John a covetous, spurious ass.

Abelard snorted and pawed the ground of the narrow dirt road, and Jamie released the tense grip of his thighs on the horse's ribs. "Sorry boy." He patted the silver dappled neck.

With Mother remarried, John now held the title of Lord of the estate. He could do what the hell he pleased. Nothing Jamie could do would stop the self-interested fool from destroying the domain their parents had spent a lifetime building. But who was more the fool—John for wasting the fortune or himself for giving his brother a reason to ban him from the only home he had ever known—Edensmouth.

Ah well. In the end it would not matter. King Henry offered marriage to a well-endowed Norman

1

heiress...if he successfully completed his mission. The young beauty brought with her a prized piece of land in France and ties to a powerful noble family.

Like armor grown too small, a heavy weight pressed against him. The successful completion of his mission might cost him the one thing he still valued on this island. The last tie to his own family. A deep sigh did nothing to ease the tightness. No reason to put off the inevitable. "Go on, then."

The horse broke into a comfortable canter.

Rain plinked on Jamie's breastplate, and he looked up at the clouds gathered overhead. What had driven Mother to move to this god-forgotten place? What had driven her to marry—a troubadour?

His mood matched the darkening sky, but a laugh escaped his lips. "'Tis not as if anyone could have stopped her, Abelard. Amye Barnard does what she pleases." Anxiety twisted his heart into a knot and pulled the ends tight. Had he known of her plan to re-marry, taken the time to come home, there might have been a way to save her. Save her from this awful mistake. Save her from marrying a possible traitor.

A few yards ahead, a figure burst through the tall pines lining the road. His melancholy thoughts were washed away like the impending rain washed away spatters of mud.

A gentle press against Abelard's flanks signaled the horse to stop, and Jamie stood in his stirrups.

The approaching runner was small. A short tunic covered oddly shaped breeches, but the thick braid, falling nearly to the waist was that of a woman. She watched behind her, all the while running as if chased by the Devil's dogs

His eyes narrowed. He scanned the thick woods, but could see no threat.

More concerned with her pursuers than where she was going, the woman ran into Abelard's flank with a loud *thunk* and fell to the ground.

The huge destrier had been taught to consider such a move an assault. He reared up to trample the perceived attacker.

Jamie nearly tumbled off, but he threw his weight forward and loosed a sharp whistle.

The well-trained animal wheeled away, missing the stunned woman by no more than a blade's width.

Heart pounding, he slid from the horse's back. "Are you injured?" he asked, using one of the few phrases of Welsh he knew.

She sat up. Strands of reddish-brown hair escaped from her braid and swirled around her face as she shook her head. The strange pants were merely the back of her kirtle pulled forward and tucked into her belt. Dark smears of dirt on her face matched those on the tan tunic, but a beautiful woman hid beneath the wild forest creature.

"Let me help you." He smiled and extended his hand, but as he stepped forward, she sprang to her feet and backed away.

Her furrowed forehead reminded him of a terrified rabbit, trapped in the open, with no place to hide, but it made her face seem somehow...familiar. Without uttering a sound, she turned back toward the trees. Before she could take two steps, the devil dogs appeared.

"Caught you at last." The darker of the two men reached out, but before he could clamp his hand on her arm, she twisted away.

Jamie drew his short sword.

Her eyes flicked from one side to the other. Short, hard breaths puffed through her slightly parted lips, forcing her nicely rounded breasts to rise and fall. Apparently deciding an unfamiliar knight would be her safest choice, she moved closer to him.

His command of the Welsh language was depleted and he was doubtful they spoke French so he changed to English. "What business have you with this young woman?"

She inched closer, yet stood well out of reach.

"We want only to take our sister back home, m'lord." The answer came in English, but the cadence definitely marked him a Welshman.

"You lie." Her voice crackled with the fire of hatred. "This man is no relation to me. He wants only to take advantage of me, my lord."

He glanced at her from the corner of his eye. She spoke French as clearly as he did. The woman was obviously not Welsh and not a commoner. He pointed his sword at the man claiming to be her kin. "If you think I believe this woman is your sister, you must consider me a fool. She is much too pretty to have come from the same stock as you."

The two *brothers* eyed each other. An unspoken consideration passed between them and the dark one finally spoke. "We want back what she stole."

"And what is it she is claimed to have stolen?" He looked the man straight in the eyes.

The Welshman stared back, like an old dog challenged by a new male in the pack. "'Twould be no business of yours, Englishman."

Anger boiled inside Jamie's gut. At any other time the insolence would have earned the man a bruised chin, but he dammed his temper. Little use would come from stirring up trouble with the folk of Mother's domain. "Can you give me further proof?"

The red-haired man danced from foot to foot, and a muscle flicked at the corner of the dark one's mouth.

Jamie was not surprised when after a few moments there was no response. He had them at the game's end. "Then I shall have to ask you to be on your way." He turned his most intimidating stare on them. He had used the look a hundred times in his work for the King. It had yet to fail in unnerving an opponent.

They glared as if sizing up their chances against him.

He shifted his sword in his hand, ready to take their charge, but the dark one jerked his head and the other trotted back into the woods. The remaining dastard turned a menacing stare toward the woman. "I will finish with you later, whore."

The terror on her face breached Jamie's carefully constructed dam, and anger flooded out in a torrent. He crossed the road and thumped the man in the chest with the pommel of his blade.

The force of the blow knocked the big man to the ground and before he could recover, Jamie's knee pressed against the coward's chest.

The pinned man laid statue still, his only movement the stretch that shifted the skin of his throat away from the pressure of the blade at his neck.

"'Tis never wise to threaten a woman in the presence of a knight." Jamie whispered, but displeasure laced a menacing undertone through the words.

He slowly slid the tip of the sword up. The chin above tipped heavenward at an ungainly angle. "One never knows how chivalrous that knight might be."

The rustle of the trees, drew his attention back to the watcher in the woods. He stood and hauled the captive to his feet by his tunic. "Apologize to the lady for lying about her, and for offending her sensibilities with your foul speech."

"She be no lady." The big man struggled to twist from Jamie's grasp.

Jamie's jaw clenched tight, and he brought the edge of his sword to the man's ribs. "I said apologize."

The worm stopped wiggling and words spewed from his mouth quick as a rain-filled brook. "Beg pardon, if I have done offense."

Jamie eyed the woman. "Does such a weak utterance satisfy your honor?"

She stood half hidden in the ditch, mouth agape. Behind her blank expression, darting eyes showed her mind was at work.

"Is the apology acceptable to you?" He prodded.

A soft curve touched her lips. Not quite a smile, but no longer the thin, tense thread of uncertainty. "Aye, my lord."

"What are you called?" He asked his prisoner.

"Llwyd." The once brash voice now mumbled.

"Is that true?" He asked the woman.

"'Tis what he has told me, my lord."

"*Chsuwid.*" His tongue felt like thick twisted rope as he tried to pronounce the name. "Should I hear again you have been threatening women, you shall need to have a more thorough conversation with my blade." He released his hold and the man dropped to the ground before scampering into the woods to join his companion. He returned to the woman.

"I thank you, Sir Knight." Despite her appearance, her curtsy was steady and deep. Too formal for a common churl. "Your rescue is much appreciated."

What was an English woman of breeding doing out here unaccompanied? He moved closer, but she backed away, keeping the distance between them. "Where is your father—"

"Dead and buried, I hope." Her voice burst forth with such vehemence, he stepped back, as if instead of words she had flung a dagger.

"Your husband or brother then. A pretty maid like yourself should not pass through these wilds without escort."

"I am a free woman. In this land, I need tell you nothing unless you intend to force me—"

"Nay. That was ne'er my intent. Only to see you safe."

She dropped her guard enough to give a slight smile and he returned in kind.

"I thank you for your service, but I must be on my way. I am overdue. My mistress will be worried."

"Where do you go? I will attend you."

"Nay. After their encounter with you, they will not soon return."

"And why would they not come back after you?"

The pink tip of her tongue slipped out and wet her upper lip as she considered her response. "They will not want their deeds discovered. I am certain they return to their master for further instruction. Again, thank you and farewell." She turned to go.

Master? Instruction? What ill deed was afoot?

"Wait!" He hurried after her, hoping to glean more of the situation.

"Yes, my lord?"

His feet stopped moving, no longer obeying his will. Eyes the color of a field of bluebells gazed at him as she glanced back. He had seen eyes like hers before, but where? His heart could not pound harder if he had just run a league wearing full armor.

The blue eyes remained fixed on him until her stare went from expectant, to perplexed, to irritated. A cough failed to clear the lump that kept his mind from connecting to his mouth. "A knight usually receives a...a boon for his services," he stammered.

The corners of her mouth turned down. She tromped back toward him, halting so near he could have reached out and touched her. Her scent was faintly familiar. Reminded him of...Edensmouth.

The rough cloth pouch she pulled from the neck of her shift stood out against the delicate skin of her throat. She emptied a few coins into her palm and let the pouch drop against her full bosom. She thrust her dirty hand forward. A few light calluses showed where there should be work-hardened fingertips. "'Tis all I have." Her words were sharp and terse. "Those varlets took the rest."

"Nay!" He held up his hands and shook his head. "I want not your coin." He reached out, thinking to wipe a smudge from her cheek, but suddenly withdrew his hand. The forwardness of the action surprised him, but he felt as if he knew her somehow.

Her fingers snapped shut over the coins, and although she stepped away from him, her familiar scent lingered.

"What then, *do* you want, Sir Knight?"

"Being a *free woman*, perhaps you might give me your name."

One corner of her mouth slipped up into a mischievous half smile, making her even more appealing. "Alice."

"Alice." The good, solid, English name rolled easily from his tongue.

"And now, good knight, I must be off." Before he could stop her, she bolted into the forest and disappeared.

Stubborn woman. He gave a long, shrill whistle, and Abelard trotted to him. He no longer felt anxious. He no longer felt angry. He no longer felt restless.

He felt recharged. Recharged from the adrenalin of the confrontation. Recharged with the hope of finding pretty Alice. She said her mistress lived around here somewhere. Perhaps his mother would know the lady. He whistled a jolly court tune as they cantered toward Cilgerran.

By the time they wound through the surrounding village and up the hill to the castle, the clouds had vanished. The entrance to the castle grounds was unlike any he had ever seen.

A short set of stairs led up to a bridged moat.

The unusually formed steps did not provide easy access. Too tall for most men to easily step up and too wide to take more than one at a time. Even on Abelard, he tread carefully, lest the horse twist a leg on the odd placement of the risers.

A wide path ran alongside the bridge, but he noted it turned directly beneath a looped barbican before ending at the gate. Anyone who could not climb the steps would be forced to pass beneath the armed post. Someone, be it a Welsh Prince or his new stepfather, had put an impressive amount of thought into creating a well fortified entrance to this castle.

The afternoon sun shone brightly on the front gate. The wood looked new compared to the weathered stones of the gatehouse. Before Abelard could step from the bridge into the gatehouse, two stocky men approached.

"Hold, Sir Knight. State your business with Lord Cilgerran," one of the men said in Welsh.

Jamie understood enough to figure out the meaning of the statement, but not nearly enough to respond. "My business is with *Lady* Cilgerran," he shouted in English. "I am Sir James Barnard, son of Sir Thomas Barnard, knight in service to King Henry of England." From the corner of his eye, he saw a soldier slip away from the postern and hurry through the archway.

"I have come to visit my mother."

Chapter Two

Jamie studied the weathered stone gatehouse.

A wave of whispers passed through the guards and soon the men stationed above were looking down. He counted four above and six below. Ten men. A lot for such a small castle.

"Wait here, sir, while the captain is called," the guard said in carefully formed English.

Jamie dismounted.

The two burley Welshmen now stood on either side of him.

The discipline of the guards gave him a measure of relief about his mother's safety. They were serious but not rude. Respectful, but not distracted by his claim of being a family member. Still, something in their stance set his nerves tingling.

He removed his gauntlets, stuffed the mail gloves beneath the handle of his buckler, and loosened the cinch of Abelard's saddle.

"Jamie?"

Delight burgeoned in his chest at the sound of the familiar voice. He looked up. The hair was a bit shorter, and the beard was a new addition, but the one person he least expected to see stood before him.

"Wil? Is that you?" He clasped the arm of his best friend since boyhood, William de Chasson, Lord Evermoor.

"Aye, you son of a Saxon." Wil's hearty hug was the first earnest welcome he had received since his return. "It has been too long since our last meeting."

The words rang more than true. Six years was so long that he no longer had a home, and hardly much more of a family. Rash pride had cost him much. His friend's wedding. The birth of children. He had robbed himself of the joy of such events. Perhaps he could somehow manage to make up for the loss.

"How come you to be here, Jamie?" Wil's puckish grin was one thing that had not changed. "I thought you were at court with the King."

"I was, but nothing there needed my attention." To have to lie to his best friend pained him, but he had been sworn to secrecy. The King had only agreed to allow him to return if he took on the special mission as well. "All the court folly became wearisome." That part was no lie. "I thought it time to come…" He started to say "home", but the word stuck in his throat. "…to take care of my mother."

A brazen burst of laughter drew startled stares from the guards. "Lady Amye will box your ears for even thinking she needed to be taken care of." Wil laughed so hard he could barely speak.

The infectious mirth tickled at Jamie's gut and a small chuckle soon turned into a roar. Many months had passed since laughter had come so easily. "If you dare to tell her, I swear I will kick your bony arse to the woods and back."

Wil turned to the nearest man. "Daed, take Sir James' horse to the stable."

"Make sure he has a good ration of grain," Jamie said as he handed the reins to the soldier.

"Come." His friend slapped him on the back. "Let us go to the hall." They crossed the bridge into the squared yard of the list. The clang of metal drew his attention. A corps of yeomen sparred with various weapons.

"What are *you* doing here, Wil?"

"My Maggie wished to come to Wales with your mother. So when Cilgerran agreed to take my fealty, we came south."

"Ah, yes. Mother wrote you married one of her ladies. And what of your holdings in Evermoor?"

"We usually spend the winters here and a month or two of the summer in Cumbria, but the impending birth of our second child prevents us from traveling this year. My sister's husband acts as castellan while we are away."

"I congratulate you on your good fortune, my friend."

Wil had done well by coming home after his training. A fief and vassals. A wife and two children.

By King Henry's own words, Jamie was a knight of renown, yet he was beginning to believe he would have done better to return to the family estate rather than join the ranks of the King's Knights. "'Tis a relief to my mind to have you here, Wil. I have to say I worried about Mother being in the wilds with a sotted songster."

"You need not have wasted a thought on that account. Lord Cilgerran knows more about fortifications than any troubadour I have ever met. He must have some kind of military experience."

Wil sounded so certain, but the reassurance did little to bolster Jamie's opinion of his mother's second husband.

"And every day your mother teaches me something new in the ways of politics and diplomacy. Her sharp wit and honeyed tongue convinced the Welsh t'would be a benefit to willingly accept an English lord."

"I have no doubt she could turn them in her favor. She always had a way of helping people see her truth." He gestured toward the dozen soldiers training with side weapons. "Most of the guards look to be Welshmen."

"Aye. Those who could speak English well enough were immediately offered positions in the castle garrison," Wil shouted over the noise of the sparring swordsmen. "And Lord Cilgerran promised promotions to those who learned to speak French. Lady Amye arranged lessons for those who wanted to learn."

Such a plan was no surprise. Mother was always thinking about improving the lives of her charges, be it her serfs, her vassals, or her children.

At the far end of the hard packed dirt, another group threw javelins. The spears thunked into bales of hay lined along the far wall. Their skill was impressive. From experience, Jamie knew long pole weapons were difficult at best. Yet, nary a throw missed the target.

The feeling that Wil had not been forthcoming about the need for concern stood at the edge of his thoughts. The readiness of these men was well beyond that of a simple castle garrison. These men readied for battle.

He followed Wil through a tunnel in the wall of the inner curtain.

"When it comes to dealing with the villagers, Lord Cilgerran gives Lady Amye most anything she desires," Wil said.

"Father was the same." They emerged into a small bailey. "I cannot recall more than a time or two he said no to her plans." The calm words hid concerns at what he saw. A stretch of white stone marked a wide repair in the gray outer wall of the yard.

Breached? No recent hostilities he knew of would cause such a gap. Surely King Henry would have mentioned a major assault.

His gaze turned to the great hall. His mouth tensed as he spied the tall, stately woman standing at the bottom of a short rise of steps. He took a deep breath and put aside thoughts of treason. For the moment.

Amye de la Vierre, Lady Cilgerran, his mother,

waited, her hands folded at her waist. Obviously, she still disliked wearing the wimple most married women wore. In her surrender to modesty, a linen veil, crowned with a circlet, covered her head and shoulders. With the exception of a few more strands of silver in her long brown hair, she remained as beautiful as the day he last saw her—six years ago.

"My lady," Wil bowed politely, but the corners of his mouth inched up. "I found this stray cat scratching at the gate."

She chuckled. "Thank you for being so kind as to take him in, William. Margaret is searching for you. I believe she is in the laundry."

"Thank you, my lady. I shall find her posthaste." Wil winked at Jamie and turned toward the buildings at the back of the yard.

"My darling boy." She kissed both his cheeks, and gave him a hug that nearly knocked him off balance. She stepped back at arm's length and brushed a lock of hair from his forehead. The twinkle in her violet eyes cooled his burning concerns to a spark, and a smile forced its way through the serious mask he tried to hide behind.

"Auch, 'tis so wonderful to see you. I had news of your return from court..." She looked down at her feet and folded her hands in front of her. "But I thought mayhap you would not come here."

He had not realized how he missed her. He had refused to come to Cilgerran until now. Her new marriage had ignited in him such anger. Six years of anger. Enough anger to make him one of King Henry's most feared enforcers.

He had turned his sense of purpose from pleasing his mother to pleasing his monarch. But even with the excitement of battle and the power of representing the King, the life he had forced on himself proved an empty life, a lonely life.

He did not know what to expect when he came

here, but it was as if the years he cut himself off from her were wiped clean in an instant. "You know I could not stay angry at you forever." He gave her the hug she deserved. "But I went to Edensmouth first."

She drew back. "Oh?" Her eyes widened, matching the surprise in her voice. "And how is your brother?"

Mother was well aware of the spite between him and John. "As well as can be expected," he answered, barely able to keep the scorn from his voice. "Being *Lord of the Manor* suits John well," he lied. "Although I think the demesne misses your steady hand."

Hoping to change the subject, he glanced at the scaffolding clinging to the walls of an adjacent tower. "You are building, I see."

"Aye." She turned and looked up as well. "Not much remained when we first came. The skirmishes ten years ago took a great toll on the structures."

His stomach tightened as the smoldering concerns flared anew. Ten years ago? Why then, would they be preparing for battle now?

"Come inside." She looped her arm through his and patted her hand against his chest as she always did when she knew he was upset. Regardless of how calm he appeared on the outside, somehow, she always knew when he was upset.

She led him up the stairs. "The King neglected to tell us Cilgerran was a rundown ruin." Again she played the bashful maiden and an alarm clanged loudly in his head.

"Of course, it might have been a punishment for all the trouble we caused at court that year."

He tilted his head toward her and raised a brow. "Trouble?"

She stopped, mid-step and turned to him. "John did not mention it?"

John had not mentioned it and neither had King Henry.

"'Tis indeed a surprise your brother told you naught of it. Well, 'tis a tale for another day." They continued up the steps.

From the top of the stairs, he looked out across the small forecourt and sighed.

"Lord Rhys, my brother-in-law, offered us a place, but King Henry offered the title as well. My lord wanted to prove himself capable without help. She laid her hand on his arm. "Just as your father did."

He snorted and his jaw clamped tight. How could she mention the troubadour in the same breath as his father?

"No one was willing to make the effort to reclaim the castle until we came."

His plan to put aside his anger crumbled like week-old bread. Even though he had yet to meet Lord Cilgerran, his opinion of the man was becoming more and more unforgiving. "Certainly your husband did not bring you to a place with no protection and no roof over your head?"

"Until the breach in the wall could be mended and the gate rebuilt, Marie and I stayed with my husband's family to the south."

A puff of air flared his nostrils as he folded his arms across his chest. He would never bring *his* wife and child to such a place, even after it had been repaired. What kind of man would have her give up the grandeur of Edensmouth for this? "And where is your husband? I would meet the man who has taken my mother from her rightful home."

Her back suddenly stiffened and a deep line creased her brow. The playful twinkle in her eye became a searing flame. "This is my rightful home, and my husband is away, just as your father often was." She spun and hurried through the archway into the hall.

Cilgerran was away? Why would he be gone when the garrison was on high alert? This did not bode well.

Jamie followed her rigid frame toward a hearth set at the end of the long room. A small fire burned, radiating a circle of warmth into the front of the hall.

She abruptly stopped and stretched her hands toward the flames. "Though you were yet to be born when we began to build Edensmouth to what it is today 'twas hard work," she said, not even looking back to see if he was there. "I know you recall how, even after so many years, your father could find little time to spend at home."

His hand found the knot at the back of his neck. Why could he not just be satisfied to enjoy being reunited with his mother? Again he had allowed his anger to rob him of what should be a joyous moment. "You were saying you affected repairs?"

Her shoulders softened, and she turned to face him. "Yes." A smile eased the tension in her forehead, and he felt as if his *faux pas* might be forgiven. "By that time, your sister was more than two-years-old and I could help more. So we moved here." She sat on a bench and patted the space next to her, but he ignored her invitation. "We have done much in just four years. Do you not agree?"

He had to admit the place looked better than he'd expected from John's description. In the current fashion, the walls of the hall were washed white with lime and a good artist had drawn in false bricks. What must be the Cilgerran Coat of Arms was painted behind a long wooden table that sat behind the hearth.

He did not miss the meaning in the heraldry. A simple escutcheon with the field split *vert* and *rouge,* charged with a falcon facing a dragon over a bar *blanc.* English and Welsh shielded together in harmony. Beneath it a hopeful motto unfurled in French. *Grâce à la force de paix et de prospérité—* Strength Through Peace and Prosperity.

The words shattered his perspective like the iron ball of a truncheon cracked through bone.

The same philosophy his father had believed in. Even here, she carried forward his memory.

He gave in and sat beside her. To give further sway to his judgment before he even met Cilgerran was foolish. "I heard you used your wiles to lure the countrymen over to your side."

"At first, 'twas a battle of wills, but in time, we convinced many clan leaders to accept my husband as the lord. And I think Marie won over the rest of the folk. She is their little—"

A flurry of energy, in the shape of a young girl, burst into the room. The child ran to his mother, and without even a curtsy, began to speak. "Mama, I want to ride the mare." The miniature replica of his mother swayed forward and back, excitedly swinging the skirt of her kirtle like a bell ringing the call for mass.

The child was tall, though she could have been no more than five or six years old. She had their mother's oval face and full lips, but the green eyes must certainly have come from her father. Dark brown hair, braided in two plaits, bounced around her head as she looked between her mother and the door.

He turned to see what the girl was staring at and spied a young woman rushing across the hall.

"Marie, you know you are too small to ride a big horse." Mother's tone reminded him of times when he had tried to do things beyond his ability. "Papa brought you a pony all the way from Brittany..."

Recognition of the approaching woman forced aside any interest in the troubadour's daughter.

Alice? She was Mother's servant? He leapt from the bench as if it had suddenly burst into flame.

Alice slid to a halt. Her tempting lips pressed into a thin line, and her pale blue eyes held a question. The soiled tunic had been replaced by a kirtle that nicely matched her eyes. She turned to his mother and curtsied, giving him a more prominent view of her full round bosom. "My apologies for the interruption, my lady."

Jamie smiled. Her voice was so proper, so controlled, compared to the way she had spoken when they met on the road. As drawn as he had been to that Alice, this woman took him even more.

"None necessary." Mother rose. "I was telling Marie if she wants to learn to ride, she will have to start on the pony. Are we all agreed?"

From experience, Jamie knew the last was more a statement than a question.

Alice and Marie both nodded.

Mother turned the little girl to face him. "Marie, this is your brother, James."

He looked down at the child, trying not to let his dislike of her father taint his impression of her. Yet his face must have betrayed his hostility.

She backed away as if he was a giant dragon come to eat the princess. She looked up at their mother, who nodded and pushed the child toward him.

"'Tis a pleasure to meet you, Marie." He reached out, his palm up, offering to take her hand.

She timidly laid her tiny fingers on his, and he placed a gentle kiss on her knuckles. She snatched her hand away and turned back to hide her face in their mother's skirts.

"Marie!" Mother scolded. "That is no way to greet a guest."

"But Mama, you said he was my brother." She turned an eye on him from the hiding place. "I do not like brothers. The last one was so mean."

"Marie Johanna Eleanor Nasrin de la Vierre!"

The sound of his deep hearty laughter echoing off the walls surprised Jamie as much as anyone. Marie had obviously met John.

"Apologize to Jamie this instant." Mother's stern voice silenced his laughter, but try as he might he could not stop smiling. This little one had courage, even if she did lack a bit in manners.

Marie inched toward him until she stood just within arm's reach. "My apologies," she squeaked.

"Now, how do we greet a guest?" Mother's question drew an uncomfortable silence as answer. She cleared her throat and familiar with the warning, Marie thrust out her hand. "'Tis a pleasure to meet you...sir."

He knelt and clasped her hand. "I thank you for the apology." He spoke loud enough for all, but then he winked and whispered so only she could hear. "Worry not. I, as well, like not our elder brother."

A frown wrinkled her forehead, but she suddenly drew her mouth into a smile as understanding dawned on her.

He stood, still holding her tiny hand. "Mother, would you allow me to teach Marie to ride the pony?"

"Your brother is a very fine knight. Would you like for him to teach you to ride?"

He looked down.

The little face looked up and smiled. "Yes, please."

"Very well." Though Mother's voice remained firm, she smiled. "You may start tomorrow. 'Tis time for your lessons now. Brother Jacob is surely waiting at your room."

The adoring look became a disappointed pout.

He picked her up and gave her a kiss on the cheek. "I shall see you at supper, will I not?"

She turned toward Mother, who smiled and

nodded.

"Yes!" Marie threw her arms around his neck and kissed him excitedly.

He set her down and she hurried from the room. Alice started to follow, but he stopped her with a touch to her elbow. "And who is this lovely creature?" He asked his mother though his eyes remained on Alice.

"Do you not recognize Sela?"

Confusion swept through him. "The girl you brought home from Crecy?"

"The same."

No wonder she seemed so familiar on the road. The last time he saw Sela she was no more than a slip of a maiden. Now, she was a woman. A woman who made his heart tap at the door he had shut it behind.

But why did she tell him her name was Alice? Why was she on the road alone? If caught, she certainly would have been killed. What secret did she hold worth dying for?

"A pleasure to see you again, Mistress Sela." He took her hand, and she curtseyed. He pressed his lips to the soft fragrant skin. Now he recognized her scent. The scent of lavender. The scent of the fields surrounding Edensmouth. The scent that reminded him of the time they had spent together long ago.

Chapter Three

"Welcome, Sir James." Sela rose from her curtsy, but his fingers gently squeezed hers before he released her hand.

He had grown into a striking man. Dark brown hair, neatly trimmed around his face, fell to his shoulders in soft waves. A slightly ragged, but stylishly shaped beard covered his strong jaw. The resemblance to his father was so apparent. Why had she not recognized him?

"Are you hungry, my son?" Lady Amye reached to ruffle his hair as if the man before her was a small child rather than a tall, well-muscled knight.

He tensed and she drew back her hand, but before he could answer, she turned to Sela. "Would you please see to Jamie while I prepare a room for him? Take him to the kitchen. Have cook fix him something."

"Certainly, my lady. This way, Sir James." She led him through the small portico at the back of the hall then down the long path to the kitchen.

"Tis quite a walk to get a meal, *Mistress Alice.*" He clasped his hands behind his back as he walked.

The embarrassment of her trickery heated her cheeks, and she turned her head to hide. "The yard at Cilgerran is smaller than the one at Edensmouth. The kitchen was re-built at the far corner to keep the danger of fire away from the living quarters."

"Makes good sense, *Mistress Alice.*"

The quip poked at her like a shepherd's crook at a wayward lamb. She could ignore his reference to her deception, but she could not ignore the man walking beside her. Her memory held nothing of his chest being so broad or his arms being so muscular or his...their eyes met.

Eyes of such unusual color, light brown with specks of violet. Eyes that had first entranced her so many years ago. Eyes now focused intently on *her*.

The smile she thought she had gotten over graced his lips, and she touched her own, wishing she had not backed away when they met on the road.

She stepped away, trying to distance herself from the heat she felt rising inside her, but her foot caught on a cobble and she began to tumble backward.

The arm around her waist took her by surprise. He pulled her close to him. His face only inches from hers, he whispered, "Take care, *Mistress Alice.*"

His hand lingered at the small of her back longer than necessary, and the warmth of his fingers reminded her of time spent with him long ago.

She pushed free of the embrace. "Had I recognized you when we met on the road, I would not have deceived you."

He smiled and the dimples she remembered appeared on his face. "I suppose we both have changed quite a bit since last we saw each other."

"Yes, I suppose we have." She wrapped her arms around herself, and squeezed her chest. "You have become a great knight like your father."

"And you have become a beautiful woman." His finger slid across her shoulder and down her arm.

His touch stirred feelings she thought she had put aside long ago. Heat filled her belly.

No. Not again. There was no place for such feelings in her life. She was a grown woman of five and twenty, not the maiden of two and ten who foolishly lost her heart to the lord's young son.

The deep breath she took barely focused her thoughts. Balling her hands into fists, she shoved the emotions back into their box and hurried to the kitchen door.

"Genevieve?" she called as they stepped into the pantry.

"*Oui,* Sela—Master James! Your *mère* did not tell me you were coming." The tall, Norman cook gave him a hug. "I would have made a cherry potage."

Genevieve's cherry potage was his favorite sweet, if Sela remembered correctly.

"Only one?" he responded. "You will have plenty of time to make three or four." His hearty laugh made Sela's heart thump against her chest, but then her stomach flopped and her breath caught in her throat. Did he say there would be plenty of time? He intended to stay.

"Come, come." The cook excitedly led him toward her inner sanctum, the spice pantry. Genevieve never let anyone into the room tucked away at the far back of the kitchen. Lady Amye was the only other person Sela had ever seen enter the room. Apparently, Jamie also held the privilege.

The urge to flee tugged against her obligation to fulfill her lady's charge. In the end, duty won out and she followed behind, but the cook shut the door before she could enter.

Relief flooded through her, and she returned to the great hall. If he was going to be here a long while, she must take hold of her feelings. Just as she reached the tower, Lady Amye came out.

"We have made up the small room on the second level. 'Tis the only room complete enough for a guest." A sad smile tugged at her lips. "Once Lord Cilgerran returns, we shall have to finish up the others. Then we can call the clans here rather than my lord having to be away."

Even after five years of marriage, Lady Amye was still so much in love. Lord Cilgerran had been away for nearly three months, longer than any other period. For the first time, the melancholy in her mistress' voice made sense to Sela. Jamie Barnard had been out of her life for more than six years, and still she had feelings for him. "His lordship will return home soon, my lady."

Lady Amye nodded and squeezed her hand. "Please make sure Jamie's belongings are taken up."

"Yes, my lady."

"He has come alone. Is there a boy who can serve him?"

Most of the boys left in the village were either too young or too old...perhaps—

"I think I know just the person, my lady."

****

Sela wound her way through the narrow streets of the village to a little house that sat at the far west end. The home of Rhiana merch Blaidd, the village healer. Her very best friend.

Rhi had taught her all about the local plants and cures and in return Sela happily shared her own healing recipes. Before she could knock, the door swung open and she was greeted by sparkling brown eyes and a wide smile.

"Sela!" The dark-haired woman gave her a hug and kissed her cheeks. "What brings you out from the keep?" Rhi led her to a seat in front of the fire then dipped out a cup of brew from the cauldron bubbling on the hearth.

Sela was glad she'd come. Bundles of herbs, hung from the roof beams to dry, released a pleasant combination of scents into the warm room. She felt centered, calm, almost cheerful, when she was here. And she certainly could use a bit of composure right now. The smell of sweet mint and betony flowers filled her nose as she fanned the steam of the drink toward her face.

Rhi filled a cup for herself and sat on a stool by

the hearth. "Was it something special you needed?"

"Well, yes." A sip of the tasty drink soothed away uncertainty about how Rhiana would react to her next words. "Lady Amye's son has arrived. I was hoping Bleddyn would come to the keep in his service."

Rhi grimaced. "If you recall, my brother and Lord High-and-Mighty did not get along well last time his lordship was here."

Sela released the held breath initiated by Rhi's frown. "No, not Lord Edensmouth. 'Tis her younger son, Sir James, the King's Knight."

"Well, that would be different."

"I know Bleddyn has talked of fostering with a knight."

Rhi's eyes sparkled with the laugh she held back. "'Tis near all he has talked of since he turned seven. And that was the best part of ten years ago."

"He is a bit old to start, but I think Sir James might be open to the suggestion if Bleddyn could prove himself worthy."

"Worthy for what?" Bleddyn stepped through the back door with an armload of firewood. He set the logs by the hearth, then stood and brushed the dust from his shirt.

"Sela brings tidings. Lady Cilgerran's younger son has come. He is a knight."

"A knight!" The young man's eyes sparked to life. "A true knight?"

"Aye. A King's Knight." Sela said. "He is just returned from service at the court in Anjou."

"And he would take me on as a squire?"

"Well, what he needs right now is someone to help him dress, deliver messages, care for his belongings..."

His dark eyes drew down to slits. "He needs a page?" He folded muscular arms across his chest and leaned against the wall.

"A servant," Sela said, hoping to soften his reaction.

"'Tis not a job for a man."

She feared this would be his response, but she had one more piece to play. "Aye, but you would also be required to do things like help with his armor and weapons."

The moment she mentioned armor and weapons he stood straight and a grin wide enough to crinkle his eyes appeared. "That I can do!"

"Thank you, Bleddyn. I know not another I could trust with the task had you said no."

"Nay, Sela. 'Tis me who owes *you* thanks. I had given up thinking to have such a chance. I promise I will not disappoint you."

She set her cup on the table and stood. "Get your things together. We must return to the keep and get you cleaned up."

He frowned. "I am cleaned up. I just had a bath two weeks ago, at the first of spring."

"I meant no offense. Only that you shall need proper clothing for service." She ran her hand through his thick unruly locks. "And I shall have to do something with your hair."

"'Tis naught wrong with my hair." His chest puffed out like a cock marching before hens. "The girls in the village like it just fine."

"'Tis all well and good, but if you aspire to be a knight's squire, you must look like one. Make haste. We must return."

He nodded and hurried through to the back room.

Sela turned to Rhiana. Though her friend smiled, some sadness showed on her face.

"Rhi, if you need him to stay, I will find another."

"No, no. 'Tis all good. I know he wants this more than anything. He has just grown up so fast. I shall miss him."

"You can see him anytime you wish. You are always welcome at the keep. And I am sure he will have time to come home."

"Aye." Rhiana lifted the edge of her apron and dabbed at the corner of her eye. "I am just being a foolish older sister."

"He will be fine." Sela took Rhi's hand and gave it a gentle squeeze. "I promise."

Bleddyn returned carrying a small sack and a sword half as tall as himself.

"Mercy. I do not think they will let you into the bailey with that." Sela nodded at the leather-sheathed blade.

"I cannot go without it." He clutched the sword to his chest. "How will I train? How will I protect my knight if I have no weapon?"

Such eagerness could only be a boon in convincing Jamie to take him on. "For now, let us assure you will be acceptable to the knight."

"You can leave the sword here, little brother." Rhi walked to him and wrapped her fingers around the leather sheath. "I will make sure 'tis safe 'til you need it."

After a moment's pause, he released his grip. She gave him a hug, and a pat on the shoulder. "Now run along. Do not keep your knight waiting."

****

Cilgerran Castle was nothing like Edensmouth. There, Jamie's suite was three times as big. He looked around the small room and was glad he'd left most of his belongings in Cumbria. The light armor he wore when traveling rested in a corner, his mail hauberk and a pair of chausses draped over one of the two chairs. Since he traveled alone, he would have to diligently care for the few clothes he brought. Perhaps Wil would have some things he might borrow.

He picked up his broadsword, the very first thing he bought with his earnings as a knight. From the length of the blade down to the carvings on the hilt, the weapon he commissioned from the armorer was a precise replica of his father's. When Father died in the Holy Lands over thirteen years ago, the original had been lost, but Jamie knew every turn of the weapon from memory. To this day, the thought that some Saracen might possess his father's sword galled him.

The last time he saw his father, Jamie had been five and ten years old. Nearly a man, but not quite old enough. He wished he was the one asked to serve as Father's squire, to fight alongside brave men beneath the Barnard standard.

John *had* been old enough to go, but the coward chose to remain behind.

Father had always been proud of his family. They had been raised to make their own decisions. Jamie knew the refusal hurt Father's pride, but he stood by his first-born's right to choose. Others may have thought it weakness, but those under Barnard rule remembered a man whose strength came not from his iron fist, but from his concern and kindness toward his people. Jamie hoped to someday inspire only half the respect his father had earned.

A knocking brought his focus back to the present. Mother would not have bothered to knock. There was no bolt. He leaned the sword in the corner by his breastplate before opening the door. His mood lifted when it was Sela who stood outside...with a young man? "Good day, mistress."

"Good day, my lord. May we enter?"

"Please." He pushed the door back as far as the hinges allowed, leaving it open in deference to modesty.

"This is Bleddyn." She gestured toward the boy, who stepped forward and bowed stiffly.

"He lives in the village. If you approve, he would serve as your personal servant."

Jamie studied the boy from head to boots. The lad stood straight, shoulders back and chest thrown forward, his face cast in a serious mask. He seemed of sturdy build, though he lacked a bit in grooming. Someone had attempted to tame his curly red locks into a plait that fell past his shoulder. A sparse growth of fine hair covered his square jaw, reminding Jamie his own beard needed grooming. "And you recommend this young man, mistress?"

"I do, my lord. I have known his family since the day we came. I am certain he will meet your needs."

He turned to the youth. "Have you been in service before?"

"Nay, sir."

"Why would I choose one inexperienced in service?" He questioned, testing the boy's mettle.

"I have a bit of knowledge of weapons," came a quick response. "I can mend your armor too, and my sister taught me somethin' about the healin' arts—"

"We have not many so qualified available at the moment," Sela interjected.

"I promise I will do my best for ye, sir," the boy added.

"Please, my lord, would you allow him a trial?" Sela's voice held a note of a plea.

Perhaps, by taking the boy on, he might curry her favor. "For you, of course, mistress, I will give young Bleddyn a try."

"Thank you, my lord. I am sure you will not be displeased. If I may, I leave you to become acquainted."

"Yes." He nodded, and smiled at her. "And thank you, mistress," he added as she closed the door behind her.

"Well, Bleddyn, I have not much for you to do, as most of my belongings are at Edensmouth. Do you know of it?"

"Aye, m'lord. 'Tis where Lady Cilgerran lived before she came here to us."

"Aye. My father and mother made Edensmouth into a strong holding. She will make this place strong as well. You are fortunate to have her here."

"Certainly we are, m'lord."

"But come, I must prepare for supper. I could use a shave. Have you ever shaved a man?"

"No, m'lord."

The down along the boy's jaw was so soft Jamie did not think he had even shaved himself before. Could he be trusted with a knife? Sela must trust him or she would never have brought him into the household. It was worth a try.

"Go to Mistress Sela and tell her you need hot water, a towel, and soap for shaving.

"Yes, m'lord." The boy started out the door but turned back. "Thank you, m'lord, for taking me on." The door closed behind him, and Bleddyn's hurried footsteps retreated down the stairs.

Jamie shook his head and rolled his eyes heavenward. What had he gotten himself into? He pulled out his travel sack and dug through to find his shaving knife and the round of polished metal he used as a mirror.

The two were a gift from his aunt. When he began to foster with his uncle, she encouraged him to be presentably neat at all times. Her advice played a part in his rapid rise in status. Many knights were skilled with a weapon, but King Henry took note of deportment and manner as well.

The boy returned with a clay ewer of hot water, a piece of soap, and a linen cloth. Sela included a knife as well, but Jamie preferred his own.

"Come then. All you need do is scrape away the hairs on the cheeks and make the jaw line neat and straight. An easy task if you have a steady hand."

31

Steam rose from the water poured into the basin. He wet the soap and rubbed it between his hands until a thick lather formed. As he spread the foam along his jaw, a familiar scent filled his nose. Sweet mint and spicy carnation. Just like the soap his father had used. He sat back in the willow chair and waited for the boy to begin.

The first tentative scrape of the blade nicked his cheek and he flinched.

"*Chyfrgolla at annwfn.*" The boy jumped back, holding the knife out at an odd angle.

"Watch your language, boy." Jamie had no idea what was just said, but the tone told him it might not be the courtliest of expressions. "You cannot serve a knight if you cannot control your manners."

"Your pardon, m'lord."

He stood and took the knife from the boy's hand. "Hold it like this, at a slant."

He wet his fingers in the basin, rubbed them around on the soap, then spread the foam in a line along the boy's round cheek.

"On the face take short strokes." He lifted the boy's chin then drew the blade two short moves. "It might take a bit longer, but that way you will not nick the skin."

He wiped the scrapings on the towel, flipped the knife, and laid the handle back into the boy's hand. "Give it another try."

After re-wetting his face with soap and water, he sat again, trying to look comfortable as Bleddyn approached with the knife.

Chapter Four

"My son, how handsome you have become." Jamie's mother appeared by his side as he entered the hall. He absently accepted the kiss she offered, and she patted his clean-shaven cheek. "Just like your father."

Pride puffed out his chest, but the pleasure he felt deflated as he scanned the room. Barely a quarter of the hall was set with tables. "Not many for supper tonight, Mother."

"Half departed with my husband. Half remain here."

"Indeed," he responded, hopeful that disapproval did not leak into his voice.

"Come. I will introduce you." She guided him to an older knight standing near the washbasin.

"My son, may I present Sir Gladus of Penwydd."

Jamie bowed and crossed his arm over his heart. The other knight returned the salute.

"Gladus was the first to swear allegiance to us."

"A pleasure to meet the son of such a magnificent woman." Gladus extended his arm, but his eyes looked past Jamie to his mother. A lecherous look that left a lump of indignation in Jamie's chest.

His grip tightened well beyond that of a normal greeting as he clasped the outstretched arm.

Gladus' eyes returned to Jamie. Though nearly hidden, there lingered a spark of challenge.

This country baronet thought to back down a King's Knight? Jamie leveled a searing glare at Gladus.

"Come, dear boy." The lilt of his mother's voice broke the loggerhead. "You must meet our steward."

He could feel Gladus' eyes on his back as she steered him toward a group standing near the front table.

Unlike the dais at Edensmouth, no platform separated the high table from the gallery but the hearth burned brightly and a half circle of tall sconces circled the tables, filling the front of the room with light and warmth.

The round of introductions drifted into Jamie's consciousness, but his attention focused toward the other end of the table where Marie stood chatting with Sela. He nodded at what seemed appropriate times, but as the discussion turned to the happenings of the day, he edged away from the group.

"Please excuse us," Mother finally said. "I must see to a few things before supper."

They all bowed politely and she lifted her hand.

Jamie gratefully offered the support of his arm, but this time he guided her—straight to Sela.

"My lady. Sir James." She curtsied deeply as they approached, and a cascade of tresses tumbled over her shoulder. When she rose, the fabric of her tunic draped pleasantly over the curve of her hip and he recalled his attraction to her had been more than a youthful longing.

"Please stay with Marie a few moments more," Mother said. "I must see Genevieve."

"Certainly, my lady," Sela replied as Mother hurried away.

He thought to kiss her hand, feel the soft skin against his lips, smell the delicate scent of lavender, but Marie clasped one. The other clutched a handful of her blue linen kirtle into a ball.

"Fare thee well this evening, mistress?" he asked.

A tight smile forced itself to her lips. "Well and good, my lord." Her short reply left no room for response, as though she did not wish to talk to him.

Her blue eyes flitted about the room like a dragonfly darting amongst blades of grass, but his eye landed on only one person in the room.

The hearth fire outlined her figure like an angel's halo. The glow highlighted her beautiful red-brown hair and accentuated her soft moist lips. Would that the dragonfly should rest on his blade. At that moment her eyes locked on him.

A pink the shade of the roses at Edensmouth colored her cheeks. Long ago, he'd seen that blush on her cheeks for the first time. He had thought her pretty then. Now she was beautiful.

"Might I ask if your shave went well?" She blurted into the threads of silence strung between them. "Are you satisfied with Bleddyn?"

"Aye." He had not the heart to tell her the boy had been unable to produce an even line and the beard had had to be shaved off. 'Twas only hair. It would grow back. "Thank you for obtaining his service for me."

"You are most welcome. You look quite handsome."

Perhaps she was just minding decorum in public, but the compliment quickened his heartbeat.

"Jamie?"

A tug at his tunic drew his glance down. Marie's outstretched arm awaited. He smiled. At least he would get to kiss someone's hand tonight.

"Good evening, Lady Marie." He bent low and brushed her hand with his lips. "How fared your lessons?"

"Brother Jacob says I draw very well for a girl of only five years, and I learned a whole new poem today..."

He lost track of the lessons as he focused on the

beautiful woman standing behind the child.

Sela's mouth curved into an affectionate smile as she watched Marie talk. She looked up and the beautiful smile again became a worried, thin line.

"Jamie?" Marie again tugged at his tunic.

"Oh. Aye, Marie?"

"I asked why you wear lions instead of falcons like my Papa does."

He looked down at his crimson tunic, emblazoned with a diagonal row of golden lions. "Well, little one, I am a King's Knight. My first allegiance is to the King, so I wear his colors."

She tilted her head to the side. "But Papa swears allegiance to the King and he wears falcons, not lions."

A bright child for her five years. When she grew up, she would be like their mother. Too smart for her own good.

He sat on a nearby bench and helped her onto his lap. "Your father is different because he is a landed lord. He has his own colors and others swear allegiance to him."

"Oh. Will you swear allegiance to Papa?"

Her precocious nature drew a smile from him. "I already have an allegiance to the King. Had I not already so sworn, I might consider it."

"You could be my knight?"

"I could."

"You swear it?"

He laughed to himself. Marie was persistent. Another of Mother's traits. He stealthily avoided her trap. "If I could, I would."

She leaned forward and kissed him on the cheek.

Mother swept back into the room and returned to the table. "Come, my darlings." She lifted Marie from his lap. "'Tis time for supper. Thank you for watching Marie, Sela. You may go."

Go? "Will you not join us for supper, mistress?"

"I am a servant, my lord. 'Twould not be proper for me to sit with the nobles."

Her excuse confused him. "You sat with nobles at Edensmouth."

"If you recall, my lord, 'twas only on special occasions, the servants sat with the nobles."

"But—this *is* a special occasion," he countered.

Her brow creased, as if she was unsure of what he meant.

"'Tis my first night..." Again the word "home" stuck in his throat. "...back with my family." He turned to his mother. "Is that not so?"

Her brows drew together, and her eyes darted back and forth between him and Sela. "Yes, this is indeed a special day," she said, though her words were tentative. "Sela, please find a seat and sup with us."

Sela curtsied. "Thank you, my lady." Her terse response sounded none too eager.

His mother took Marie's hand and walked toward the two high backed chairs at the center of the table. A smaller chair, piled high with pillows, was placed between the two settles.

"You, my son, shall sit at my right hand, and my daughter, you may sit next to papa's chair on my left." Her voice brightened. "I shall be surrounded by my children for the first time in many years."

Before seating his mother, Jamie lifted Marie onto the pillows. He eyed the seat next to her. Left empty for the absent lord. Too much was going on for Cilgerran to be away. What plan was afoot that the lord needed to go himself?

He looked out over the gallery, searching for signs of discontent. Gladus sat at a table with four others. Their raucous laughter and merry faces showed nothing unusual.

The only displeasure he saw was Sela sitting at

the table nearest the back portal. She nodded uneasily and made a response when one of the young nobles spoke to her.

Jamie frowned when the man slid closer to her. Sela glanced toward the door, then slid further away. Perhaps he should not have made her stay.

Wil and his wife joined the front table. "Sir James, this is my lady wife, Margaret."

Lady Evermoor was a small woman, very full with child.

He kissed the hand she offered. "A pleasure, my lady."

She pushed back a dark curl that escaped her wimple. "A pleasure, indeed, to at last meet my husband's most trusted friend." She frowned and rubbed her well-rounded belly. "Husband, I think I must sit. Your son is quite unruly today."

Wil took her hand and the nearly new mother eased onto the bench. She did not look very comfortable. Odd that she should attend the meal so far along in her time, but Jamie sat and they chatted amiably while servants poured drink.

His mother stood and the room quieted. "It pleases me that you sup with us this night. We celebrate for I have been reunited with my beloved son." She lifted her cup. "To Sir James Barnard. Hail and welcome."

All drank the toast, but Jamie saw only the cup Sela held. To be that cup. To have her hand wrap around him. To press against her full lips.

"Have you enjoyed your time in the King's service?" Lady Margaret interrupted his fantasy.

"Indeed, my lady. I have gained much experience and a bit of stature as well," he answered as servants replenished the wine and brought the first course. The bowls of stewed fish smelled delicious. The lightly seasoned sauce rolled smoothly across his tongue. He had forgotten what succulent food came from Genevieve's kitchen. Throughout the remainder of the meal he conversed with Wil's wife, though his attention was not fully upon Lady Margaret. His eye wandered to the table nearest the back door.

Sela politely picked at her food, speaking only to say thank you when a server brought a dish or to reply to the man sitting next to her. Instead of Lady Margaret, he imagined *Sela* sitting beside him, her belly beautifully rounded with *his* son.

The young noble put his hand on the bench next to Sela and leaned to whisper in her ear. Her expression changed from anxious to offended.

A hand squeezed his thigh before he could rise from the table. "Do not toy with her," his mother whispered in his ear.

A blush heated his face as he stared into her piercing eyes. *How did she always know his thoughts?*

"I would not have her hurt," she finished curtly.

"I had no intent—"

"I know you my son. You are like me. Willful, when there is something you desire." She stood. "Come." She extended her hand toward him. "Walk with me."

Courtesy demanded he rise also. He slipped his hand beneath her palm and they left the table—abruptly ending the meal.

She led him through the front arch, ending any chance for him to talk with Sela tonight. As they marched through the courtyard and into the tunnel leading to the list she said not a word. Halfway through, she released his hand.

The orange-yellow flame of a small oil lamp cast a pattern of light and shadow across her face. The dimness deepened the displeasure showing there. "I am not blind, my son. I see the way you look at her, but you cannot think to marry her." The dark whisper matched her face.

"But *you* married a commoner," Jamie tossed back.

She rubbed her fingers against her forehead, stretching out the wrinkles of her frown. "My life was at a place where the status of the match did not matter so much. My husband is recognized as part of a noble family. Yet, many frowned upon it when I married him. With no such ties, how difficult would it be for Sela?"

How would it affect Sela? He thought only of the family he had begun to want. He had known her since they were young. Even though he had been away for six years, the desire for her lingered in his heart.

His mother grasped his arm. Though he could not see them, he knew her violet eyes were fixed on him.

"You are not landed, but you are a King's Knight. Though you live at court, you are gone more than you are home. You will not be there to protect her from the barbs of courtiers and ladies. Laughing behind her back. Teasing her about what trick she used to snare you. Aside from which, do you think the king will allow such a match?"

He had not forgotten his liege. The king would not take kindly to the refusal of the prominent match that had been offered. But what had prominence brought him? High praise? Shallow flirtations?

Gall rose through his chest and into his throat, forcing the thoughtless words from his mouth. "Yet, he allowed you to marry a troubadour."

He regretted the barb as soon as it crossed his lips.

She released his arm and backed away. Lamplight bathed the solemn mask of her face. "As I said, I can be willful, and the circumstance was well beyond normal." The pain behind the mask shot from her eyes, piercing his heart like an arrow.

"I do *not* want Sela hurt. Do not raise her hopes only to dash them against the ground. She has suffered enough for one lifetime." She pushed past him and started back toward the courtyard."

Sela suffered some ill fate? The ache that welled up shocked him. He had been such a fool. He should have been there to protect her. He hurried to catch his mother, but stopped mid-step. When did Sela become *his* to worry about? To protect? On the walk to the kitchen? As she sat at supper? Or now, when Mother made her unattainable?

His mother had reached the tower before he caught up to her. "I would never hurt her, Mother. I knew when first we met on the road—"

She spun to face him and her voice dropped to a whisper. "You met her before this afternoon in the hall?"

"Aye. In the forest, not far from the castle. She was pursued by two men."

"Do not mention this to anyone else."

"What is it?"

"Come to my chamber."

****

Preparing Marie for bed was always a challenge. When the child began to sing a song about a knight courting a peasant girl, Sela dropped the braid she was twisting. "Where did you hear such a thing?"

Angelic eyes looked up from the dressing table, but the smile belonged to a little devil. "I sneaked into the hall one night to listen to the knights sing. Have you ever heard them sing? They have such beautiful voices," Marie prattled on, barely stopping for breath.

The things the child could remember. Sela took up the unraveled plait and began braiding again. "'Tis not a fit song for a lady to sing. Aside from which, you should not be roaming the castle alone at night." Though Sela was certain no harm would come to Marie while she was within the keep, a more careful watch would need to be kept on her young charge.

"But I wanted to hear them." Marie sighed. "They sang so beautifully."

Willful child. Just like her mother. Well meaning, but stubborn.

The braid was quickly finished and Sela tied a short strip of cloth around the end to stop it coming undone. Marie was a sound, but restless sleeper. If her hair remained unbound it would be a tangled mass in the morning.

"Come, now. Time to rest, little one." She followed Marie to the bed and stood patiently while the child knelt and said her prayers.

She asked blessings on her mother and father, and all the family, on both sides, and all the household servants, and the people she knew from the village. The list was always long. Marie never wanted to forget anyone. Tonight it was a bit longer, as she added "...please God, bless extra well my new brother, Jamie, who I like much better than my old brother, John. Amen."

Silly child. Though the thought was not far from Sela's own. "Up we go." She lifted Marie onto the featherbed then tucked the covers around her.

Most every night, Lady Amye sat with her daughter spinning tales of great knights and beautiful ladies until the child fell asleep. The time seemed a balm to the lady's heart. Especially when her husband was away. Sela sat and waited for her mistress to arrive.

Marie yawned and picked at the shiny black hairs of the fur bedcover. "Tomorrow, my brother will teach me to ride."

"Yes, darling. He will."

"I shall have the finest horse."

"When you are big enough, you shall."

"I like my brother. Do you like my brother?"

"Yes." Sela rubbed her heated cheeks, thankful for the dimness of the single candle on the table. "I do like your brother."

"He likes you too."

A breath caught in her throat. "How can you know such a thing?"

"Because he was looking at you all through supper."

"Do not be foolish."

"I am not foolish." Marie's eyes began to close as the late night overwhelmed her excitement. "Will you marry my brother so he will stay?"

The hand pressed to Sela's chest barely kept her heart from bursting through her breastbone. "I...I cannot marry your brother," she stammered. "I am a commoner. I cannot marry a noble."

Marie's eyes popped open. "My brother, the one I do not like, says Papa and I are both common and yet Mama married Papa," she said as she drifted back to the edge of slumber.

The knot in Sela's chest dropped to her stomach, a twisted ball of anxiety and anger. How could John say such a thing to a child? "Go to sleep now. Even if I could marry your brother, I have only just met him today," she lied. "'Tis too soon to speak of such things," she lied again. Such things would never be spoken of.

Ever.

****

The climb to the antechamber of his mother's solar was quick. Unlike her rooms at Edensmouth the walls were cold, bare stone. No tapestries to warm the walls. No coverings on the floor save the rushes. The only furnishings were a table, a bench, and a few stools.

Unlike the door to his room, this one had a bolt. She slid it into place then hurried into a second chamber. She returned, tightly clutching a key.

"Here." She thrust the black metal at him, hurried to the hearth, and swept back the rushes with her foot. A heavy stomp tilted up one of the boards, revealing a compartment. She knelt and dragged a small chest from the hole.

"Let me help you." He handed her the key, lifted the box, and followed her to the table. "What is it, Mother? What is all this about?"

"We have discovered a plot to take Cilgerran Castle." She unlocked the box and pulled out a handful of papers and maps. "Though many are loyal now, many still chafe at English rule."

"And your lord is not here to deal with this treason?"

"Stop! You know nothing of our lives here." Her bitter words stunned him to silence.

He had never seen such anguish in her eyes, not even when his father died.

"*My lord* is out *there*." She swung her arm wildly toward the window. "Away from the safety of the keep." She slumped onto the bench. "Trying to deal with it."

Jamie sighed and sat on a stool across from her. What kind of man was he to let his anger hurt her again and again? Not a man worthy of his father's pride. He knew nothing of substance about Cilgerran. He had not even met the man. Still, the fact that someone other than his father possessed his mother's heart galled him.

"What has Sela to do with all this?" Though he hoped the change of subject would ease his self-reproach, it was of little help.

A heavy sigh lifted her breast and she looked up. "Sela can go where I cannot. She went into the viper's pit and brought back the proof we needed."

She handed him a letter.

"This was what they wanted from her on the road today?"

"Yes. I have sent messengers south to my brother-in-law and east to my lord that the attack is imminent."

From the few words of Welsh he knew, he was able to determine a plan had been set in action. He looked at the signature.

Carrecosh. Redstone.

It was not among the names on King Henry's list of traitors. Perhaps it was an epithet or a false name.

"I am glad for your presence, my son. Another trustworthy knight will add to our success." The corners of her mouth turned up a bit, but her eyes were not included in the gladness. "My husband hopes to convince the clans that King Henry will crush them if they rise up now. The fact that you are a King's Knight will help convince them the King is watching. Hopefully, enough of the clans will see reason and stand with us."

Could she know the King expected this insurgency? No. No one yet knew of the suspicions except the King, the Queen and himself. His current mission was to observe and report, but he could not just stand by and watch with an attack at hand. Nor could he leave to report to the king. Surely Lord Rhys would send word.

Jamie looked at his mother. She was as strong as ever. Even in this place, away from all the comforts she knew at Edensmouth, she showed the courage of a knight and a leader's wisdom. He handed the parchment back to her. "I will stay as long as you need me."

****

Her mistress did not come, so Sela stayed until a quiet rhythm of sighs assured her Marie slept. She

45

reached the door of Lady Amye's suite, just as Jamie came out.

"My lord." She curtsied.

He took her hand, squeezed it gently between his own, then pressed his lips to her knuckles. "Thank you." The whisper set her heart aflutter like the wings of a hummingbird.

"You are quite welcome," she said as she slid her hand from his and clasped her fingers tightly in her skirt. "Though I know not for what."

He brought his face near to hers. "For the risk you took being a spy for my mother."

The flutter stopped dead. He knew?

"Your mother saved my life. There is nothing I would not do for her." She owed everything she was to Lady Amye.

"You are a brave woman to go amongst rogues and traitors who would easily kill to keep their secrets."

"'Twas nothing," she whispered. Her stomach turned as she thought of Llwyd touching her. She had given up almost all modesty to get close enough to him to get what she needed. It had taken all her will not to retch as he stroked her breasts and stuck his sour tongue in her mouth. She had managed to avoid rutting with him, yet still she felt like a whore.

Like the whore she used to be.

Chapter Five

Sela hung the burgundy kirtle Lady Amye had worn to supper on a wall peg, then brought the small jewelry casket to the dressing table.

Lady Amye tugged the ruby ring her first husband had given her from her hand and laid it in the nearly empty box. The larger pieces from her first marriage had been sold in the early years here to finance the improvements made to the castle, but a special few, like the ring, remained. She looked into the mirror and sighed before reaching back to unfasten the simple garnet pendant Lord Cilgerran had given her before he last departed. "What think you of my son?"

A chill crawled up Sela's spine, and she nearly dropped the necklace Lady Amye handed to her. Twice tonight she had been asked about Jamie. "He has grown into a fine, handsome man, my lady." She laid the necklace atop the other jewelry.

Lady Amye stroked the ring on the thumb of her left hand. The golden band was engraved with two facing falcons, their tails knotted into a Celtic heart. Sela could not recall her mistress had ever removed the ring since Lord Cilgerran placed it there.

"Aye," Lady Amye sighed. "He reminds me so much of his father...both in form and character."

"Even as a youth, he always had great character, my lady." A warm feeling filled her heart. From their first meeting, over twelve years ago, Jamie Barnard had made her feel comfortable.

Lady Amye closed the lid of the jewelry box and handed it back. "He will go far in this life. His father would have been so proud of him."

As quickly as she tucked the jewel cache beneath the false bottom of the armoire, Sela tucked away her happiness for Jamie. She was no Pandora. The boy who had befriended her so many years ago was destined to become a great man. She could never share his happiness. To open herself to such thoughts would only be a source of pain.

By the time she returned, Lady Amye had pulled out the pins holding her hair in place. The undone twist fell in a pretty snarl down her back.

Sela picked up a silver-gripped comb and began to smooth the tangle.

"He is a fine man," Lady Amye continued, "but you must not let his charms beguile you."

Sela stopped combing. How could Lady Amye know? The feelings had barely begun to rekindle, but the truth her mistress spoke made it no easier to smother the tiny flame burning in her heart. "No, my lady. I would not think of such a thing. Though I am free, I am of such low birth I would never aspire to such a high position."

"But he might aspire to you." Lady Amye turned and took her hand. "I wish it could be, for I love you like a daughter, but I do not believe the King would allow it. Jamie is too useful a match."

"I know this, my lady." The soft words masked tears that fell not from her eyes, but from her heart.

Lady Amye turned back to the mirror. "You could be nothing more than a mistress to him. You deserve better."

In Sela's eyes, no one could be better than Jamie Barnard. She ran the comb through her lady's shroud of long dark hair. "I would not be so foolish as to think of having a chance with him, my lady."

"Jamie has come to help us, but he will return to the king once he is finished. Do not let him take your heart with him. Please. Guard your heart as I did not. Though all worked out well in the end for me, you alone know what terrible pain I suffered for my willfulness."

"Yes, my lady. I do."

****

Jamie had been surprised when Sela slammed shut the door to his mother's room without even a goodnight. Had he seen a tear on her cheek as she turned away? What had he done to make her run from him?

By the time he returned to his room, Bleddyn was asleep in a chair, his head resting on the table. A fire in the small brazier fought against the chill of the spring night, and an oil lamp cast a halo of light from a table set near the bed.

When the door closed, the boy jerked awake and stood. The downy beard was gone from his face, making it appear even rounder.

Jamie stroked his own clean-shaven jaw. "I see you have been practicing with your knife."

"Aye, m'lord. I apologize for my poor skill earlier. I will do better next time."

The long day caught Jamie up in its grasp and his loud yawn filled the tiny room. To sleep on a good feather bed would be a true pleasure after a dozen nights spent on the lumpy straw pallets of traveler's way stations.

"What is this?" He picked up the lamp and bent to look closer. A *rôbe de chamber,* a few linen shirts, and a pair of braes sat in a neatly folded stack on the bed.

"Lady Cilgerran sent these things to you earlier, m'lord. I was told to tell you they belonged to your father and they should fit you now."

Jamie's heart swelled as he ran his fingers over the soft, smooth robe.

"May I take your tunic, m'lord?"

He allowed Bleddyn to help him undress down

to his undershirt, but when the boy held up the robe, the hurtful words he had spoken to his mother came back, sitting like a lump of day-old porridge in his gut. She had thought him enough of a man to own his father's belongings, but he was not. Not yet.

"M'lord?" Bleddyn lifted the robe a bit higher.

"Put it away." He could not rightly bring himself to wear the robe until he proved a worthy man inside as well as out.

The boy folded the silk into a semblance of a square and carried the clothes to the corner where a small chest had been added to the meager furnishings of the room.

"Anythin' more I can do for you, m'lord?"

"Aye. You can call me Master Jamie in private. No need to be so formal when 'tis just us two."

"Yes, m'l...Master Jamie."

The room was small for two men. No place had been set for Bleddyn to sleep. Jamie pulled one of the covers and a pillow from the bed and held them out. "Unfortunately, tonight you shall have to sleep on the rushes. I am certain they are clean. My mother would have it no other way."

"I can sleep in the great hall—"

"What if I should need you during the night? Should I run searching the hall for you? A knight's man should be with his master."

"Yes, Master Jamie. Thank you."

****

In just three days, Marie proved to be a bold and confident rider. Jamie watched carefully as the little pony galloped around the list. His sister had taken instantly to the horse's back. He expected no less. All the women on Mother's side were expert riders. "Marie, slow down," he shouted over the clop of the pony's feet on the hard packed earth. "Watch your form. 'Tis not a race. Sit up."

She straightened her back and pulled on the

reins to slow the pace of her steed. Today she looked a proper lady; wearing a tunic over her linen kirtle, hair plaited in a single braid that reached nearly to her waist. "'Tis not game to go slow," she shouted as she passed round the bales of hay set up as a make shift riding circle.

"A canter is not slow. If you want to ride you must learn to control your mount."

She cantered perfectly around the yard three times.

"Good. Now walk." Each time he turned to follow Marie's progress around the ring, he caught a glimpse of Sela sitting on a bench at the edge of the list.

She watched patiently as Marie put the pony through his paces, as though his sister were her own child. Did she long for children of her own? She would be a wonderful mother. She'd learned from the best. She had been with his mother for more than a dozen years, grown up in a warm household, been almost like family.

They had once been close. Though she was in service to his mother, they had formed a special bond during their years at Edensmouth. He wanted that closeness back, but she seemed reluctant to give it. He had been away a long time. Perhaps the feelings were lost. Or perhaps they were just hidden under the passing years, waiting to be uncovered.

His mind wandered back to the conversation with his mother. *I do not want her hurt... She has suffered enough for one lifetime.* The warning only increased his curiosity. What hardship had she endured? Surely mother would have said if something had occurred in his absence. However, the life Sela led before she was brought to Edensmouth had *never* been spoken of.

The pony passed by again.

Marie's mouth was pinched into a tight frown.

"You have done well today," he shouted after her. "Let us give your steed a rest."

She turned the little horse and they trotted back to him. Not waiting to be lifted down, she slid to the ground. No worry of her falling far enough to be hurt. At the shoulder, the pony was barely taller than his waist.

"Come. 'Tis time you learn how to care for your mount after a ride."

"But should not the grooms do such?" she asked.

"What if you are somewhere without a groom? Who would care for him then?"

She turned her head to the side, as she was wont to do when thinking.

"Your horse is your friend." He clasped her shoulder and she looked up at him. "Nay, he is like unto family. If you take care of him, he will always take care of you."

"I see." She nodded in agreement.

"Do you have a name for him yet?"

"Yes!" Her excited reply popped out like a newborn robin fresh from its egg. "I shall call him Falconer, after Papa."

"'Tis a fine name. Let us get Falconer settled and fed."

"Come, Sela," she shouted across the yard. "You must know how to care for Falconer, too."

Sela slowly walked toward them.

Marie reached for her hand.

"Here." Jamie held out the reins toward his sister. "Take charge of your mount."

She took the leather straps and started toward the stables.

"Mistress?" He lifted his arm toward Sela. Would she take it?

She paused a moment before placing her long, graceful fingers on his forearm.

He folded his free hand over hers. Though not

small, her hand was delicate and warm beneath his palm. "Do you ride, mistress?"

"I do, but not nearly as well as my lady." Her magnificent blue eyes remained toward the ground, as though she knew if he looked into them, he would kiss her right there.

"Not many ride as well as my mother." He would never forget his mother and aunts embarrassing full-grown men during family gatherings, beating them in horse races. Father had taken it all in stride. At first, Jamie had thought Father ofttimes *let* Mother win, but she had proved herself a rider of note even after Father's death.

"'Tis true." Sela said. "The mounted hunt has always been her favorite sport."

He stopped walking and she was forced to stop as well. "In a day or two, I should like to take Marie for a ride. Might I convince you to join us?"

She looked up, but the look in her eyes troubled him. "I really do not think—"

"You would merely be our guide." He squeezed the hand resting on his arm. "Perhaps a short morning ride? Back in time for dinner?"

She pulled her hand from his and tightly clutched the skirt of her kirtle, but her blue eyes were now leveled at him. "I was going to say, my lord, with all that is happening I fear my lady would not allow Marie to leave the keep."

"Would a ride within the village be a danger? I will be with her."

"Perhaps not, but caution might be of best service. You would have to ask your mother, my lord."

Indeed he would.

She turned toward the stable.

He hurried to catch her. "Then mayhap I might prevail on you to show *me* the village. I shall be here for a time. I will need to know my way about."

She took a step back. "Bleddyn could do that for you. He has lived in the village all his life."

Damnation! How could he learn if her feelings for him still existed if she cut him off at every tack? Perchance an appeal to her sense of duty might work. "Yes, but I would like to see it through eyes I trust. Through your eyes."

Pink tinged her cheeks and, again, she looked down "I have duties with your sister."

"Mayhap we could go during her lessons with Brother Jacob?"

She hesitated, frozen like a fawn in a break. "Perhaps." She hurried ahead.

He stopped her before she could step through the open door. "Think on it, mistress." He lifted her hand and politely kissed it. "I would appreciate your view of things here."

****

Sela spent nearly half an hour untangling Marie's hair and picking out pieces of straw. After Jamie had shown his sister how to groom and feed the pony, a game of chase had ended with a session of tickling in a pile of hay. How delightful to see the big knight pretending to miss the spry child as they ran through the stables. What a good father he would be some day. Playful, patient, and kind.

"I am glad *this* brother has come to live with us." Marie fiddled with the tiny ring on her left hand. "He is wonderful nice."

"Aye, darling. He is nice." Sela smiled. *So very nice indeed.*

"I think it makes Mother happy."

"Yes, dear, it does. She loves your brother very much." *How could she not love him?* And it was good to see how much he loved and respected his mother. Lady Amye said he would stay as long as she needed him. Such help would never be offered by Lord John.

A sharp rap sounded at the door.

"A moment please," Sela called out while she quickly finished Marie's hair. "Make haste," she whispered. "Get your slippers."

Marie pulled the shoes from beneath the bed while Sela pulled a clean kirtle from the chest. She slid the dress over Marie's lifted arms and pulled tight the laces while Marie smoothed the front of the skirt. Marie hurried to the table while Sela rushed to answer the now persistent knocking.

"Good afternoon, Brother Jacob."

"Mistress Sela." The monk shuffled into the room carrying an armful of parchment scrolls and a heavy leather-bound book. He hefted his burden onto the table with a huff. "Good afternoon, Lady Marie."

Marie stood and curtsied to the wiry, old man. "Good afternoon, Brother Jacob. Thank you, Sela. You may go."

Excellent. Marie was learning when to be familiar and when the situation called for formality. Sela nodded, then closed the door behind her, leaving them to their work.

She did not envy Marie the task of sitting through the afternoon lessons. After the passage of five summers, Lord and Lady Cilgerran had insisted that a young lady should begin her education. But Marie did not learn just the normal things a lady should know. Sela knew the tedium of learning to read and write. Lady Amye had insisted that she learn. And there must be some way to make geography and literature more interesting than sitting through Brother Jacob's boring lectures.

Sela hurried down the steps into the bright afternoon sun. Though she loved Marie as if the child were her own, she coveted her hours of freedom. Caring for such a lively little girl took a lot of vigor. During the afternoon, Sela could walk in the garden, or like today, take care of her own interests.

The courtyard was quiet now except for an occasional string of birdsong, but as she got closer to the kitchen, she could hear the banging of pots and smell the sweet scent of baking honey cakes. Hopefully, Genevieve would not be too busy to talk. They had become friends of a sort. The only other servant who came from Edensmouth, the cook was a confidante Sela trusted.

"Genevieve?" No answer came, so she walked through to the back of the pantry. "Genevieve, are you here?" She knocked at the spice room door.

"She is at the ovens," a male voice sounded as the door opened.

"Sir James."

His tall, muscular frame filled the arch of the door.

She curtsied, but nervously lowered her eyes when he smiled at her. "Your pardon, my lord." Her heart drummed against the wall of her chest. "I was not expecting you here."

"Have you time for our walk, now?" Though he did not move from the doorway, he leaned forward and the spicy smell of the soap she had given him for shaving enticed the feelings she buried into the open.

"Tomorrow might be better." She feared to look up, lest the feelings pounding at their prison door might break free. "'Tis market day. There will be much more to show. More people to meet."

"Tomorrow, then." He lifted her hand. "After the mid-day meal?"

She nodded, her words suppressed by his closeness.

"Though I hoped it might be sooner..." His thumb slid across the breadth of her hand.

Her heart quivered like the plucked string of a lyre.

"...until then." His lips lingered on her fingers

for a moment, then he turned and strode down the path toward the tower.

The flex of his muscular arms. The movement of his broad shoulders. The powerful stride. All masculine, yet he moved with the same grace he'd had as a boy.

Despite her lady's warning, she found it harder and harder to put the childish daydreams from her head. Pandora's Box slid from beneath the armoire, and she felt the lid lifting. Felt the feelings refusing to stay inside. *Dear God in Heaven. Help me,* she prayed as she slumped against the spice room door. She was falling in love again with a man she could never have.

Chapter Six

Two portly women carrying a large basket of linen turned to stare as Jamie hurried back to the tower. He felt as though the pounding of his heart must be so loud everyone could hear it.

He had gone to speak to Genevieve about Sela. After Father's death, the Barnard vassals had focused all their attention on John, the probable next lord, and Mother had been overcome with grief. The cook had noticed Jamie floundering in his own sorrow and taken him under her tutelage.

She shared with him some of the small things he would have learned from his father, given the chance. She taught him how to clean a wound on the battlefield. She taught him how to be safe with women and not leave bastards across the countryside.

But today, when he'd shared his interest in Sela, Genevieve had responded with "What are you thinking, *mon petit*? Sela is not a match for one such as you." When he pressed the issue further, she lifted her nose and sniffed the air. "I must go and check the ovens." She patted his cheek in that way she always had when she was trying to avoid telling him something, and hurried from the spice room.

Then, like a wish magically granted, Sela's call had drawn him from the room like a moth drawn to a candle.

His quest to be like his father had taken him far from home. He had buried the feelings he'd once had for her, but he knew now that they still smoldered beneath the surface.

In the time since he'd left, she had become everything he sought in a woman. Smart, strong, brave, loyal, independent...beautiful. She was a free woman. She had no attachment, yet she risked her life for the safety of her lord and lady.

Now, more than before, he wanted her, but the yearning had changed. It was no longer the courtly love he had put to page as a youth of six and ten. He leaned against the arch of the tower door and closed his eyes, trying to bring back the words he had written, but never shown her. They would not come, but it mattered not. Those words were meant to impress a pretty girl.

His love was different now. Grown stronger like the man he was now. The man who wished not for a wife who brought just power or wealth, but for a woman who was a real help-mate. The man who hoped to find what his father had found in his mother. A true soul-mate. Deep within himself, in the place he shut away from the outside world, Jamie knew Sela could fulfill those desires.

On the way up the tower stairs, he considered that the war to win her would require multiple fronts. To win over his liege would be the easiest challenge. He could think of a number of ways to help King Henry see merit in the decision. To win over his mother was no small task, but it could be done. To win Sela's heart, however, would be his real battle. Though he was still a man of small wealth, he was a man of power. He directly served the King. Perhaps she thought herself beneath his notice. Perhaps she thought he idly toyed with her. He must find a way to show her the error of her thoughts. To show her that to him she was the world.

Bleddyn was laying a fire in the small brazier when Jamie entered.

"How long have you known Mistress Sela?"

"Why, almost since she came here, Master

Jamie. She and my sister came to be friends within the first month."

"I should like to meet your sister. Tell her what a fine job you are doing." Mayhap Bleddyn's sister could tell him something of Sela's mysterious past. Something that might help him gain her trust. "Might we visit your home?"

"'Tis no castle, but if you desire to go, certainly I will take you."

****

Sweet smelling smoke curled from a hole in the thatched roof of the small square cottage they faced. The rest of the houses on the row were like most others Jamie passed on the walk through the village; crowded close together, some even sharing a wall. But the house of Rhiana, the healer, stood in the middle of a large open plot, surrounded by a low stone wall.

Plants of all kinds, from twisted vines to tall fruit trees, filled the yard. A cluster of berry bushes surrounded the wooden door.

Bleddyn made a tisking sound and bent to retrieve a small basket resting beneath the bush nearest the door. The white petals of the fallen blossoms that should have littered the ground had been gathered up.

"Why she leaves it out I shall never ken." He shook his head. "She knows the birds steal the petals for nesting. These will barely make enough of the cure to get through the winter." Before he could knock, the door swung open.

The low door blocked Jamie's view of her face, but he could see the slim figure of a woman standing with her hands on her hips just the other side of the threshold.

"Bleddyn, what are ye doin' back here so soon? Did you make a cock-up of it already?" The brash words countered the musical voice.

60

"Nay, Rhi." Bleddyn shoved the basket into his sister's hands. "My master wished to meet my family. See where I live." The boy turned. "Sir James, this scold is my sister, Rhiana."

She stepped outside, revealing features clearly resembling her brother's though much more delicate. Unlike Bleddyn's curly red hair, hers was straight and raven black. "Your pardon, m'lord." She curtsied, then stepped back to allow them entry. "You are most welcome in our home."

"Thank you, Rhiana." Jamie had to bend to get through the door, but once inside, the room opened into a high ceiling.

Bleddyn set an elaborate chair by the hearth.

Jamie looked doubtfully at the thin branches that had been braided and bent into an ornate settle with a high back, but the only other seat was a stool that would have his knees to his chin. The wood creaked as he settled himself onto the chair, but it held his weight.

"Can I get you something, m'lord?" Rhiana had folded her hands neatly in front of her. Her tone was now quite proper. "The mead is not yet well aged, but I do have a bit of ale left in the barrel. Or I could brew a fresh elixir."

"Ale will do just fine, thank you."

She went through a door at the back of the room then returned carrying a short cup and a clay ewer. A flowery fragrance wafted toward him as she poured the bubbly beverage and handed it to him.

He took a sip. *Mmmm. A strong, pleasant taste.*

"No cup for me?" Bleddyn asked.

"You know where the barrel sets," his sister replied, no longer using her speaking-to-nobles tone.

Bleddyn snorted at her, but remained otherwise silent at Jamie's side.

"I ask your pardon, m'lord. The place is such a sight." She backed toward the hearth. "I am the village healer and tomorrow is market day."

"No need to apologize." He took a large gulp of the tasty brew. "You need to ensure you have all the necessary goods to ply your practice. I merely came to meet you. I fear I did not think to send word in advance of our coming." He drained the last bit in his cup. "This is quite good."

"Thank you, m'lord." She came forward and poured more.

"I am pleased with your brother's work. If you have no need of him at the moment, I should like to take him on for the time I am here. Shall we say room and board at the keep and earnings of two silver pieces per month?"

"M'lord, you are far too generous."

"Rhi," Bleddyn squeaked. "Do not disagree with my master. He knows my worth."

"You should be compensated for the loss of having his strong arm to help you." Jamie turned to the boy. "Your brother will give you half his earnings to put aside for any costs you might incur due to his absence."

The look on Bleddyn's face was not one of joy.

Jamie turned back to Rhiana. "And I think I shall be able to spare him to help you at market time."

"Thank you, m'lord, but you do not have to—"

"I insist. A man must fulfill his family duties. Is there something needs doing while he is here?"

"I suppose I could use help loading the cart for tomorrow's market."

"Be a good lad. Go do that for your sister."

Bleddyn looked between the two, and though his face twisted with distaste, he bowed and went to do the task.

"Please sit," Jamie said as she nervously fumbled with the edges of her apron. "Tell me how you came to be the healer in Cilgerran."

She sat and folded her hands in her lap. "Someone from Mother's side has been the healer 'round here as far back as any can remember. I inherited the gift of talking to the plants from her." She stirred a small cauldron that bubbled on the hearth and Jamie noticed her stature soften.

"When I was old enough, she showed me how to mix the herbs and make the powders, what leaves to use to heal a wound. When she died, 'twas then I took her place."

"I see you grow your herbs right here in the center of the village. Most healers I know gather their wares from the woods around the area."

"Aye, m'lord. Many do, but our family is different. The tale my grandmother told was that long ago our ancestors did search the forest for the 'helper plants.' But the prince of the forest plants fell in love with my namesake, the first Rhiana, and followed her home. Now, the plants choose to grow in the yard...to be near us. I know it sounds a silly story, but sometimes when I am out there tending them, I feel like...well, like they protect me."

"Your knowledge of healing must be impressive. Mistress Sela speaks highly of your skill."

"Mistress Sela is a fine healer in her own right."

"You have known each other quite a while, I have heard."

"Aye, m'lord. Nearly since the day she arrived."

"And you know each other well?"

"Well, enough." She leaned back and raised a brow.

"Then you know of her service with my mother."

"I know she is dedicated to your mother beyond measure. 'Twas what convinced many of us that Lord and Lady Cilgerran were worthy of *our* loyalty. For once, your King Henry sent someone wise and fair to govern us." She sat silent for a moment then added, "I meant no offense to his highness."

A smile pursed his lips. "I assure you none would be taken." In fact, after all the rebellion in the northern shires, he was sure the King would consider her words a compliment. But his real concern was how much Rhiana knew about Sela. How much would she tell? "Mistress Sela has been with our family for many years."

"So she said."

"Ah, she's told you of how she came to us?"

"Aye, she has."

"And of her family in Crecy?"

She straightened on the stool, but did not answer.

He could see her mind working and felt his opening slipping away. He leaned forward, hoping to maintain any advantage. "I am told you are closer to Sela than anyone."

"Nay." Her face suddenly set and she folded her arms across her chest. "There is one closer. Mayhap you should ask Lady Cilgerran about her."

He looked for a moment into her unwavering eyes, then leaned back in the chair. He would get nothing more from this source.

What dark secret could Sela have that no one was willing to even speak a word about it? He finished the ale in a single gulp. "Well, I suppose we should get back to the keep. 'Twas a pleasure to meet you." He stood and she did like. "I will take good care of your brother."

"Thank you, m'lord." She curtsied. "I am sure Bleddyn will take good care of you as well. I shall fetch him." She turned and went out through the back room.

Jamie walked around as he waited. He sniffed at the various bundles hanging from the hearth. He was unfamiliar with most of the herbs, but he did recognize the scent of heather, and another bunch smelled spicy-sweet, like Sela. Lavender.

Rhiana's angry voice stabbed through the air.

He went through to the second room. It was empty, save two cots and a small table. At the far end, a leather flap fell nearly to the floor, blocking the view through an opening.

Bleddyn answered his sister in like tone.

Though Jamie could not make out the words, the anger was apparent. Could his questions about Sela be the reason for this fight? Footsteps drew near, and he hurried back to the hearth.

When the two returned, Bleddyn carried a long bundle wrapped in woolen cloth and bound with a coarse woven rope. He looked uneasily at his sister.

She did not look pleased.

"What might this be?" Jamie nodded toward the mysterious bundle Bleddyn clutched to his chest.

"M'lord, may I take my sword with me?" The boy's eyes pleaded.

"I told him 'twould not be sensible to take the sword into the keep." Rhiana's stern frown showed her concern.

"You have a sword?" Jamie had not even thought to ask if Bleddyn had any training.

"Yes, m'lord."

"Let me see it."

Bleddyn carefully laid the bundle on the table between them. He untied the rope and folded back the cloth, revealing a well-wrought hilt and a quality leather scabbard.

A common man could not afford any steel, much less a weapon of this quality. "How did you come by such a sword?"

"'Twas our father's." The surety in the lad's voice evidenced his pride.

A pang of jealousy lanced through Jamie's heart. If only he could have *his* father's sword. He noted the awe in the eyes he met as he looked up.

"How could your father—"

"He made it." Bleddyn interrupted. "Father was the chief armorer to Cilgerran Castle."

"May I?" Jamie asked, honoring the unspoken rule regarding another man's weapon.

"Certainly, m'lord."

The blade sang the sweet note of well-honed steel as Jamie pulled it from the scabbard. It had been well cared for. Cleaned and the edge kept keen.

"Can you use it?"

"Aye, m'lord. Since I was old enough to hold a stick, Father taught me, and when he was killed, I kept on practicing with this sword. Every day."

Jamie could not deny to someone else the very thing he wanted so much for himself. "By all means, bring your sword."

Chapter Seven

The next day, when Sela came to get Marie after the mid-day meal, Jamie reminded her of their afternoon appointment. He managed to find a few flowers in an untended garden along the west wall and went to Genevieve, hopeful she could help turn the handful of small blossoms into something more presentable.

She produced a blue ribbon of silk and told him how to tie them into a posy, but as was her usual way, she made him do the work himself. She told him it was as easy as tying one's own lacings, but his large fingers were no match for the delicate fabric. Now, he sat on the steps of the great hall, nervously playing with the awkward-looking bow.

"Sir James."

He jumped to his feet and hid the flowers behind his back as Sela hurried toward him.

The afternoon had warmed nicely and she wore no cloak, merely a wine colored surcoat over a flaxen colored kirtle. His eye followed her long braid across her shoulder and over the curve of her bosom. The garter at her waist slightly nipped in the sides of her coat, barely revealing the curve of her hip. Simple and beautiful. Did she realize the effect she had on him?

"Please forgive my tardiness, my lord."

"I was beginning to think you changed your mind." He fingered the silk behind his back. A poor offering compared to her loveliness.

"I promised to come. I keep my promises. Brother Jacob was a bit late today."

"I see." He passed the flowers from one hand to the other. He wished he had not picked the damn things, but he could not get rid of them, now. May well just give them to her. He held out the small gathering of yellow, white, and blue. "A bouquet for a beautiful flower."

"Thank you, my lord." A rosy pink tinged her cheeks as she took the gift, but her voice was easy and light. No hint of worry.

"You are a native to France?" He knew for certain she came from Crecy. He just wanted to hear her speak.

"Yes my lord. I was born in France, but ...*Cymru ydy m addef.*"

The change to the more guttural sounding Welsh tongue caught Jamie off guard, but he knew *Cymru* was Wales and *addef* meant home. No wonder she had been able to go amongst the traitors without difficulty. Her Welsh flowed as easily as that of the guards around the keep.

"Shall we go, my lord?" She easily slipped into back into French as she put the flowers in the basket she carried.

"Aye, mistress." He offered his arm.

She smiled and laid her hand lightly on the sleeve of his tunic. "Thank you, my lord."

"Thank *you*, mistress, for your time."

No longer quite so nervous, Jamie turned toward the front gate—wondering if the day could become any more pleasant.

****

Sela waved as she and Jamie passed by the shop of the cooper. Bridget, the barrel maker's wife, stopped her sweeping long enough to wave back, but a customer walked up before they could cross the road to speak and she hustled the man inside.

They continued through the narrow streets of the village, and she introduced Jamie to all who stopped her. Most showed due respect to "Lady Cilgerran's son," but a few of the more common folk spoke as familiars. No matter how he was greeted, he took it well and each person was left on good terms. Finally, they reached the village center.

Farmers, merchants, and tradesmen packed the wide, open space around the well, leaving just enough room for prospective customers to wander through and find what they needed. Sela searched among the farm wives selling vegetables they had grown, and the tradesmen fixing a cauldron or mending a boot. From a distance, she spied a tall, thin woman holding out a piece of green cloth to a customer just beginning to show the impending birth of a child.

"Wyn!" Sela shouted over the noise of the crowd.

Her friend looked up and smiled, then turned back to her customer.

Sela looked over her shoulder at Jamie. "If you mind not, I have a special errand to take care of for my lady."

He smiled and the dimples graced his face. "Please. Whatever you need do, mistress. To disrupt your customary market day was never my intent."

They wove through the crowd to Wyn's cart. Sela looked through the lengths of linen and wool laid out, while the weaver finished collecting payment from the woman who decided to buy the green cloth.

The hairs on her arm suddenly stood to attention like the yeomen of the guard. A quick look around and her eye fell on a man standing three carts down. His ice-blue eyes stared at her, intent and focused.

She knew those eyes, but she could not think where she had seen them. She thought she knew most everyone in the village, but she did not recognize him. He pretended to be a serf, though he was not. His clothes were too clean. Too new. And his beard was too well shaped.

"Hello, my girl." Wyn grabbed her shoulders and kissed both her cheeks.

Sela peeked over Wyn's shoulder as they hugged, but the red-haired man had vanished. Before she could wonder further, the weaver turned her attention to Jamie.

"Well, then." Wyn's eye roamed down from his face to his middle then up again to his chest. "Who'd be your fine looking companion, dear?"

Sela blushed. Wyn was a terrible tease. Always trying to match Sela up with every man they passed on the street. She cleared her throat to get Wyn's attention. "My lord, Sir James Barnard, might I introduce Maudwyn merch Griffydd, of the weaver's house."

"Oh, my..." Wyn clumsily dropped to one knee, steadying herself with her hand on her leg. The din around fell silent as everyone nearby turned to stare. "I beg yer pardon m'lord."

Sela hid a smile behind her hand—it was now Wyn's turn to blush.

Jamie took the hand draped across Wyn's knee. "A pleasure," he said. As he had done at least a dozen times that day, he kissed her hand then helped her stand. The noise closed about them as everyone turned back to their own business.

"Wyn is the best weaver in the shire," Sela bragged. "She can make any kind of cloth, from the sturdiest wool, so tightly woven as to shed water, to linen so soft it feels like silk."

Wyn laughed at the compliment. "Mi Da' would have somethin' to say 'bout that."

"Your father has not worked in almost two years now," Sela said. "Surely he would not have given his loom over to you if you were not good enough."

"He did na' have much choice in the matter. His

70

hands said no to the loom, so now he just stands over me jawin' while I work. But, I know you did na' come to hear me wailin'."

"You finished it?" Sela eagerly leaned forward.

"Indeed I did." From the bottom of a pile at the back of the cart, Wyn pulled a bundle wrapped in linen and tied with un-dyed wool yarn. "Here it be."

Sela could hardly wait as she undid the yarn and folded back the linen, revealing a stunning length of brocade. She rubbed her hand over the cream-colored cloth. Intricately woven embossed flowers had been hand painted golden yellow with green centers. "Oh, Wyn! 'Tis the most beautiful piece I have ever seen."

"Indeed." Jamie's deep voice interrupted her reverie. "'Tis very pretty. I cannot say I have ever seen better, even on the ladies of the King's court."

"Thank ye, m'lord." Wyn wobbled through a curtsey, but her smile was big enough to bridge a moat.

"Should you ever wish to make your fortune, I know several court ladies who would pay very well to have you as their exclusive cloth maker."

"I do na think I shall be leavin' Cilgerran, m'lord, but I thank ye for the offer."

Sela re-wrapped the beautiful fabric. She could never afford such exquisite cloth. Aside from which she had no reason to wear such a dress. Perhaps Lady Amye would like it. She sighed and handed the bundle back to Wyn. "This one is beautiful, but I need another piece. Lady Marie's birthday is coming soon. My lady would like for her to have her first surcoat."

"Ah. I think I know just the thing. Where is it now?" Wyn counted through the stacks until she found the one she wanted. She flipped over the pile and held up a piece of finely textured dark green cloth with yellow and white lilies sewn into the borders. "There is no other like it."

"Your weaving ever amazes me," Sela said as she ran her fingers over the cloth. It was smooth like silk, yet thick like wool. A perfect choice for the overdress. "How do you make such a heavy fabric so soft and fine?"

"Tis the thread. My brother wanted to try spinning linen fibers with the wool. The threads were thick, but wonderful' smooth and easy to bend into a heavy damask. But he only made enough for this one piece."

"The family Gryffydd are all involved with clothmaking," Sela explained to Jamie. "The two oldest brothers grow flax and sheep. Delwin is a master spinner. Wyn here weaves the threads into cloth and her twin brother Lyn makes the most wonderful dyes. Think you your sister might like this, my lord?"

When he did not answer, she looked back to find him staring attentively at her. She repeated her question. "My lord, think you this will suit Lady Marie?"

He turned his eyes to the cloth Wyn held outstretched at arm's length. "Yes, 'tis fine work." He reached for his pouch. "How much do you want for it?"

"Nay, my lord." Wyn shook her head. "'Twould be an honor to make this a gift."

Jamie could hardly believe what he heard. A merchant giving away her wares? Mother had said something about how the village folk adored Marie. The look of pure joy in Wyn's eyes as she folded the cloth was proof.

"It must have been meant for our Lady Marie." Wyn held out the fabric like a foreign ambassador presenting an offering to the King. "There is not enough of it to make anythin' fit for a grown person."

"The house of Cilgerran thanks you." He bowed

in acceptance. He was not truly a relation to Lord Cilgerran, but such loyalty made him proud to be akin to the family in any way. "Perhaps Mistress Sela could select something my mother would like?"

Sela nodded and began looking through the bolts of fabric. She bent over the cart and her hips stood out nicely rounded against her tunic. The creamy white bottom he imagined beneath the offending cloth stiffened his cock until it strained against the lacings of his braes. He looked away, glad he had worn his surcoat.

She straightened, holding two bolts of fabric. "My lady might like either of these very much."

"Excellent." He reached in the pouch and pulled out two silver pieces. "This should cover both." He handed the coins and Marie's gift back to the weaver. "Please have everything delivered to the keep when the market is done."

The extravagance of his payment had the desired effect. She smiled and bowed twice. "Aye, m'lord. Thank you." She would certainly remember his generosity should he approach her for information about Sela in the future.

"Come, mistress." He offered his arm to Sela. "I promised to have you back before supper and we have barely begun."

****

Jamie could not have gotten more satisfaction from their day at the market. She asked his opinion as they selected fabric, fruits, and boots. They bought healing herbs from Rhiana to replenish the castle stocks, and Sela helped him pick out a small gift for Marie's upcoming birthday. All things that reminded him of family.

More importantly, he got a chance to see her among the people of the village. She showed kindness and respect to every person they spoke with. In return, they respected her—not just because of her position, but because she was a caring person. Just like they respected his mother. As they walked up the hill toward the castle, he recalled the look of pride on her face as she introduced him. Especially to those she seemed to consider her friends.

As much as he was physically attracted to Sela, even more, he wanted her to feel safe and happy. As she had been with the people in the market today. He would do anything to keep her safe, but could she be happy with him?

He could be happy with her. Each day on waking, he imagined what she would look like lying there next to him. Each moment alone, he wished he was with her. Each time he saw her, he wanted to know her thoughts. "May I?" He offered his hand as they approached the tall steps leading to the drawbridge.

She looked at his upturned hand and then to his eyes. Her lips parted, as if considering whether or not to accept his simple offer.

"Fear not, mistress." He held his breath, thinking she might leave him standing there, looking the fool.

"I do not fear you, my lord. You have been naught but kind to me since the day we first met." She reached out and grasped his fingers.

Relief burst the chain binding his chest. He thought back, trying to remember that first day...

"What do you there?" Jamie questioned the thin slip of a girl cowering before him.

"I am sorry, sir." Her head tilted forward, hiding her eyes. Wind ruffled wisps of red-brown hair, escaped from the two braids looped on either side of her head.

"And what have you done to be sorry for?"

"I seem to be lost, sir." She looked like a scared rabbit cornered by a hawk. "My lady bade me go to the kitchen and bring her back something to eat...but

I seem to have lost my way."

Jamie shook his head. *"Come."* He took her hand and walked. *"I shall show you how to find your way."* He pulled the girl along behind him until they reached the courtyard. *"Look up."* Jamie pointed to the sky, but the little rabbit continued to keep her eyes on the ground. He slid his finger beneath her chin and lifted it.

Breath caught in his throat as the bluest eyes he had ever seen stared back at him from a perfect, oval face. He nearly forgot what he was going to say as he stared into those blue, blue eyes.

"Look up toward the sun," he finally uttered.

She lifted her eyes skyward and he continued.

"In the morning, the sun is toward the gate. After noontide, 'tis toward the kitchens. Since 'tis late in the day, we walk toward the sun to get to the kitchens."

"Thank you, sir. You have surely saved me from a beating."

He looked at her in disbelief. *"No one here will beat you, little rabbit. I will not allow it! Whom do you serve?"*

"Why, Lady Jehanne."

Jamie laughed aloud. *"My sister will not harm you."* He took her hand and continued toward the kitchen.

She hurried her steps instead of dragging behind him.

"Jehanne likes to believe she is already in charge of the household."

"But my sisters said the English are monsters and savages and that I would come running back home once I saw them," the girl said as she ran behind him.

Jamie stopped and turned.

She crashed into him with a huff.

"Do I look like a monster?"

"Nay." *She lowered her eyes again. "I suppose not."*

"*I am English. I am a Norman Englishman.*" *He pounded his fist to his heart. "Like my father and his father and his father before him. At the root, we come from the same place as you." He stood tall and puffed out his chest. "We are civilized unlike the Saxons and Picts."*

She looked up. A shy smile and a twinkle in the blue eyes brightened her face.

Jamie swallowed hard.

"*Aside from which, Mother would never allow anyone to beat a servant," he continued, though the lump in his throat still stuck tight. He suddenly felt uncomfortable. He had never been nervous with the servants before. What charm did this little girl cast over him? He continued walking, no longer holding her hand, though in truth he very much wanted to continue. "Jehanne is just trying to frighten you."*

She silently followed after him.

They arrived at the kitchen door and feeling more in control, he turned to her. "What is your name, little rabbit?"

"*Sela.*"

He repeated the name. It rolled smoothly from his tongue. Sounded pleasing to his ear. "I am Jamie. Come, Sela. Genevieve will give you a tray."

****

The memory brought a smile to his lips. He had forgotten that first pet name he called her. They reached the bridge and she released his hand.

An urgency to know everything about her pulsed within him, but he could not find anyone who would tell him anything he did not already know. The only way he was going to find out was to ask. Here was his chance—before they crossed to the gate. If he kept his distance, under the eyes of the guards at the far side of the bridge, this would appear just a simple conversation between a noble and a servant.

"Mistress?" He called as she started to step onto the wooden planks.

She turned toward him. "Aye, my lord?"

He folded his arms across his chest and leaned back, but his voice pleaded with her. "Please, Sela, will you not tell me of your past?"

She lowered her eyes. "You know most all of it. For me, life truly started when I came to Edensmouth."

"I seem to recall once long ago you spoke of sisters. Do you not miss them?"

She turned and started across the bridge. "I have not seen them since I left my father's house. Barnard became my family, and now, Cilgerran. I try not to think about my life in Crecy. It was not..." She stopped walking just as she stopped speaking. "...pleasant." The word shot from her mouth like a stone from a sling. She hurried across the drawbridge into the list.

He hastened to catch up and stopped her with a hand at her elbow. "My apologies. I did not wish you to recall unpleasant memories."

"I must see to Marie." She started through the tunnel to the courtyard, but he took her hand and drew her back.

He lightly brushed his lips against her knuckles. "Thank you for showing me the village today."

"'Twas a pleasure, my lord." She curtsied and as suddenly as she had shut down, a smile brightened her face, just as it had those many years ago. "Good day, my lord."

He gazed after her until she disappeared from view. He was beginning to see traits of both his father and his mother in himself. His mother was a strong woman. Yet, Father had said he never once regretted the decision to take her as wife.

Sela was a strong woman. She must be to serve

his sister, Jehanne, then his mother, and now Marie as well.

Mother was tenacious. Never giving up until she had what she wanted.

He would be tenacious, too. He would win Sela's heart. He would break through her wall or lose himself in the endeavor.

Chapter Eight

The midday meal was close at hand, when two men wearing mail shirts and carrying helmets marched into the great hall. Sela recognized them as vassals of Cilgerran. She moved closer, hoping to better hear their news.

Lady Amye put aside the plans she reviewed with the architect and waved them forward.

"My lady," The two knelt before her. "We bring word—"

"Hold." She turned to the architect. "Master Duncan, please make the alterations we agreed upon. We shall continue anon." She signaled for Sela to come closer and whispered in her ear. "Please find my son and ask him to come to my chamber."

"Right away, my lady."

Jamie had come for Marie just after morning mass. Most likely they would still be in the list. But before she left the hall, she watched Lady Amye lead the messengers out the back portal. What news did they bring?

She hurried through the tunnel in the curtain wall and over to the makeshift riding ring. Lady Amye's warning clung near the edges of her consciousness. Since market day, she had avoided Jamie except when her duties required she see him. Yet no matter how much she tried to bury the old feelings, every time she was near him they seemed to sprout like snow drops after the first spring thaw.

He stood in the center of the ring of hay bales, his back to her. The dark hair curled at his neck drew her eye to his broad shoulders and muscular back, calling forth the seedlings of desire she so recently buried.

He turned to follow Marie's progress as she galloped around the circle. The moment their eyes met his serious concentration changed to that ruinous smile, razing her meager wall of protection to the ground.

In the warmth of the early summer morning, he had tossed his tunic aside. The white linen of his gonelle came just to mid-thigh, showing red chausses covering muscular legs. The sweat-moistened cloth clung to his torso and outlined the ripples of his muscular belly.

The day suddenly seemed warmer, and she wiped the back of her hand across her brow.

"How may I serve you, mistress?" He shouted.

She had nearly forgotten why she sought him out. She drew a deep breath, hoping to calm the drumming in her chest. "Your lady mother wishes to see you in her chamber at once."

He nodded then turned back toward the pair circling the yard. "Walk him to let him cool," he shouted to Marie. "Then care for him."

Her gallop slowed to a trot.

"Mistress Sela will help you."

Marie reined the pony to a stop then slid from his back.

Jamie trotted to the opening then reached to pick up his tunic. His fingers brushed over her hand as it rested on the hay. "I hope you do not mind." He smiled at her again.

So easily she could get lost in that smile. "No, my lord. I mind not at all." The lush, deep voice that came from her throat surprised her, and she quickly lowered her eyes to avoid his reaction.

"Thank you." He pulled on his tunic, then turned and left.

She rubbed the spot on her hand that he had

touched, looking after him until his powerful frame disappeared through the tunnel.

Marie approached, leading the pony. "Where did Jamie go?"

"He had to go and see your mother." The slow clop of the pony's feet had the calming effect that she was unable to bring about on her own. "You are an excellent rider," she said as they continued around the ring.

"I love to ride the most of anything I do." A spring of excitement bubbled from Marie. "Jamie says that mayhap in a week or two I might give an exposition for Mama and Papa."

"Your mother and father will be very proud. You ride so well."

They walked the ring a few more times before Marie turned toward the stable. The stalls were newly cleaned and smelled of fresh hay.

"Would you like me to help you?" Sela offered.

"No, no. I can do it." Marie brought a stool and a currier's brush. She set the stool near the pony's backside and climbed up. "Jamie showed me how."

She began to brush the russet colored rump. She needed both hands to keep the brush steady, but by the time she finished, his coat shone like polished brass. She jumped down and moved the stool to work on his plump, round middle.

Jamie had taught Marie much in just a week's time. Clearly, he loved his sister very much. He spent more time with her than most men would give to a child. Sela could envision him teaching his own children to ride. She could imagine him telling his sons stories of conquest, teaching his daughters to dance...just like he had taught *her* to dance...

The harvest feast at Edensmouth was splendid. To sit and eat with all the nobles was more than Sela had ever expected, but apparently Lady Barnard insisted on gathering everyone to share in the bounty of the season. Now everyone was enjoying entertainments hired for the feast.

She peeked out from the alcove as Jamie danced a reel with one of the farmers' daughters. He was so good he made the gangly girl look like a princess. The bright, lively music ended, and he made a wide sweep with his arm as he bowed.

Sela sighed. Time to go back to the room. The feast was a grand time, but she had best be there and ready when the young mistress returned.

"Where are you going, little rabbit? I have been looking for you since supper ended."

She stopped, but did not turn around. "I must prepare my mistress' bed, Master Jamie."

The music began again. A slow courtly dance.

He put his hand on her shoulder.

She tried not to stiffen at his touch, but her shoulder lifted, shrugging off a hand that had shown her naught but kindness.

"We have not even had one dance," he said.

Currents of panic swirled in her stomach like eddies around rocks in a river. Of all the things she had learned in her father's house, dancing was not one of them.

"Oh, no, Master Jamie. 'Twould not be right to dance with you. You being a noble and all."

"'Tis the intent of this whole affair that we nobles get to know our people. Let me get to know you, little rabbit. Come dance with me."

She turned toward him, but could not look up.

"I should like to dance with you very much, Master Jamie, but...I fear I know not how."

He laughed, but it was not a cruel laugh. It made her feel comfortable and her melancholy instantly lifted.

"Is that all that is stopping you? Come, then." He took her hand and started toward the hall. "I will teach you."

"No." *She pulled her hand from his and wrapped her fingers tightly around a handful of her kirtle.* "I could not."

"Why not? You said you would like to dance with me, did you not?"

"I am not fitly dressed. I would not want to shame you."

"You look beautiful."

Hardly. The borrowed dress was much too large and the coarse material was anything but beautiful. She shook her head, hoping he would give up and leave her be.

The music started again.

"This is an easy song," *he said.* "If I taught you this time, would you dance with me next song?"

She should have known. Jamie Barnard was not wont to give up on anything he started. No way presented itself to get out of this dance. "All right."

He took both her hands. "First you bow to your partner. That would be me."

Sela bowed as she had seen him do many times.

"No, no." *His laughter filled her ears and she frowned.*

"You should curtsy. A bow for a girl is a curtsy." *He curtsied like the funny court jester who entertained during dinner.*

Sela giggled and curtsied, best as she could.

"Now step to the center with your right foot..."

When they finally swirled around the dance floor that night, it was the most wonderful thing she had ever done. That was the moment she first fell in love with Jamie Barnard.

Marie finished brushing the pony's mane and jumped down from the stool. She brought the specially made cover from the peg by the door and fastened it around his neck. Three falcons, representing the Cilgerran family, were stitched onto the crimson cloth. She stroked each bird with

83

her small hand, then threw her arms around the pony's shaggy neck and kissed him. "You are such a fine boy, Falconer."

The little horse nuzzled her ear and gave a snort.

Marie giggled and picked up two buckets from the head of the stall. "My friend says grain and water, please." She headed off toward the grain trough.

The groom had left a mound of fresh hay after cleaning out the stall. The pony snapped up a mouthful and started to chew.

Sela patted his rump and leaned against the wall. "You are a fine boy indeed," she whispered, but she was not talking about Falconer.

****

Jamie climbed the tower stairs by twos. He had seen two men pass through the list and wondered what gave rise to their serious demeanor. He knocked and waited to be admitted. The door was opened by a tall, muscular man. Mother sat at the table with a man of similar build and face, but much older.

"Good, my son. Sela was able to find you quickly. Sir James Barnard, this is Balstaff and his son, Godwin."

Balstaff stood and each man crossed his right arm over his heart.

Jamie returned their salute.

"They bring word of my lord's return." Her smile showed relief, but her violet eyes flashed with sparks of concern.

"'Tis good news," Jamie said, cautioned by her glance to guard his comments.

"My lady," Balstaff began, "his lordship is nearly four days ride away. But now that we know where our enemy will be, we can cut this blight from our midst."

"Truly we must if we are to survive." She sat silent a moment, tapping her knuckle gently against her lip, stirring the cauldron of her mind until a plan bubbled to the surface. She turned suddenly to the two knights.

"I thank you for bringing word to me. Go now and refresh yourselves. We are but an hour from the mid-day meal. Our ranks will be gladdened when we announce my lord's return." She waited until their footsteps retreated down the stairs before she spoke again.

"I want you to take charge of the garrison until my husband returns."

"But what of Wil?" Jamie had no desire to usurp his friend's position.

"I have no complaint with William..." She poured a bit of water into her ink pot and stirred it vigorously. "...but you are a far stronger commander in battle."

"Battle?"

She pulled a sheet of vellum from a stack on the table, dipped her quill into the ink, and wrote a few words. "Besides which," she continued, "I have other things for William to do. Though he is a good knight, he has turned out to be an even better administrator." She continued to scribble as she talked.

"When he returns to Evermoor, he will be a balanced leader. Well formed both for times of war and times of peace."

She wrote a few more lines, then nodded her head. "I need you both for what you do best." She blotted the parchment and dusted it before dripping a pool of crimson wax on it. She pulled the chain that held her signet from around her neck and pressed the ring into the soft wax. She read over what she had written once more, then handed him the document.

An order appointing him commander of the garrison troops and—he looked up. "Mother, are you certain of this?" The order also granted him charge of the castle affairs and guardianship of Marie should anything happen to her husband.

"More than certain. 'Tis important that some clear line of command and succession be established. Your father taught me that when we first married. A house without a ruler is a house doomed to fall. Marie is the key to succession here. I see how much you love your sister. You will not let anything happen to her."

"Should not Lord Cilgerran have some say in it?"

"We have discussed it. My lord trusts my wisdom in this matter. You are the best choice to be castellan until the King decides otherwise. My lord may make any change he desires when he returns."

"Very well. What would you have of me?"

****

Sweat flew from Jamie's hands as he swung around and brought his sword down against his opponent. A loud clang rang out as Wil caught the blow on his own blade and knocked it aside.

"Assure that our troops are ready," had been Mother's only request. The task was not difficult. The men were well trained, but he had spent the last two days enhancing their skills.

Jamie reached out with his free hand and grabbed Wil's sword hand, but Wil spun around and hooked his leg behind Jamie's calf. A quick pull sent both men sprawling to the ground and Wil landed with his back on Jamie's chest. An elbow to Jamie's side ended the exercise. Wil's hand-to-hand combat had improved.

Jamie took the extended hand and Wil pulled him to his feet. He could not recall Wil had ever beaten him. He hoped the awkwardness he felt was well hidden as he addressed the men circled around them. "So you see 'tis just a matter of speed and balance for a smaller man to overcome a larger one."

The men of the garrison stood, arms crossed on their chests, and silently nodded.

He could not see any disdain on their faces, but he shouted an order so they would not have too much time to think on Wil's victory. "Pair off and practice."

They immediately turned and began trying to throw each other to the ground using the demonstrated technique.

He watched their attempts for a bit, before he turned to Wil. "That was a new trick. Where did you learn that one?"

Wil beamed. "Lord Cilgerran showed me. I shall be pleased to let him know his teachings have been put to good use."

Jamie's estimation of his mother's husband improved. Strange that a troubadour should have such skills. A lot of questions remained to be answered about Lord Cilgerran.

He exchanged his sword for the towel Bleddyn held out, wiped the sweat from his chest and arms, then pulled on the tunic the boy gave him.

He took back the sword and sheathed it. "Thank you." He started toward the garrison, but then turned back to Bleddyn.

The young man had been in service nearly a month. He was never far from Jamie's side and never had to be asked twice for anything. He was a good lad.

Jamie made a decision. "Get your sword."

The boy's face lit up.

"Should we be besieged," Jamie continued, "we shall need every hand. Show me what you can do with your weapon."

"Aye, my lord." Bleddyn hurried off toward the tower.

Jamie wandered over to the archery range and to his surprise, the lauded Welsh archers stood watching his mother take aim at the target. She let the arrow fly and it hit the mark, nearly digging the entire way through the narrow straw bale. The archers nodded and murmured at their lady's prowess with a bow.

"Would you like to try, my son?" She held out the weapon.

He took the small bow and looked at it from all sides trying to discern what made it so powerful. When he drew back the bowstring the pull was so light he thought the weapon would crack in his hands, but the wood held. He released and it snapped back with a powerful twang. "What tree gives such a fine weapon?"

"Welsh Elm," she said, her eyes a twinkle with pride.

He fitted an arrow to the string and drew back. His shot hit just to the left of hers, missing the center mark by a few inches. He tried again, this time hitting to the right. The third shot came as close to hers as it could without splitting her arrow.

The archers again nodded their approval.

"Good shooting, my son! You have not lost your touch."

He handed her the bow. It was a fine weapon. No wonder the Welsh chose arrow over sword. Yet as they turned to walk across the list, he had to speak his concern. "You have so many archers, Mother. Not many infantry."

"Warfare is much different here. The gnarled land makes open battle difficult, so most fighting is done with archers or spearmen."

It seemed a cowardly way to Jamie.

"'Tis more practical," she said, seeming to respond to his unspoken thought.

He tucked the information away with the other

things he had learned about his Welsh troops. He knew now the preferred strategy was to strike and run unless they heavily outnumbered the enemy. With half of the men gone with Lord Cilgerran, the castle was short of protection.

For the last four months, Wil had drilled the men every day except the Sabbath, and all the soldiers, whether swordsman, spearman, archer or infantry seemed fit and ready to fight. The only thing that seriously worried him was their lack of horsemen. Even in wooded terrain, a well-trained cavalry could provide an advantage.

Bleddyn returned, the sword belted at his waist. He bowed to Jamie, then to Lady Amye.

"What have you there, Bleddyn?" She gestured toward the sword.

"My lord has asked to see my sword skills."

"Has he?" She smiled at Jamie, then stepped back to join the circle of fighters forming around the two swordsmen.

Jamie drew his sword and took a stance. "Well then, squire, lay on."

Chapter Nine

The waning moon sat low on the horizon, barely brightening the sky to the east. Footsteps of the guards walking the far parapet echoed off the walls of the keep.

Jamie looked out past the bulwark, past the village, past the tall growth of trees. He had walked the entire circuit of the battlement three times—trying to discern from which direction an attack might come. With Cilgerran land surrounded by thick, heavy woodlands, the enemy could come from any direction except the river. The village would be vulnerable no matter what.

To bring everyone within the castle walls would be the ideal, but unlike Edensmouth, Cilgerran Castle was too small for everyone to stay inside for long. Nor could enough supplies be gathered to feed everyone during a long siege. Even without the villagers, the enemy could starve the castle into submission within a few weeks.

Food. That was the answer. That was how the enemy would attack if he were smart. Somehow, the fields had to be protected.

He started toward the stairs but a figure standing on the platform stopped him.

Sela.

He would recognize her anywhere.

A soft breeze ruffled her hair. Undone, it fell like a cloak down her back. She stood staring out at the River Tiefi. What did she ponder so deeply?

"Are you not chilled, mistress?"

She turned and curtsied. "No, my lord. I am well

warmed." She drew her cloak tighter around her shoulders.

"Might I join you?" He stepped closer.

"Certainly, my lord."

He stood beside her and looked out toward the rushing river. "Do you come here often?"

"When I need to think. 'Tis peaceful this time of night and the river shares its wisdom with me."

"And what wisdom does the river give you tonight?" The moonlight kissed her lips and despite Mother's words nagging at the edge of his mind, he wanted to kiss them, too. "Does it tell you how beautiful you are?"

"No, my lord. I am not beautiful." She turned from the water and pressed her back against the tall stone of the merlon. She turned her face away and her hair hid her beauty from him. "I am just a plain, common woman."

He moved to stand in front of her, a hand to either side of her shoulders. "Sela, you must know I think you beautiful." He pulled back the tapestry of soft hair and tucked it behind her ear. "I always have."

Her eyes were closed. "No, my lord. You cannot think such."

He leaned closer. His lips touched her temple. A scent like a field of lavender filled his nose. "Ah my sweet, but I do," he whispered. He turned her face to him and gently pressed his lips to hers.

Sela did not want him to look into the depths of her soul and see the secrets she kept, so she closed her eyes. He could never know how much she wanted his kiss. How she longed for his touch.

"See. 'Twas not so bad, little rabbit."

Little rabbit. She had forgotten the childhood name he had called her, but she did remember the first time he'd kissed her...

"Leave her alone, Jehanne!" Jamie yelled at his

*older sister. "Mother will punish you for shouting at
the servants."*

*"She is my maid, Jamie. I shall do what I
please."*

*Sela stood frozen behind Jamie. In the year she
had been the young lady's maid, she had been
severely scolded more than once, but she had never
been struck. This felt different. She had never seen
her mistress so angry before.*

*"She broke my necklace." Lady Jehanne held up
a broken strand of beads. "She must be punished."*

*"It was an accident." Jamie turned. "Was it not,
Sela?"*

*"Yes, mistress. I am so, so, sorry," Sela
stammered as she peeked over his shoulder.*

*Lady Jehanne's face was redder than the
summer roses blooming in the garden.*

*Tears welled in Sela's eyes. "I did not mean to
break—"*

*A very un-ladylike curse flew from Lady
Jehanne's mouth as she lunged toward them.*

*Jamie pushed his sister aside and grabbed Sela's
hand.*

*The last thing Sela saw as he pulled her from the
room was her mistress fallen on the floor clutching a
half-empty strand of beads.*

*They ran until she thought she could not run
anymore. He helped her climb to the top of the castle's
small Western tower and pushed open a hidden door.
They crawled out onto the pinnacle.*

*She peeked over the wall, and her breath caught
in her throat. She had never been so high before. She
could see past the far side of the castle, but when she
looked down, the base of the tower rushed up at her,
and she backed away from the edge. Right into
Jamie.*

"Fear not, little rabbit," he whispered in her ear.

"But we are so high up."

"'Tis safe enough. I come here all the time." He took her hand and led her to the outward facing side of the tower.

Sun drenched land spread out before her, and a cool breeze tickled her cheeks. When she glanced down this time, the River Eden looked like a small stream.

"No one remembers this place is even here, except me." He sat down and leaned back against the slanted roof. "And now you."

She nervously shifted from one foot to the other. All she could think of was Lady Jehanne sprawled on the floor with her beads scattered around her.

"Sit down." Jamie leaned forward and patted the space next to him. "'Tis not so high from down here."

"I must go. My lady is already angry with me. She will flay me alive if I stay away."

"No harm will come to you, my little rabbit. Did I not promise the first day we met?"

He had watched over her. Helped her when she struggled with her tasks. Sela nodded.

"Have I ever spoken false to you?"

"Not as I know of."

"Then sit. We shall give Jehanne a chance to calm herself. Then we can go to Mother and explain what happened. All right?"

She smiled then eased down next to him. "How did you find this place?"

"I needed some place to get away. Somewhere to think."

"What do you think about?"

"I think about being a third son." He lay back against the roof again and looked off into the sky. "My eldest brother is first in line to be granted Edensmouth. My second brother will get to buy lordship of the lands left to my mother by my grandfather. There will be nothing left for me but to be a steward to one or the other of my brothers...or to *go into the church."*

"Would that be so bad?"

He sat up and looked straight at her. "My brother John is an insufferable fool. I could never serve him. Peter is not nearly as bad, but—" He lay back again and folded his arms behind his head. "And I think I would hate the church. So many rules. And the vows. Chastity, obedience, poverty—of course as I will have nothing, I would not be giving up much." He sighed dramatically, and Sela giggled.

They lay silent a long while, gazing at the clouds drifting by. Suddenly, he turned toward her. Cupping his chin in his hand, he stared at her and smiled.

She laced her fingers over her belly and nervously rolled her thumbs. "What is it?" she asked.

He stared a moment more. "May I kiss you?"

She had been kissed before, but in her father's house no one asked. They just did it. But she liked Jamie. She did not think she would mind if he kissed her. "Yes, you may kiss me."

He leaned toward her and gently placed his lips on hers.

It was nice. Not like the hard, wet, sloppy brothel kisses.

He did it again, this time a bit longer.

Her heart beat faster. She liked his gentle kisses. Wanted them. To feel his lips linger on hers raised a fire within her unlike anything she ever felt. She touched his face, then unbidden, her arms wrapped around his neck.

His arm slipped around her waist and he pulled her tight against him.

Suddenly Sela felt something she never felt before. For the first time since leaving her father's house, she wanted to let a man touch her. She wanted Jamie Barnard to hold her close.

No! Remembering herself, she pushed him away

and sat up. "We must go, my lord. I should apologize to my lady and face the consequences."

He sat up, too. "I have gone too far." He took her hand. "I apologize, little rabbit."

On the way back they spoke not a word. The punishment given for the broken necklace was minor compared to the punishment Sela gave herself. She denied herself the pleasure of ever kissing Jamie Barnard again...

This time he was not asking, but Sela wanted this kiss. The sound of the wind swirled around the merlon, but she could not feel it. His warm body pressed against her, shielding her from the cold. Though the touch of his lips was gentle, he kissed her like a man savoring a feast. Tasting first her lips, then the line along her jaw, and the skin at the curve of her neck. She shivered as his breath tickled the sensitive place behind her ear.

"You are cold, my sweet." He took her hand and started toward the stairs. "Come, let us—"

"No!" Sela yanked her hand from his and backed away. "I cannot, Jamie." She had not called him Jamie since that day on the rooftop. Since the day she had dammed away her love for him.

"Why, Sela? We used to share something special. Do you no longer like me?"

No. She did not *like* him—she *loved* him. Tears breached the rims of her eyes and rolled down her cheeks. No longer able to stand the pain, she sobbed, pushed past him, and ran down the stairs.

Jamie looked down the dark staircase until he could no longer hear her footsteps.

She was crying. The tears on her cheeks sparkled in the moonlight, and her sobs still rang in his ears.

He cursed and pounded his fist against the stone wall. She must despise him now. Yet, he had felt the passion in their kiss.

What stood between them? His thoughts turned back to the past that no one would speak of. He had to find out what had happened to her. He would not need to worry about convincing his mother or the King if he could not break through her wall and claim her as his own.

Chapter Ten

The sound of a distant horn pulled Jamie from a restless sleep into the darkness of his room. For two nights, the kiss, the tears, her sobs, had woven through fitful dreams that brought no rest. The horn sounded again and he snapped awake...

The attack had begun.

He sat up and shook his head to clear the fog from his mind. Light cleared his vision.

Bleddyn had lit the lamps and now held up the first piece of armor.

"Good man." Jamie stood, pleased with the rapid response. Since taking the boy as his squire, Jamie had taught him how to help quickly put on the armor. An easy task since Bleddyn already knew each piece and its purpose.

Enough men had been gathered to form three fronts. Confident in his mother's trust of the two knights, Balstaff and two dozen men were already on the west side of the village. Godwin and another two dozen stood ready in the eastern facing fields. They hid in the farmers' huts, waiting either for Lord Cilgerran's return or for the enemy's attack. It was not much of a defense, but it would have to do. Everyone else was on high alert within the castle walls.

Before Jamie pulled on his gauntlets, he patted Bleddyn's shoulder. The squire had proved a good swordsman. His father had taught him well. Jamie wished there was time to find suitable armor for the boy to wear. They would have to take care of that soon. "Stay here, squire."

"But, Sir James—" Since taking the squire's oath, the boy had refused to use anything but a proper title.

"I am sorry, boy. You have no armor. I need my squire alive, not dead. Stay here."

"My sister and my friends are out *there*, my lord. They will think me a coward if I stay inside the tower."

Jamie frowned and gave a sigh. He had not the time to argue. He hardened his face, but inside a smile slipped into his thoughts. "Find Lady Marie. Protect her. If anything happens to her, it will mean your hide."

"Yes, Sir James." Bleddyn belted on his sword as he followed Jamie out the door. "I swear on my life. Nothing will happen to her."

Jamie nodded his approval, and Bleddyn disappeared up the stairs toward the family's suite. Jamie went down to the yard.

The usually dark courtyard was brightly lit with torches. Already, villagers stood around small piles of their belongings. They had been warned to run for the keep at the sounding of the horn. Anyone outside when the gate closed would be left to their own wiles.

Bleddyn's sister came through. She shifted the large pack she carried to her other shoulder and headed for the great hall.

"Rhiana," Jamie shouted over the din of the increasing crowd.

She started up the steps of the hall.

He wove through the throng of people milling nervously about the yard. "Rhiana!"

She turned. Her solemn face showed concern. "Yes, m'lord?"

"Can you tell me if most are here?"

She scanned the crowd. "I see Pwell's family. They would be coming from farthest away."

Sela appeared in the door of the great hall. "Rhi, come. We must—" She stared at Jamie for a moment.

He nodded to her.

"We must ready ourselves for casualties," she continued, staring through him as she pulled the healer up the stairs.

"Over there." Rhiana pointed her chin toward the west wall. "Ask Wyn. She knows most everyone."

Jamie nodded his thanks and approached the weaver. "Can you check to see if all are here? I wish to close the gate, but do not want to shut it if many more have yet to arrive."

"Aye, m'lord. That I can do fer ye."

"Good. Make haste." He went to check the front gate, struggling against the current of people streaming in through the curtain tunnel. Barely a hundred people, still it would be a feat to get everyone in and have the room necessary to defend the castle.

His mother stood on the front battlements, bow in hand, a quiver stuffed full of arrows on her back. The archers looked uncomfortable as she stood among them, but she was the least of his worries. Putting her in charge of the archers was the best use for her. He had seen her rally the troops as well as the most battle-experienced commander.

Today, that was him.

Just as Jamie ordered, Wil had organized two lines of defense. Facing the bridge, the best of the javelin men were lined along the upper battlements of the two guard towers.

The next level down, Genevieve and the kitchen staff had cauldrons of boiled water at the ready to be dumped on those the spearmen missed. The cook had been ill tempered when he took her smaller cooking pots, but she quickly changed her tone when he explained the part her staff would play in defending the castle.

The back part of the gateway was narrowed like a loophole with the bales of hay that only two days before were a riding ring. Carts stacked against the bales would keep the enemy from merely pushing the barrier aside.

Any who escaped the misery of the boiling water would have to file through into the courtyard by ones or twos. Not only would it make those who got through vulnerable, but it would back up their comrades below the murder hole, making them easy targets for archers. Wil stood to one side anxiously examining the barricade.

"Looks sturdy enough. How is Maggie?" Jamie asked, hoping to relieve some of the tension.

"Worried. It seems she has begun her labors, but she does not want to take the healer away from the wounded. Truth be told, I worry a bit myself. I mean, with just the one woman to tend her. What if something should go amiss?"

He did not need his second-in-command worried about his wife and child in the midst of battle. "I shall see to it someone is sent to help."

Wyn approached. "Seems as if all as might be comin' is here, m'lord. Most of the men will refuse to leave their farms, so's I imagine they would fight alongside the soldiers out there."

"My thanks." He turned to Wil. "Get anyone out there inside and shut the gate."

"Aye, sir."

The "sir" surprised him. For the first time, he stood next to his boyhood friend in battle.

This was what being a lord was truly about. He was responsible for all these people. His mother, his sister, his friend, all the villagers in the yard, the woman he loved... Their lives all depended on *him*.

"'Tis time, my son." His mother's shout from the battlements plunged him deep into the gravity of the situation. "They come."

He turned his face heavenward and closed his eyes. He asked for help, but not from God. "Father," he whispered, "please help me be strong like you."

He climbed to the battlement, then turned to look over the inner curtain to the courtyard. Sela hurried women and children inside the great hall out of harm's way.

God, let me be alive at the end of this day to seek her forgiveness.

He turned back toward the bridge. From the corner of his eye, he could see the dust of a skirmish already progressing to the east, but his attention focused on the three armored riders approaching the gate.

The knight in the center removed his helmet. The sky had begun to lighten, but it was still too dark to make out the culprit's face.

"Amye de la Vierre, surrender your forces and we shall let you and your English dogs leave peaceably."

The voice was familiar, but he could not be sure where he had heard it before. The slight implied by refusing to use his mother's title did not escape his notice.

"Hah! Why would I believe a traitor like you?" Mother's words came out calm and clear. "We trusted you above all others, and you betrayed us, Gladus."

A thousand thoughts raced through Jamie's mind, but only one stabbed through. *Why did she not tell me it was Gladus?*

Fire began to spread across the western field. This was neither the time nor place to address the issue. They must present a united front or they were doomed to fail.

"My lord does not look kindly on this treachery, Gladus of Penwydd," Mother said as cool as if frost ran through her veins instead of blood.

"Your lord is not here to protest, dear woman."

"My lord stands beside me." She tossed back without pause.

The whispers of the crowd crashed in his ears as loud as storm waves beating coastal rocks.

Jamie had not expected this. Never in his memory had Mother willingly deferred to one of her sons. Pride filled his heart. She had chosen to trust *him*. The sun peeked over the ridge brightening dawn into day. He knew now *exactly* what he must do.

"Gladus of Penwydd," he shouted. "I am given authority by my liege to take your surrender. I will do what I can in your favor, but I must warn you King Henry does not take treason lightly."

One of the other riders leaned toward Gladus and whispered something. Ugly laughter echoed up to them. "Lady, surrender," Gladus said. "Come out. Your fields are aflame, and by now, your poor troops have given in. We *will* treat you fairly."

The lecherous look on Gladus' face as he spoke fired Jamie's blood to a boil. Despite her bravery and strong will, she would not be safe if the castle fell to Gladus. She looked to Jamie and he nodded.

She nocked an arrow to her bowstring, took careful aim, and fired.

The missile, followed by a hail of arrows from the archers, thunked into the wood of the bridge just at the horses' hooves. The black horse Gladus rode reared up, nearly tumbling the traitor to the ground, but he managed to stay aboard. The others raced back across the bridge as the frantic horse danced around wildly.

Gladus yanked the reins to get his mount under control, but before he followed his companions across the bridge, he turned and shook a gloved fist. "If that is the way you wish it, then so it shall be."

A shout went up from the battlement, but Jamie knew the fighting was far from finished. He leaned over and kissed his mother's cheek, then whispered in her ear. "Why did you not tell me of Gladus' treachery?"

She squeezed his arm as she whispered back. "I knew not for certain who was the traitor. Only that it was one who stayed behind when my husband left."

"Mother, if I am to be your commander you must trust—"

"My darling boy, I trusted you to be prepared for whatever may have happened...and you proved me right." She reached up and patted his cheek. "Your father would have been proud."

He took a deep breath, his thoughts turning to what must be done to protect the title. "We must send help to the fields."

Her eyes fluttered shut and her brows drew together.

He knew she considered strategies, but every moment that passed made their situation more dire. "Gladus was right. Our forces are weak. We have none to spare, but someone must at least go and find out their status. I saw fire to the west. If they burn both crops we will not be able to feed everyone this winter."

"M'lady" an archer shouted. "Riders comin' fast."

She turned and stared toward the group of approaching horsemen. A smile as bright as the sun lit her face "Alain."

The name was barely more than a whisper on her lips, but it filled the very air around her with excitement. "Open the gate," she shouted.

At last he was to meet the mysterious Lord Cilgerran.

She handed her weapon to the nearest yeoman and hurried down the ladder. Jamie hurried after.

A clatter of hooves against stone echoed in the gatehouse, heralding the cavalry that streamed into the list.

Mother's smile faded as the man leading the band dismounted and removed his helmet. "Llandon, where is my husband?"

"My lady." He bent to kiss the hand she absently held out. "We met Gladus' forces on the way here. The clans of Nepth and Gareth stand solidly with us. My lord stayed behind with them to fight."

Cold, damp fingers squeezed Jamie's hand. The relief she had so recently found evaporated. She valiantly tried to hide her fear, but he caught the tiny flicker that broke through to her eyes.

"He sent us on to help you here," Llandon continued, "but I see you have managed well on your own."

"My son, this is Llandon ap Manwith, my lord's sheriff."

Jamie returned Llandon's salute.

"Here are the men you need to go and help my husband rout the traitor from our midst." She turned back to the sheriff. "I have given control of our forces over to my son until our lord returns. I leave you in his command."

"As you wish, my lady."

Before the last word was spoken, she hurried to the tower and disappeared up the stairs.

****

Though the fire had subsided by the time they arrived, smoke still swirled around the western field, giving an eerie cast to the battle.

Jamie unsheathed his broadsword from the scabbard strapped to his back. "*Ymlaen*," he shouted to the riders around him. *Onward.*

Abelard's ears lay flat against his head as the warhorse surged toward the melee. Jamie, too, felt the rush of power brought on by battle. The two had been blooded together. Too many battles had forged man and horse into a single efficient fighting unit, as if they shared one mind.

A cohort of men with axes and hay forks struggled to beat back a group of pike men. Jamie turned to join them. The thunder of Abelard's hooves against the ground bolstered the power of Jamie's war cry as they circled round the skirmish. Part of the phalanx broke off to engage him, leaving a smaller group for the farmers to handle.

The steel of his sword sang sweetly as it sliced through the air. Cracking through the wood of the first pike, the blade tinged against the metal tip of another. Abelard reared up against the closing attackers, and they scattered as his hooves came crashing down on one of their comrades.

A stone zinged against Jamie's helm with enough force to knock him sideways just as Abelard lunged forward. His head spun, his vision blurred, his body suddenly crashed against the ground. He pushed himself to his hands and knees, but the ringing set off by the sling's shot bounced around inside his helmet, confusing itself with the fog covering his eyes. He tugged the sallet from his head, and the pealing bell was replaced with the cries of battle. His sword. Where was his sword?

He staggered to his feet and drew his side arm, but between the smoke and his blurred vision, he could barely tell friend from foe. His eyes cleared too late to prevent him from wandering within arm's length of a pike. The pike man lunged forward, but from nowhere, Jamie watched his own broadsword block the thrust down. The arm holding his sword was covered in chain mail. The swordsman stepped forward, and a scarlet red tunic blocked the attacker from Jamie's view.

Red Tunic put his booted foot on the long pole, trapping it in place.

The pike man dropped the pole and ran like he had seen the Devil's own son coming for him.

Red Tunic turned and tossed the sword to Jamie.

Just as Jamie's fingers wrapped around the grip, he heard the sound of an arrow thunk into flesh. A spray of blood stained the lions of his tunic.

Red Tunic crashed against his chest.

Jamie lowered the man to the ground, and turned back to the battle. There was nothing he could do for the man, now, except stay alive.

****

When the smoke finally lifted, more men from Cilgerran were alive than dead. Several of the enemy were taken, but Gladus was nowhere to be found.

Jamie walked the edges of the western field, searching for the man who saved his life. At least he could see the man decently buried. Shiny raven feathers flapping in the breeze led him to what he sought.

Red Tunic lay face down in a trough near the edge of the forest. The fingers of his outstretched hand fisted rhythmically into the mud.

Closed...Open...Closed...Open...Closed...

As though each squeeze was a heartbeat keeping him alive.

Jamie fell to his knees and pulled his dagger. He notched the shaft of the arrow, broke the fletch off cleanly, and tossed away the black feathers. The fighter moaned out his pain. A pain Jamie knew all too well.

He rolled the man onto his side. "This is going to hurt like hell," he said, though he doubted Red Tunic could hear him. With one good push, Jamie shoved the arrow out through the front of the shoulder. Red Tunic screamed and his hand clenched onto Jamie's arm like a blacksmith's vise.

God no.

The ring on the man's finger bore a pattern Jamie recognized. It matched the one his mother wore.

Chapter Eleven

Wounded men, brought to the bailey from the battlefield, waited to be tended. Sela finished bandaging a yeoman's arm.

He nodded his thanks and trotted off through the tunnel.

She went in search of Lady Amye. Since learning that Lord Cilgerran fought in the field, an uneasiness had spun in her stomach. She knew how much her mistress feared to lose another husband. Knew what thoughts must fill the lady's mind. The same thoughts filled her own head about Jamie.

"'Tis not too bad a wound, Griffin," Lady Amye said as Sela approached. "Your leg should heal in no time."

Another cart stopped in the keep. More wounded? Or had they finally gotten to the dead? Sela looked up to see how many more bandages they would need. Apprehension pressed heavy as a granite block against her chest.

Only two men occupied the cart. Jamie, his face dark with mud and soot, knelt over the second man. He glanced up and met her stare. When his eyes turned to his mother, they filled with pain.

Sela looked down toward her mistress.

Lady Amye stared at Jamie a moment before she squeezed her eyes shut. She turned back to finish the bandage, but her fingers fumbled with the cloth as though she had never before tied a knot.

Sela knelt and finished tying the cloth.

Lady Amye smiled reassuringly at the soldier, but Sela saw the small tremble of her lip as grief formed behind moistening eyes. Lady Amye suddenly stood. She swayed forward and Sela thought she might fall. Sela reached to steady her mistress, but Lady Amye stiffened and pushed the hand away. Halting steps moved her toward the wagon as though she feared what she would find there, but could not stop herself from going. Sela followed.

Lord Cilgerran smiled up at his wife. Blood darkened his torn tunic. His hand stretched to touch her fingers. "Ah, my beautiful Amye." He labored to take in a breath. "I feared not to see you again." Then he fell silent.

****

Jamie's head pounded as he slumped back against the cart rail. He had dreaded this scene from the moment he discovered the identity of the man in the red tunic. He would never forgive himself if Mother's beloved husband died saving his life.

"Alain?…Alain?" She sobbed over her husband's lifeless body.

Sela stood beside her, helplessly stroking Mother's back. She looked up at him and her eyes begged him to do something to help.

He climbed from the cart and pulled his mother from the body. Her sobs quaked through him as if they were his own. He wrapped his arm around her. Her weight sagged against him, but he refused to let her fall. He had not been able to stop her collapse when his father died. The vision of her helpless on the floor of the great hall at Edensmouth still haunted his dreams. That day he swore to become a knight, like his father. That day he swore to protect her from such pain. But he had failed. Worse, he had let his anger overwhelm his vow. What words could he say to ease such a loss? As he hugged her tightly, he thought he saw Cilgerran's fist close. He eyed Sela.

Her pain turned to surprise. The fist opened and closed again. Her surprise turned to elation. She reached out her hand and grasped his mother's shoulder. "My lady, he lives."

His mother broke from Jamie's hold and anxiously laid her ear to her husband's chest.

"You cannot give up while breath is left in him," Jamie encouraged, thankful for even this tiny thread of hope.

"Come, my lady." Sela's voice was soft, but her tone was firm. "We can still save him."

"Yes." Mother straightened and took a deep breath. "But I fear we shall need all the help we can get." She wiped the tears from her cheeks and turned to Bleddyn. "Please fetch your sister."

The boy nodded and ran toward the list.

"Come." The strength returned to his mother's voice. "Bring him into the hall." She hurried up the stairs and disappeared inside.

Sela was not far behind, but she turned and offered a small, hopeful smile.

They carried the litter up the stairs.

"Over by the fire," Mother reappeared as they reached the top of the flight. Her kirtle skirt swirled around her as quick steps hurried her toward the hearth.

Jamie's concerns eased. This was the woman he knew. By her decree, he would have control of the demesne, but he had never run even a small estate. He was a strong warrior, but she was the diplomat and the landlord. Her hand was what was needed now. He could defend them, but she was the one who could hold the fief together day to day. What would he have done had she not recovered her wits?

Genevieve came in carrying a kettle of water. Sela and his mother busied themselves cleaning Lord Cilgerran's wound. Rhiana burst into the room, followed by Bleddyn. She hurried to the hearth and knelt next to the other women.

Jamie watched as they tended the lord. There was nothing more for him to do here, so he took Bleddyn and went to help bring back the casualties from the western field.

****

Sela looked up just as Jamie left the hall. Thank God he was all right. As she had watched him ride from the list at the head of the garrison, feelings had spun about her like Pandora's demons, taunting her, laughing at her inability to stop the torture. He could die out there. Die without knowing how her love for him filled the empty places inside her. But it really did not matter. He could never know.

"Damnation, Sela," Lord Cilgerran cursed as she pressed a cloth against the puncture in his shoulder.

"Hush, Alain," Lady Amye whispered. His head now rested in her lap, and she gently stroked his cheek.

At least he had regained consciousness. The arrow he had taken had been removed, but blood still leaked from the wound.

Sela lifted the cloth. Tiny droplets of blood beaded on the surface. "Apologies, my lord, but—"

He nodded and she pressed the cloth back against his shoulder. He closed his eyes, his breath coming heavier with each exhale.

"Rhi, we need the elixir," Sela called to the healer who busily tossed herbs into a cauldron on the fire.

"I work as fast as I can. 'Twill be a few minutes more."

Sela lifted the cloth. The blood seemed to have stopped. She hoped it was because of the pressure and not because too much blood was lost.

Steam from the vessel Rhiana brought filled the air with a sharp odor. "We must pour a small bit along the wound, then, he must drink the rest."

Lady Amye bent to whisper in her husband's ear, then grasped his head tightly between her hands. Genevieve held down one shoulder, and Sela leaned her full weight against his torso. Lady Amye nodded, and Rhiana slowly tilted the bowl.

The roar as the hot liquid washed over the wound jolted through Sela and echoed off the walls. The sudden silence was as jarring as the scream. They all looked down wide-eyed with fear, until finally the sounds of Lord Cilgerran's heavy breathing filled the stillness. Rhiana handed the cup to Lady Amye.

"My darling, you must now drink. We cannot finish otherwise. 'Twould be too painful."

He let out a weak chuckle. "Cannot be more painful than what I feel this moment."

She smiled. "I know. But drink anyway." She held the cup to his lips and managed to get most of the brown liquid into his mouth. In a short while, he fell into a deep sleep.

Rhiana brought a red-hot dagger from the hearth. Sela pulled the bloody compress away. As the healer pressed the hot steel against the oozing flesh, a sensation shivered through Sela like a newly hatched nest of spiders. Most hated the smell of burning flesh, but the sizzling sound always affected her the most.

Rhiana removed the knife. The wound was ugly and black. Hopefully the arm would not have to be taken.

Lady Amye took the sewing needle from Genevieve.

Sela admired her lady's ability to close a wound. She had learned to stitch wounds, but no matter how she tried, her stitches were never as neat as those of her mistress, and the wound never healed as nicely as with Lady Amye's needle work. This time the lady's practiced hand trembled as it threaded the silk through the eye. "Would you like me to do it, my lady?"

"No. I will do it." She pulled the edges of the gaping wound together and began to stitch.

Sela had watched the task many times, but this time was particularly difficult, down the length of the wound and back, forming a tight, even seam.

Finally the last stitch was sewn. Lady Amye cut the thread with a knife and knotted the two ends. Rhiana brought a clump of the bladder moss used to draw out bad humours that had been soaked in more of her healing brew. Lady Amye carefully placed the moss over the silk threads, then covered the whole of it with a clean cloth. Sela helped Rhiana wrap the shoulder. And they all sat back.

Lady Amye's puffy, red eyes remained fixed on her husband. "Genevieve, please see everyone within the walls is fed."

"Yes, my lady."

"Sela, you and Rhiana please assure everyone who needs help is tended to."

"Yes, my lady." Sela looked back as she walked out the door.

Lady Amye was bent over her husband, stroking his face.

Sela sent a prayer for Lord Cilgerran's recovery skyward then descended into the melee of the yard. A woman so good as Lady Amye did not deserve to lose love twice in a lifetime. They were so tender with each other, even in this brutal circumstance.

Her mind flashed back to that night on the parapet. To the words Jamie spoke. To the way love showed in his eyes. To how gently he kissed her. Just as she had seen Lord and Lady Cilgerran kiss so many times. Sela wondered if she would ever have a chance for such a love.

****

"So many losses, my son."

The crunch of the floor rushes told Jamie his mother paced the length of the anteroom. He had seen a hundred times as many men die in a battle, but in such a small holding even the loss of a few could seem large.

He turned from the narrow loophole overlooking the courtyard. His mother had not left Lord Cilgerran's side for two days, yet she had her finger on the pulse of the domain. She seemed haggard and worn, but knowing she would ignore his concerns about her, he was loath to mention it. "Ten from the garrison. Another eight from the clans, including the one clan leader."

She stopped pacing. "Gareth was a very good friend and one of our most loyal clansmen." She sighed. "His son might not be so inclined."

"The men of Cilgerran clamor to fight, Mother. Your husband is their leader. He acquitted himself bravely in battle. I can barely keep their ire in check."

She rested back against the table. "But you must. We need to make sure we are protected before we can go after the traitors."

"We should strike while we—"

"'Tis not the same as if we were in England or Normandy. We cannot go chasing off without thought to the care of our domain."

She was right, of course. As much as he knew about battle, there was ten times more he needed to learn about ruling.

"We love our people," she continued. "I do not doubt they would fight for us to the last drop of blood, but we are at the edge of hostile territory. Once we leave our lands, we are surrounded by many uneasy alliances. Surely they know my lord was cut down in battle. Yet, they must not be sure if he is alive or dead. Otherwise they would have rejoined their attack. If our fortifications are weak in any way, the wolves will pounce on us."

"But to wait would show weakness as well," he countered.

She drew a deep breath and set a hand behind her for support. Dark circles stood out beneath the brightness of her violet eyes, but the finger of her other hand rapidly tapped against her lips. "Is it safe to have people stay in the village?" she finally asked.

"I believe it is. Men are posted around the outskirts to keep watch."

"And the garrison? Is it strong enough to provide both defense and attack?"

"It can be made so."

"All right then. As you wish." She eased onto the small stool beside the table.

Jamie took her hand and gave it a squeeze. "Please rest yourself, Mother. It would not do to have you fall ill. I need you well."

Tears rolled down her cheeks as she slumped against the wall. "I cannot rest until my husband is out of danger."

Jamie knelt beside her. "All will be well. With a love as strong as yours to hold him here, he has no choice but to recover."

She patted at her cheek with the sleeve of her kirtle. "Thank you for the courage, my son. You have always seemed to know the truth in my heart even when I did not." She sat up pretending confidence, though her eyes still showed concern. "'Tis why I know I can depend on you so much."

"Mother...?" Jamie lowered his eyes, ashamed to look at the strong woman before him.

"What is it, my darling boy?"

"Please forgive me for being angry with you."

"Auch. There is naught to forgive. I know you love your father." She opened her arms wide, and he hugged her just as he had when he was a boy. "I love him too. Not a day goes by I do not think of him. I could never replace what he gave to me." She braced his shoulders in her hands and looked him in the eye. "But my second husband has made me happy too. Happier than I thought I could ever be again."

"I know now my father holds no less a place in your heart. You deserve every bit of happiness you can find."

"Thank you, my son." She brushed his hair away from his eyes and kissed his cheek. "Now I must return to my lord." She slipped off the chain that held the signet ring, placed it in his hand and folded her fingers over his. "Though the decisions you make must be your own, you do not have to rule alone."

The tension in Jamie's forehead defeated his attempt not to look anxious.

"Even the King has advisors." She stood and started toward the bedchamber. "You too have a wealth of resources. You need only remember to use them well." She opened the door and whispered a few words inside.

Sela appeared in the doorway. At the sight of him, her body stiffened. Still, dressed in a pale yellow kirtle and a green wool tunic she was simply beautiful.

"You are in charge of the household as Jamie is in charge of the garrison," Mother said to her. "See that he has whatever he needs."

Jamie's heart almost stopped beating. Sela had avoided him for nearly a week. He had not seen her at all for the three days since the attack.

His mother's request brought a frown to her face, but she responded, "Yes, my lady." Her tone quelled his hope of quickly breaking through the wall she had built between them. She came and stood before him, but refused to look at him. "Your servant, my lord."

Chapter Twelve

Torn between a warrior's penchant to strike back and the words his mother imparted, Jamie paced the length behind the table in the great hall.

Wil patiently sat on a bench pulled up to the other side.

Each time Jamie turned back toward his friend, Mother's words about his father being away from the family picked at his conscience. Even though Jamie told Wil to take some time with them, his friend had spent more time seeing to the affairs of Cilgerran in the last few days, than with his wife and new-born son. Wil insisted that Margaret understood that his duty to his lord came first.

As well, Mother had said *Use all your resources...Wil is a better administrator...* but Wil was also a knight. He could command the castle defenses just as easily as Jamie.

Jamie stopped pacing and sat opposite his friend. "You know these people better than I. They chomp at the bit to go after Gladus and his rogues." He leaned in close. "And I must say I agree. But Mother says protect the castle first."

"The Welsh have strong family bonds," Wil replied. "The people who live under Cilgerran's protection consider him like unto a father. 'Tis why those who are loyal take such affront at his injury. Yet, Lady Amye makes good sense. We have built a few strong alliances, but nearly as many are tenuous. And obviously there are those who refuse to stand with us."

A strong argument. The people may *want*

retribution, but what they *need* is leadership. "We know we are a small holding," Jamie said, "but we cannot be seen as weak. We must quash the rebels, but we must also ensure the safety of the title. Revenge alone will not serve our cause. We must refocus our efforts into two fronts. I need time to strengthen the garrison."

Jamie chuckled to himself when Wil put his chin in his hand and began to tap against his lip. His friend had been in service to Lady Amye long enough to pick up one of her habits.

A light suddenly sparked in Wil's eye. "Mayhap we might quell them with some physical labors. Some project to restore the village."

"Perhaps a wall..." Jamie began.

"Or we certainly need to clean up the western field," Wil interjected. "The crop cannot be saved, but at the very least we can ready the field to lie fallow."

Mother was right. Wil was a knowledgeable resource. Perhaps, between the two of them, they could serve as well as one Lady Amye. His decision made, Jamie stood. "'Twill be the quickest thing to do. Make arrangements to get people out in the field."

Wil stood. "At once." Before he stepped through the archway he turned and shouted back. "To arrange food and such, you shall need to talk to Sela."

A knot wound itself in Jamie's gut. Though Sela completed her duties with the utmost speed and efficiency, she made a point of only being around him when necessary and only speaking to him when he directly addressed her. He had yet to discover anything he could do to make up for his transgression on the parapet. A deep breath did nothing for the knot, but he would have to approach her. Now was as good a time as any.

He went through the back entrance to the

service room. Though it was hours until the next meal, three women stretched and folded table covers, fresh from the laundry.

"Have you seen Mistress Sela?" He asked the short, plump woman nearly hidden behind a stack of snow-white cloths.

"Aye m'lord. She be in the buttery drawing out wine."

Suddenly, he realized he did not even know to whom he spoke. Mother would certainly know every person working in the household. When he thought back on it, Father called everyone by name as well. The laundress, brown eyes wide with worry, looked up as he stood awkwardly over her.

"Though I should, I know not your name." He smiled and a wide grin replaced the wide eyes.

"I be Heledd, m'lord. The castle laundress."

Using a trick his father taught him, he filed the name away in his mind along with the fact that Heledd's curls were blond instead of the usual dark color of the Welsh. If he was going to remember all who worked here, he would have to find something singular to go with each name.

"And these hard workers?" He gestured toward the other two.

"Girls," Heledd called to them.

They put down their work and turned to face him.

So much for unique characteristics. Two robin's eggs could not have been more alike.

"These be my daughters Eiddwen and Cainwen, m'lord."

Two pairs of doe-eyes stared blankly back at him

"Eiddwen." He spoke to no particular girl.

The young woman on the right curtsied.

"Cainwen," he nodded to the one on the left. "I thank you for the work you do for us."

"'Tis a pleasure to work for such kind people as

Lord and Lady Cilgerran," Heledd answered for all three.

He nodded and returned to the task at hand.

The cool dampness against his face as he entered the buttery reminded Jamie of the smuggler's caves along the Brittany Coast. Barrels filled the dark, musty room. As he walked down a wide path, he noticed the markings on each cask; a letter and some numbers. A51...A52...A53. He turned to the barrels on the other side. M51...M52...M53. The same system Mother used at Edensmouth. "A" marked barrels of ale, "M" was for mead. Surely somewhere there would be a very small number of barrels marked "S" for spirits and a goodly store marked "V" for wine.

"I am back by the old wines, Branwen," Sela shouted.

The sound of her voice set his heart pounding, and he stood a moment as the ever-tightening knot in his stomach moved up into his chest. He turned down an aisle of barrels marked with a "V" and before long he could see a light ahead. Around the next corner, he found Sela bent over a barrel.

Bathed in the yellow light of the sconces, she glowed like an angel. He wanted to touch her, hold her, but feared to do further damage to the relationship he, with all his heart, hoped to mend.

"Sela?"

She jumped as she looked up, but quickly recovered her composure. "A moment, my lord?"

He nodded his consent. He wished she would stop calling him "my lord." Even "Sir James" was better. He pushed aside a pile of stained rags and leaned against a trestle table set up in the tight space between the wall and the barrels. He watched intently as she continued decanting the wine.

She dipped out a small amount from the open barrel and poured it into a cup. She sniffed the liquid then took a small sip.

The wine served here was sweet and flavorful. Better than anything he had tasted, even at the King's table. What did she smell that told her the wine was ready? Could she make sweet wine for the meals served at his table? Their table.

The taste of their kiss on the parapet flooded his thoughts. Her lips, parted to accept the gentle probing of his tongue, had tasted as sweet as the wine she now poured into the jug.

His cock twitched to life and he crossed his hands over his groin.

She brought the jug to the table, wiped the outside with one of the cloths, and set the ewer next to several jars at the other end. She turned toward him, but her eyes remained lowered toward the floor. "How may I be of service to you, my lord?"

He stood, still covering his hardening cock. The last thing he desired was to drive her further away with un-chivalrous behavior. "I must speak with you about provisions, mistress."

"What type of provisions would you need, my lord?" Her tone was steady, but her eyes still remained lowered.

"The burned field to the west must be cleared. We shall need to feed the workers and the guards. Though I think we shall not need an overnight encampment," he added to impress her with his thoroughness. "We should be able to return home by nightfall."

"Certainly, my lord. Just food and drink then. Would you like some kind of celebration once the task is completed?"

He had not thought about such, but it seemed a good idea. "'Twould be a boon to celebrate our quick recovery from our enemy's attack. Show them they have not beaten us."

"How many do you think there might be, my

lord?"

"The whole village would come for such."

"Aye, my lord. Some might not be able to come, but most would be there. What of the allies to Cilgerran? Would they be invited to celebrate with you?"

It would be wise to invite their allies, but...

"Considering our damages, will we have enough for them as well?"

Her eyes though lowered, moved back and forth as she silently pondered his question. By the time she answered, she had inched away from him and stood by the wine cask. "We can make do."

Not a resounding endorsement, still an indication of what needed to be done.

"Perhaps just those allies who came to our aid. We will summon all for a feast at a later time."

"Yes, my lord." Her eyes focused on the barrel as she dipped out a ladle of wine and poured it into a waiting jug.

"Please arrange both a day of provisions and a feast," he said as she emptied a second ladleful into the jar. He stood silent, intent on making her look at him.

Dread filled Sela's mind as she realized she could not avoid looking at Jamie. Each time she saw him, her fingers longed to caress his face. Her heart begged her to go to him.

When she looked up, his expression was not that of a lord speaking with a servant, but of a man longing for a woman. Like she always hoped he would look at her.

Her chest felt as if an iron band was strapped around it, but she forced herself to speak. "The western fields cover a larger span," she responded, though his face said the field was not the thought foremost in his mind.

Even in the dim candlelight, the eyes she knew

so well held her, drew her deep into his soul. A soul where she saw only want. The want of her.

Sela closed her eyes. She hoped he could not see the small tremor of her lip as she took a deep breath. She turned back to filling the wine jug.

"My lord, it may take two days work to clear—"

Sela jumped back as wine spilled over the top of the jug. The stain would never come out if the drink got on the linen sleeves of her shift.

In the crowded space, there was no place to go except against Jamie.

His arm wrapped around her waist from behind, drawing her close against him.

His breath warmed the side of her neck but she shivered, fighting to hold back the longing she had to sweep away after every time she saw him. His hard erection pressed against her bottom.

She felt a need unlike any she had felt before. Moisture slickened the place between her thighs, and her one desire was to feel his warm hardness within her. She reached back to touch his leg.

His lips pressed against the curve of her shoulder.

She could have the very thing she wanted most. If she would only turn to him. This was insanity. No matter how much she wanted him, his honor must come first. Should anyone ever discover the truth of her past life, he would be ruined.

His fingers gently swept up her torso, grazing the underside of her breast. She wanted to put aside his touch, but the hand she folded over his merely cupped his palm more firmly against her breast.

Approaching footsteps broke the spell.

Sela pushed herself from Jamie's embrace. She took a rag from the table and nervously wiped the sticky purple drink from her fingers.

"Over here, Branwen," she shouted, backing further away from him.

"When would you like to begin work, Sir James?" she asked as the serving girl came around the corner.

"Tomorrow, if possible. If not, then the next day will do."

She kept her eyes lowered, afraid that if she looked at him again, all prudence would be lost. Lost to the willful heart beating in her chest.

Chapter Thirteen

Jamie's spirits soared as he stepped into the bright morning sun. It was all he could do not to dance down the path toward the tower.

Though she had been hesitant at first, Sela's reaction when she'd bumped into him proved that the spark between them still existed. The moment she'd touched him, the connection was undeniable.

He loved the way her hair shone just a touch red when the sun beamed on it. He loved the full pout of her lower lip. He loved the way she felt in his arms.

Just as much, he loved her strong, yet gentle way with the household. She knew things about running a holding that he had not taken time to learn. He wished, now, he had come home to work with Mother, but Sela would teach him what he needed to know. She had learned her ways from the best possible source. They could be a powerful pair, like Mother and Father. Jamie felt it in every measure of his body.

He needed to write the command to come to the field. What should it say? Anxious to begin, he reached for the latch on the tower door.

Four purple stains marked the back of his hand, left by her fingers, a sign from heaven branding him as her own. He lifted his hand to his lips, promising with a kiss to never lose heart.

She would guide his hand, help him to be the strong, yet kind, ruler his father had been. He climbed the stairs to his room.

Bleddyn sat by the fire, mending the missing rings in an old mail shirt Jamie had found in the armory for him to wear.

"Squire, see to whatever tasks Mistress Sela needs done."

"Aye, Sir James." The young man draped the hauberk over a chair and started for the door.

"But return in an hour," Jamie said before Bleddyn could leave. "I shall have a message for you to deliver."

"Aye, Sir."

Jamie began to compose the charge to report to the west field. He got halfway through, then read what he had written.

No. It seemed *too much* like an order. These were not soldiers, just ordinary men and women, subject to the whims of feuding lords.

He started again and soon had a more engaging dispatch. Although he left room for those tending the injured or caring for small children, everyone else was strongly urged to be present at the field on the morrow.

Bleddyn returned just as Jamie pressed the Cilgerran signet into the soft, red wax dripped onto the bottom of the parchment.

"How goes the preparation, squire?" Jamie loosely rolled the document, then tied it.

"If you do not mind, Mistress Sela asked me to help with the kitchen encampment."

"Whatever she needs. Make sure 'tis well done." Jamie held out the scroll. "See this gets to her post haste."

"Aye, Sir." Bleddyn took the missive and departed.

Jamie wished he could have delivered the order himself. Seen her again. But he should not interfere in whatever plans she made.

A corps of fighting men he could command without much thought, but how to manage the relationship between a lord and his non-military subordinates was something he had yet to work at, especially when it came to Sela. Though he hoped for more in the future, she was in service to his family. It was his duty to determine what needed doing. It was her duty to see it was done.

Jamie smiled. For the first time, he felt like more than a soldier. Never before had he been so intimately involved with the running of an estate. Until now, his concern had been becoming a warrior. Skill with horse and sword had won the king's respect, thus the offer of the Norman heiress and her property.

The moment of satisfaction vanished.

In order to gain the precious parcel of land, he would have to marry the heiress. That would mean he could *not* marry Sela. Perhaps she would come with him to Normandy—

Damnation! What was he thinking? Mother would disown him if she even knew he had such a thought.

That aside, he knew in his heart he could not cheapen what he felt for Sela by asking her to be his mistress.

At court, more than once wives had destroyed the lives of mistresses. Two otherwise civil women were turned into vicious animals by jealousy. Even the Queen had been accused of being bitten by the green dragon.

He could not make Sela hide in the shadows while another woman ruled his household. He could not make the woman he truly loved watch another bear his children. It would be torture for Sela, and for him. She deserved to be in the light. She deserved his full devotion.

Yet he had no suitable prospect to offer her. Without property, he served at the pleasure of his king, constantly going where his service was needed. He would not have Sela leave behind the comforts of service with his mother, only to follow him from place to place. No home to call her own. She deserved more.

As he looked out the window, he rubbed at the knot that plagued the back of his neck since he took command of the castle.

In the courtyard, Bleddyn oversaw a group of young boys hard at work. Carts lined the outer wall, waited to be loaded with baskets of vegetables and sacks of flour.

Jamie grunted and turned toward the door. Such an opportunity to learn something about the administration of an estate should not be wasted. Perhaps if he could manage to rein in his enthusiasm, go slowly and patiently, he could learn a bit more about Mistress Sela as well.

****

Sela suddenly turned and Jamie found himself within a hair's breadth of her. It seemed to happen a lot of late.

"Your pardon, my—" she began an apology.

He stepped back and locked his hands behind him, cutting off her apology with his own. "I meant not to intrude." He looked nervously at the ground in front of him. "But I wondered if there is some way I might contribute."

Her eyes darted quickly around the yard. "You might help Bleddyn."

He glanced over at the wagon where his squire guided his *battalion* in loading the pavilions, some small barrels, and an assortment of table planks onto a large farm cart. If Jamie remembered correctly, the tents would be the center of distribution at mealtime.

"If you would not mind, I would rather let him try it alone. 'Tis his first *command* since becoming a squire. I should like to see how he handles himself and his...*men*."

"Until we are ready to leave, there is naught else to do but bring out the provisions and stack everything in the carts, my lord."

"I think I can handle a bit of lifting." He forced a smile to his lips as his heart beat a familiar pattern. Hard and fast.

Now it was her turn to look nervously down. She shuffled through the sheaf of parchment scraps in her hand and pulled one free. "Perhaps you could help with this task?"

He read the list she handed him.

"Take a few men and bring these barrels from the buttery to the yard, please."

"Certainly I can, mistress. Though I must admit, I am ashamed to say I know not the name of any man here. Would you be kind enough to introduce me?"

"If it would please you, my lord, certainly I can."

"Indeed, 'twould be a great relief to me." He walked with her to the foot of the courtyard steps.

"Huw, Madog, Owain," she called to three men resting on the stairs. All three stood and bowed to her.

"Aye, Mistress Sela?" the largest of the three answered.

"Please would you help Sir James bring the wine and ale we need."

"For you I would do anything, Mistress Sela," a younger blond responded with a showy bow.

"Sir James, these are the sons of the village blacksmith. Huw ap Pwell, Madog ap Dielyn and Owain ap Dielyn."

Each man bowed courteously as Sela spoke his name. They certainly looked like blacksmith's sons. They were nearly as tall as Jamie, and their thick arms stretched the fabric of their shirtsleeves tight. The same blue eyes, prominent nose, and strong chin marked each as coming from the same stock. Though the younger brothers were fair-haired, the oldest had dark hair and carried a different family name. No matter though. "Come," Jamie said as he turned toward the buttery. "Mistress Sela has set us a task."

The brothers seemed to be good men. Once Jamie set them at ease with the fact that he was their lord, they were jovial as they worked. He enjoyed their company and by the time they brought out the fourth barrel, he had them laughing with him.

Jamie and Huw rolled the last of the barrels through the buttery door. Eight in all. Six Ale and two wine.

"You seem to know Mistress Sela well," Huw said as he turned to shut the door to the storeroom.

"Aye, I have known her since we were children," Jamie replied, keeping the half-truth to himself. He had barely a fig leaf of an idea about Mistress Sela these days.

"She is quite a beauty."

"Aye, she is." The sparkle in Huw's eye caught Jamie's attention and he stared at the man beside him. He had blocked the thought of any other man's interest in her from his mind, but Sela was a beautiful, unmarried woman with high status in the lord's household. Any man with sense would want her.

He could see it now. Each brother had shown his interest back at the water barrel. Outgoing Owain tried to make her laugh with his bright wit and manner. Madog, the quiet one, stood rod straight, but his eyes showed he hung on her every word. Huw most of all. The look of awe and respect when she called his name.

No wonder she had been put off by the uninvited kiss on the battlement. She might already have a dozen suitors to choose from. She would be much better off married to a man with a place in the community. The home might be modest, but at least it was a home for her to go to. And her place as Mother's servant would raise the status of her husband as well. Why would she choose a landless knight like him?

Jamie rubbed the back of his neck. The knot that had been worked loose by hard labor began to tighten again. He was about to question Huw on his intentions when Owain blustered into their exchange.

"What are you sluggards just standin' about for? Mistress Sela will have our hides if we do not get these barrels loaded."

Jamie puffed out his chest and squinted at Huw. "Your brother has a bit o' nerve talking to his lord in such a manner."

The smile fell from Owain's face. "Please, I...I beg your pardon, m'lord."

Jamie could barely keep the laugh from bursting out, and he slapped Huw on the shoulder.

The younger man's brows drew together.

"You are right, Huw," Jamie said. "Maybe we ought to teach him some manners...before he gets himself in trouble."

"Too late for that." Huw smiled and cast a sideways glance at Jamie. "'Tis nothin' but trouble he has been since the day he was born."

Owain suddenly raised his hand in a sign of disrespect.

Jamie laughed and leaned his weight against the barrel of ale.

Chapter Fourteen

Sela returned from the scullery pulling a handcart full of kitchen tools. A few small cauldrons and the metal parts for the roasting spit rattled as the cart bumped into a rut and came to a stop just outside the curtain tunnel.

She bent forward to assess the problem. Some missing cobbles had left a handy trap for the cart's wheel. She would have to let Wil know the path needed mending. He would find someone in the village to do the work.

A hard yank freed the cart and it lurched forward with an awful clatter. As she trudged through the dark tunnel, her mind roamed back to the encounter in the buttery. To Jamie's soft whisper in her ear. To the sparks that surged through her as his hand found the curve of her breast.

She emerged into the list to find the women standing still as stones. *What in God's name...?* Suddenly, she saw what the women were staring at and the handle of her cart slipped from her hand. The tools inside clanged loudly and four men, naked from the waist up, looked in her direction. Their torsos shined with the sweat of their labors and with every movement, muscles rippled beneath bronzed skin.

The barrel they had just lifted began to fall. Huw's muscles bulged as he strained to keep the burden aloft. He shouted at his brother to pull the barrel onto the cart.

Jamie helped lift the burden, then rolled the barrel to the front of the bed.

Freed from the weight, the blacksmith's sons all hurried toward her.

Jamie merely jumped down and stood beside the cart, his arms folded across his chest.

She knew how it felt to have them folded around her.

Some of the women scattered back to their tasks. A few of the younger ones stood staring at the brothers as they passed.

Huw reached her first. "Mistress Sela you should not be pulling—" but his words were lost in a jumble with those of his brothers.

"Please continue your work." Her sharp tone silenced all three. "The barrels must settle before they can be tapped. And we need yet to fetch water from the river for cooking and for mixing with the wine."

She pulled her cart to the front of the list. As she passed by Jamie, the memory of his hot erection pressing against her in the cool darkness of the buttery found its way to the surface of her thoughts, and the most private part of her began to throb.

She quickly turned the cart and set it next in line with the others, then started back to the kitchen.

Two girls remained in the yard, gawking at the men.

Sela's scowl chased one girl into a storeroom, and she grabbed the hand the other. The girl stumbled after her as Sela marched toward the kitchen. "Genevieve, have you nothing for your workers to do?" She pushed the girl through the door before turning back toward the courtyard.

Halfway down the path, Sela stopped. Breathing hard. Squeezing her hands into tight fists. Why was she was so upset? It could not be because other women stared at her Jamie. She shook her head. What had come over her? He was not *her* Jamie.

"Are you unwell, mistress?" The tenderness in his voice drew her back from the edge of despair.

She uncurled her fingers and looked up into a face tense with worry. "No. I must be a bit...tired. It has been a hard week." Hard to deal with the aftermath. The aftermath of the attack. The aftermath of working side by side with him.

He took her hands between his.

She thought to back away, but her feet would not move.

"I should never have asked you to prepare for tomorrow," he said. "The next day would have been fine." Even with his brow drawn together, his face made the heat rise inside her.

"No." She straightened and slid her hands free. "You have commanded that everyone come tomorrow. We shall be ready. Could two of you take the first cart of barrels to the site? I shall find others to help finish with the loading."

"I will make it so, if you wish it, but pray, mistress, do not tire yourself overly much. We need you still to run the house after we have finished in the field."

Sela nodded. "Once the kitchen pavilions are up, and the provisions are at the site, I shall rest. I promise."

"Then we best be on our way with those barrels, so you may be at rest all the sooner." He bowed and turned toward the courtyard.

Jamie wondered if Sela was as well as she said. He had found her staring at the ground, her hands balled into fists, chest heaving, as if she had trouble drawing breath. He looked back.

She stood for a moment, then turned toward the kitchen. She must be in dire need of rest.

He should get her into bed. An image of her lying naked in his bed flashed through his mind. He shook his head to erase the lovely vision. *No.* He meant he must get her to rest.

"Is she all right?" Huw asked as Jamie reached the courtyard. "I have never before seen her in such a mood."

"She seems a bit tired," Jamie answered. "Why did I not have the good sense to give a reasonable deadline?" He uttered the words aloud, more to himself than the man beside him.

"She is a strong, capable woman," Huw answered. "I am sure she can do whatever you ask of her."

Huw was right, but she might place her duty above care of herself. He was the one at fault. She should not suffer for his ignorance. The sooner they finished setting up the encampment, the sooner she would be able to rest. "She bids us take the barrels to the field." Jamie nodded toward the younger brothers. "You two, finish loading the second cart. Be quick about it. Follow as soon as you are done."

Huw handed him the tunic he had tossed aside while they worked. He pulled the linen over his head, and climbed onto the back of the farm wagon. "Hear me now," he shouted.

Work halted and everyone in the yard turned toward him.

"I am your lord and by my word, I swear this insult to Cilgerran will be avenged, but first we must care for our own needs. We've much work to do. Make haste." He jumped from the cart, took hold of the horse's halter, and walked toward the gate.

"Come," he said firmly and Huw fell in beside him. "Wil should have the guards set and Bleddyn should already be there with the tents and tables. We must get them up as quickly as possible." He picked up his pace once they crossed the bridge and entered the village. "I want everything done by the time she arrives."

****

The list was a hive of activity by the time Sela returned. Huw and Jamie were already gone with the first wagon. Madog and Owain were just leaving. Everyone hustled about their tasks with a renewed urgency, loading baskets and sacks and tools into carts.

She should have returned sooner, but an apology was due to both Genevieve and the maid. Her appalling behavior had been unbecoming to herself and to her mistress. Lady Amye had taught her better. Never before had she experienced such a jolt of jealousy. She had no reason to be jealous. Jamie Barnard could not be hers.

Ever.

Still, he filled her thoughts. Her body craved him. Craved his kisses. Craved his touch. Craved to have him within her. As he had held her against him in the buttery, her soul had come to life. Though she could never have Jamie, deep inside, she knew there was no other man she could love.

She would have to content herself with the exquisite pleasure of looking upon him each day until...her heart sank...until he returned to the King's court. The fire he lit in her soul refused to die, but Cilgerran needed her now. She dragged her thoughts back to the task before them.

Within the hour, the trip to the field was begun. She hoped to get there before the sun set. Much work needed to be done to get the encampment ready by tomorrow. Despite her promise to rest, a long evening lay ahead.

She had made the walk from castle to field many times before. Lady Amye had instilled in her a sense of the importance of walking. Each step made one more familiar with the land. Gave a sense of love and pride for the earth that supported and provided for them.

But today the accustomed beauty of this land

was marred. Her stomach clenched tight as the harsh stench of stale smoke stung her nose. Visions of broken crops and scorched earth flooded her head and silence blanketed her heart as she led the carts the rest of the way to the field.

Clouds grayed the afternoon sky by the time they reached the first of the furrows. She looked on the western field for the first time since the attack. Her heart might just as well have been stabbed through with a dagger.

Fire and hooves had made a charred mess of the once neat rows. The young wheat she'd helped plant not long ago was trampled flat. People would go hungry this winter if they could not find a way to replace the loss. An additional tax on the vassal lords or perhaps one of the allies would be willing to sell or trade for the extra supply.

On the far side of the field, two white pavilions jutted up from a small area untouched by the battle. As the procession approached the camp, she could see that even the trestle tables had been put in place.

The smell of roasting meat brought a rumble from her stomach. A dozen or so rabbits and a like number of squirrels roasted on a row of sticks over a bank of fires. Ten barrels sat to the side of the main tent. Ten? She had only asked for eight and only eight had left the yard.

Jamie hurried toward her, his wide smile lighting her heart like the sun, exposing the feelings she tried to keep in the dark. With his boots muddied and his shirt un-tucked, he almost seemed like a common man, but his strong Norman features and his bearing said otherwise. Everything about him spoke of nobility.

"Welcome, mistress." He took her hand and gently pressed it to his lips. "Are you hungry? May I get you a cup to slake your thirst?"

Sela's heart fluttered, but reminding herself of her promise to merely enjoy his presence, she willed its beat to slow. "My thanks, but no. Perhaps anon." She looked around the busy campsite. "You have done much work."

"Aye, mistress. Since we have so little time to prepare, we should use it wisely. I thought we might need something for an evening meal, so I sent the young ones off to catch what they could for supper. They did quite well, I think."

"Indeed they have. I did expect to prepare an evening meal. Your forethought has saved us a great deal of time."

He smiled. "We await your command, mistress. What would you have us do?"

"Everything must be unloaded from the carts. Genevieve will see to it, she knows where best to put everything. Also, we do need to have water brought—"

"We have two barrels," he interrupted. "I borrowed them from the farm nearest the field and filled them. Will we need more?"

Ah. The two extra barrels. He *had* been busy.

"Thank you." She released a small smile, grateful for the time saved. "We shall need at least two more. Usually Cullein, the farmer by the river, lends to us when we have need. 'Tis closer to the water source and makes for less travel. If you take the horse cart over there, I am sure he will be pleased to help."

"Thank you, mistress. I shall see to it right away." He gave a slight bow, then trotted over to the wagon.

What a pleasant surprise. Much of the work she thought would need to be done was already finished. Jamie Barnard was as thoughtful as when he was young. Even though he had become a strong warrior, he had not lost his kindness.

Perhaps that was why she found it hard to let go of her childish desire. Why it was so hard to make herself stop loving him.

She watched his easy way with the smith's sons as they harnessed the horse to the cart. The brothers jumped into the back as Jamie took the reins and turned toward the river.

Sela sighed as she started toward the cook tent to see what help Genevieve might need. "Bleddyn." She stopped the young squire as he passed.

"Aye, mistress?"

"You have done a fine job getting everything put to order."

"Thank you, mistress, but 'twas in truth Sir James who made everything get done. Once he arrived, the work went fast. I have ne'er seen anything like it."

"Oh." Sela smiled at the thought of Jamie shouting orders to the hapless men and boys.

"Between my master and the smithy's sons, I have never seen men work so hard," Bleddyn went on. "We went to the woods to find rabbits for dinner, and by the time we returned, they had the small tent up. Me and the boys had to help with the large one, but everything was all set out and ready to go. Taught me a thing or two about planning ahead."

"Well, my thanks to you and your men for the food you have provided."

"'Tis my pleasure, mistress. Is there aught else we should do?"

"Perhaps you might help Genevieve with the supplies."

"Certainly, mistress." He bowed and moved off toward his group of charges.

Sela made her way to the fire pit. Two young boys went down the smoky row of roasting meat, turning them one by one. They reached the end of the line, then hurried back to the beginning to start again.

"You boys are very busy," Sela said to the taller of the two.

He stopped a moment and gave an awkward bow. "Aye, mistress. Sir James said we must turn them so they will not burn."

"Sir James is right, *mes enfants*." Genevieve stepped up beside Sela. "'Tis the way I taught him and now he has taught you. Remember this lesson well." The cook crossed her arms and smiled. "Master James has always been so good with the children," she whispered to Sela. "He will be a good father, just like Lord Thomas."

"Yes." Sela recalled how he played with Marie in the stable; how he had helped *her* in her first days at the castle.

"And a good husband as well." Genevieve added.

The words ripped her already torn heart. "Yes, he will," she answered. *But not for me. Not for me.* Her heart filled her chest until she thought it would burst. Instead, tears spilled from her eyes as she turned and walked away.

Chapter Fifteen

The barrels, heavy with water, made the journey back to the field much slower than the trip to the river. Twice the men got out to push the heavy cart from a rut in the road.

Huw suggested they lessen the load by walking alongside.

Owain complained, but Huw's squinted eye silenced the grumbling.

"Jamie," Huw said as they walked side by side. "What think you of Mistress Sela?"

"She is a fine woman," Jamie answered, all but certain where Huw would turn the conversation.

"Aye, she is."

Jamie looked straight ahead and said nothing, uncomfortable with the thought of giving information to a rival.

Huw ventured into the silence. "You have known her since childhood?"

"Aye."

"What was she like as a girl?"

Jamie frowned. He wished he knew the answer to that question. It might help him understand why she kept him at a distance, but he answered Huw's question as earnestly as he could.

"I really could not say. She came to us at the age of twelve, almost a grown woman. Until my return it had been over six years since we last saw each other. Unfortunately, I have more understanding of horses than women."

"Aye. I fear the same lack of knowledge," Huw said and they shared a laugh.

Huw folded his hands behind him exposing a broad chest and accentuating his strong arms. The blacksmith would be a good match for Sela. Better than a knight? A landless knight, Jamie reminded himself. If her heart was set on another...To think of such brought back the knot at the base of his skull.

But what if she wanted Huw? The right thing would be to put aside the need he felt for her. His need to have her. His need to keep her safe.

His lament was pierced by a sob. The sob he had heard that night on the rampart. He stopped and searched the woods.

"What is it?" Huw asked.

Suddenly, in the far distance, she came clear. Sela sitting amongst the trees. Why was she out here...crying?

"Nothing." Jamie stepped off the path. "I need to attend to personal business." The "personal business" was not really a lie. Sela was his business and he must tend the anxiety created in him by her sob. He started into the woods.

"Do you want us to wait?" Huw called after him.

"No, take the barrels to camp and see to whatever Genevieve needs. I shall return shortly. Make sure the boys stay busy."

****

Sela sat on the fallen oak, curled forward, hugging her arms tight about herself. Tears flowed down her cheeks unbidden. Though she tried to stop them, they slipped through her lips, salting her tongue with the bitter taste of disappointment. Genevieve meant no harm by her praise of Jamie as a father and husband. Still the words hurt. Hurt deep in Sela's heart.

How could she have let this happen? How could she have fallen in love with Jamie Barnard again?

'Tis just a girlish dream, she had told herself over and over. The wish of a young girl to be loved by

a handsome boy. Only now the girl was a grown woman and the boy was an important and powerful man. She sobbed again, trying to release the ache deep in her chest, but it only worsened.

"Sela?"

The gentle sound of her name on his lips tore at her even more. What had she done to have heaven torture her so? She turned away, afraid he might see her pain.

"What is it?" He knelt beside her and placed his hand on her shoulder. "Why do you cry?"

"'Tis nothing, my lord."

"It must be something of import to make you cry so."

She turned and found herself staring into an ocean of love. Kneeling beside her in a plain shirt and dirty braes, he looked a man with whom she could have a life. A life filled with passion.

His body stiffened. The comforting warmth of his hand fell away from her shoulder, leaving a coolness to shiver down her spine. "Is it what happened—on the turret? Please, forgive me. I should not have kissed you, but—"

"No," she smiled at his apology. "I minded not the kiss." She'd loved the kiss. She wanted more of his kisses, but the truth clouded out all hope. "'Tis just that I know it can lead nowhere."

"What?"

"You are a noble, Jamie." She stood and walked away, leaving him kneeling on the ground. "And I...I am just a common woman. Too lowly for a man of your stature."

"What do you mean?" He came and stood behind her.

Though she did not turn, she could not help but feel the warmth of him. So close. Yet further away than ever. Her stomach twisted as she thought of her time in her father's house. She must tell him the

143

truth. Only then would he leave her to recover her peace. "Before I came to Edensmouth, I lived and worked in my father's house. It was…" She could not bring herself to say the words. To blacken herself in his eyes.

"But since that time you have raised yourself to be a woman of great worth." His voice was solid and sure. "You are no more considered a household maid than the steward of Edensmouth was considered a common beefeater."

Sela spun and gazed at him, pleading with every fiber within her. "Please stop."

"What is your dark secret, little rabbit?" he whispered. "What keeps you fighting against me?"

She shook her head and tears stung her eyes before rolling down her cheeks. "I am not a fit bride for a powerful noble. I am…I was a—"

He lifted her chin and looked into her eyes. "And who are you to say who is fit and who is not."

"I would ruin your chance at a title. I could not do such a thing to you. You are on the verge of greatness—"

"But what would greatness be without someone to share it?" He took her hands and squeezed them gently. "Someone to guide me in the best direction." He stroked his thumb along her cheekbone wiping away the moistness of a tear. "Someone to help me when I fall."

She pressed her cheek against the warmth of his cupped hand; gently pressed her lips against his palm.

He leaned close and kissed her.

She tried with God's strength to stop her lips, but they melted against his. His kiss reached down into her soul, and the ache in her chest vanished.

His arms encircled her, his hands pressed her tightly against him. Soft kisses covered her neck and warmed her throat. "Share greatness with me, little rabbit. Be mine."

His breathless words unraveled her resolve and wove it into a new pattern. The pattern of love she had hoped for her entire life.

She closed her eyes and rested her ear against his chest. Her heart raced in time with his. The beat quick and strong. If only she could... But she knew better. She pulled herself from his embrace and wiped her sleeve across her mouth, failing to remove the sweet taste of him from her lips.

"I am sorry, my lord. This can never be."

Jamie knew he must do something as she walked away or he would lose her forever. "Wait, Sela, please. Listen to me." He ran to block her way.

"There is nothing more to be said, my lord." She went around him. Kept walking.

What could he do to show her she meant life itself to him? To make her listen? "Then you leave me no choice, mistress. I shall have to inform my mother that I shall seek to join the Order of Solomon's Temple."

She stopped, but did not turn around. "The Templars? Surely you jest, my lord. You hate the church."

"There would be no other choice for me. If I remain a royal knight, the king will require me to marry. There is no woman I want other than you." The chill in his voice belied the fiery battle raging in his mind. To give up everything he ever wanted...land, title, family... was a fool's quandary. But what value was any of it without her?

She spun to face him. "My lord, your mother has such great hopes for you. This will break her heart."

"And what of your heart, little rabbit?" A quiver in his voice cracked the icy reserve he fought to maintain. "Will not it break if I leave this mundane world?"

She took a step toward him.

The sadness that filled her eyes stabbed a dagger of hopelessness through his heart, but he held out his hand. A moment passed when he thought she would turn away, but she came forward.

"Please Jamie." Her blue eyes sought the ground, but tears wet her lashes. "Please, do not do this." The hand she laid on his chest could just as well have squeezed his heart to a stop. "Do not force me to make this impossible choice. There is no way—"

He lifted her chin before the words he refused to believe could pass her lips. The bluebell color of her eyes seemed suddenly dark as night, but he dared not turn back. "There is always a way, Sela. If you will let me, I will find it."

Her eyes search for something.

He could only hope it was something he had in him.

"I want you to find that way, Jamie." She reached up and drew him into a tender kiss.

Did she say yes? *She'd said yes.* He put his hands about her waist and lifted her toward the green forest canopy, spinning and dancing with her above him.

The sweet blue eyes he loved sparkled down at him like the brightest stars and her laughter filled his ears. "Auch, Jamie Barnard, put me down. You make me dizzy."

He set her back on her feet, and lightly brushed his lips against hers. "I will tell Mother when we return."

The smile flattened into a thin line, then dropped into a sad frown. "Jamie, your mother will not approve."

"How do you know?"

"She as much as told me so."

"She has little say in the matter."

"I cannot go against my lady's wishes. I owe her

my life." She turned and hurried toward camp.

He rushed to catch up with her. "But if she approved?"

Sela stopped. "If she agreed, I would gladly—"

"Then I will gain her consent."

She looked up. The dark eyes returned. "Until then, no one must know. I will deny any promise until my lady approves."

"All right," Jamie reluctantly agreed to the painful condition. "But each day until then you must grant me a few moments. I should die to know you are mine and not be able to even touch you."

She smiled shyly. "I think my lady shall not need me tonight. She has not left her lord's side since he was struck down. Perhaps I could meet you once Marie is settled in bed."

"Perhaps I could take the evening watch on the western rampart."

"Aye, perhaps you could." The eyes that had captured his heart when they first met more than twelve years ago twinkled with excitement. "But come." She took his hand and walked toward the field. "We shall never get to the western rampart if we do not finish with the encampment."

They were nearly running by the time they returned.

Chapter Sixteen

Much of what Genevieve needed done was
finished by the time afternoon drew down to dusk.
Workers sat around the fire eating the roasted meat.
With the complement of men from the garrison to
protect the camp, Genevieve suggested the kitchen
staff remain so cooking could start with the dawn.

Jamie suggested that Bleddyn remain with
Genevieve. The squire did not seem pleased, at first,
but once Jamie mentioned the time *he'd* spent under
the cook's tutelage, he was readily able to convince
the squire of the value of what Genevieve might
teach. The camp was completely set when the small
contingent left the field.

On their return to the castle, Sela went up to
assure that Lady Amye had no need of her. Lord
Cilgerran sat up, bolstered all about by pillows. The
arm of his damaged shoulder was swaddled against
his chest with linen. Lady Amye sat next to him on
the bed, holding his good hand.

"I am glad to see my lord is so well recovered."
Sela smiled at him and he nodded back.

"Aye. We are most thankful for this quick
recovery," Lady Amye said, never taking her eyes
from her husband. "God has blessed us with a great
healer in Rhiana."

"Indeed, my lady. She is very knowledgeable."

"How goes the work in the field?" Lady Amye
asked.

"Very well. Sir James was quite efficient in
getting the encampment set up. We shall be well
prepared on the morrow."

Lady Amye finally turned toward Sela. "I knew he would do well."

"Will you need service of me this evening, my lady?"

"Please, could you see to Marie? 'Tis nearly her bed time." Lady Amye turned back to her husband and gently stroked his free hand.

"Certainly, my lady. I shall go right away."

As she crossed to Marie's suite, she smiled. Soon Jamie would be waiting for her.

"What do you there, little one?" Sela asked as she shut the door to Marie's room behind her.

"I am writing." Marie sat hunched over the parchment with quill in hand.

"What are you writing, my young scribe?"

"My name."

Sela looked at the parchment. It was nearly half-full with lines of carefully written, long, neat rows.

Marie Johanna Eleanor Nasrin de la Vierre.

"Very good, my darling," Sela praised the work. "Now, 'tis time for bed."

Marie looked up and wrinkled her forehead. "But I hoped to finish my hundred lines," she whined.

Sela took up a brush and began to smooth Marie's hair in preparation for braiding. "You will have time to finish in the morning." She quickly completed the plait while the child tried to finish a few more lines. "Come now."

"Must I?"

Sela folded her arms over her chest. "You must. Your mother says 'tis time for you to rest," Sela said, though the uppermost reason in her mind to hurry was not her lady's bidding.

Marie sighed and cleaned the quill before laying it on the writing desk and hopping down from the tall stool.

Sela readied the bed while Marie undressed, knelt down, and said her bedtime prayers. The list of people to bless was long as always, but she was quick to sleep once her head touched the pillows.

Sela went to her quarters, just off Marie's room, and lifted her cloak from the wall peg. She checked Marie one last time and she smiled as a whisper caught her ear.

"Marie Johanna Eleanor Nasrin..." The words repeated over and over while busy little fingers wiggled against the bedcover.

Perhaps Marie had the markings of a scholar, but Sela could not believe a child so full of life could be tamed by a nun's habit. A beautiful, smart, well-spoken woman was worth her weight in gold to a powerful noble. Finding a match for Marie should not be difficult.

Careful not to wake her charge, she slowly lifted the latch, stepped into the stairwell, and quietly closed the door behind her. She wrapped the cloak around her shoulders and fastened the silver clasp at her throat. Anticipation thrummed in her chest as she made her way down the stairs and into the cool night air.

She recalled how excited Lady Amye had been on her return from her rendezvous with Lord Cilgerran before their marriage. Now she understood how thrilling it was to steal away to spend a few moments in a lover's arms.

She hurried to the top of the staircase as quickly as her skirts would let her climb, and when she stepped through the portal Jamie stood looking over the wall.

The moonlight outlined his handsome features against the darkness. He turned toward her, and she ran into his arms. Before he could speak, she pressed her lips to his in a hot, passionate kiss.

He broke it with a chuckle. "I suppose I need not

ask to kiss you anymore."

"I would always say yes, so why ask."

He slipped his arm inside her cloak and drew her close.

Sela slid her arm around his waist as they walked to the far end of the battlement. The air was still and she could feel the warmth of his body pressed close to her. She spread her cloak by the far crenel and they sat, hidden from the view of those below. "Would that we could stay like this forever, my lord."

He frowned at her. "Why do you insist on calling me 'my lord'? You know I have never liked the title."

She sat up with her face next to his. "I call you so, because I very much want you to be my lord, Jamie Barnard."

"Oh." He smiled.

Sela leaned forward and kissed him before curling comfortably against his side.

"You shall not have to wait long," he whispered against her hair. "I shall seek mother's approval on the morrow. Then you must keep your promise to be mine."

Her stomach began to twist and turn. "What will you do if my lady says 'no'?"

"I will not give up until she says 'yes'. I will vex her until she cannot stand to see me coming. It worked when I was a lad. If, as you have said, I am still her favorite, it will work now. She always gave in to me in the end."

Sela looked up at him as if he were crazed.

"Well, it worked some of the time." He brushed his lips against hers and smoothed her hair. "I shall return." He stood and started a slow steady turn along the battlement. Keeping the watch.

She sighed and wrapped her arms around herself to keep the joy from bursting out of her chest. The lady's son, the boy she thought she had no chance with, loved and wanted the serving girl.

He returned and sat next to her. "My little rabbit." He scooped up her hands and kissed them. "We will have such a grand life together. I promise you."

She leaned her head against his shoulder.

"It may take some time," he continued, "but I promise you, in the end, it will be good."

"However long it takes, I will be with you."

Enjoying just being together, they silently sat in each other's arms until the moon moved behind the stone of the merlin.

Jamie stood to walk his post again and Sela stood too.

"I should go now," she whispered.

"Too soon you fly, my sweet." He stroked her cheek.

"Would that I could stay, but—"

"The next guard is due soon. Would you wait for me below?"

Tomorrow would be a busy day. She should go to her room and rest, but she wanted to stay with him, to lie in his arms, feel the warmth of him beside her. "Yes, I will wait."

Jamie smiled and bent to pick up her cloak. He draped it around her shoulders and gave her a soft, quick kiss. "There is no bolt on my door. I shall not be long."

She clung to his hand a moment before starting down the stairs. The walk back seemed longer, but Sela felt excitement as she danced past the kitchen. She spun about, barely able to believe she stood a chance to have her dream. To have the man she had loved for more than twelve years. She sat on the steps of the great hall, looking up at the moon. A prayer formed in her heart.

Please let this be. She closed her eyes for a moment. *Please, God, let us be together.*

Chapter Seventeen

"I must go," Jamie whispered. "I cannot stay."
"Take me with you," Sela pleaded.
"I cannot."
What? He had made her promise. He could not now leave her behind. She tentatively reached forward to touch him.

His face suddenly hardened like stone, his beautiful smile, and even the dimples in his cheeks, frozen in place.

"No! Jamie!" Her heart froze. She stepped back from the statue before her. This could not be happening. Ragged fingers of fear ripped at her gut.

The entire figure cracked like a pillar of ash. The dark lifeless effigy crumbled before her into a mound of charred black earth.

Sela looked down at the ruin. Her heart pounded loud in her ears. "Oh, Jamie. Please, please let me go with you."

She fell to the ground splaying her body across the black dirt. Wanting to feel him. Needing to feel him against her skin.

But she felt nothing. Not even the essence of him remained. He was gone. Gone from her forever.

The tortured wail that tore from her throat scared her, but what could she do but mourn?

Suddenly, her ears heard one thump. Then a second.

Two beats of a heart. Now a third.

She pushed herself up and began digging at the mound. Her fingers were black by the time she reached the bottom, but there, beating loud and strong, was a heart. His heart. She held his heart...

Sela's eyes snapped open. The bright eye of the moon glared down at her from the deep blue of a midnight sky. Her body ached as she pushed herself up from the cold stone. How long had she lain on the courtyard steps? Had she missed him? She ran to the tower, but he was nowhere to be seen.

She hurried up the stairs to his second floor room. Light glinted through a small opening in the door. She reached to push it open, but hesitated. She had promised to meet him, and had not come. Would he be disappointed? What would he think of her, coming to him now?

She turned away, but determination to thwart the loss prophesied by her dream, overcame her fear. She turned back and opened the door.

He stood, half naked, staring at the flames of a small fire in the hearth. The dim light outlined his muscled arms and tinted his broad chest a flame orange. The smile that brightened his face when he turned toward her removed any doubt Sela felt. "I thought you must have tired and gone to your bed," he said.

She unfastened her cloak and let it fall to the floor. "Nay, I have come to yours."

He came and took her by both shoulders. His hands slid down her arms, and his fingers twined with hers. His breath warmed her lips and they parted of their own accord.

His kiss ignited the flame deep inside, and she stepped back from him. She should tell him the truth, but the truth would quell the moment and she wanted this moment, needed this moment, to make her feel...whole.

Many years ago, she had felt the lust of a man's hardness inside her. In the brothel, a man had taken her body without asking. The touch had made her feel...soiled.

Now she wanted to know what it was like to feel a man inside her with love. Her head told her it was wrong to be here, but her soul told her *his* touch would make her feel...clean.

"Are you certain, Jamie? I could not forgive myself should I hurt your chances in any way."

"More certain than when I took my vow of knighthood. You will be my only wife."

She looked into his eyes as she slid her arms free from her sleeves. Baring her torso to him, she closed her eyes. "Please...touch me."

His lips covered hers and she felt as if the hosts of heaven filled her. He fell to his knees and clutched her to him. Trembling hands squeezed her bottom as he kissed her belly. "I will make you my wife this moment if you wish it." He paused and looked up. "But I will wait as well if that be your desire."

She looked down into a pool of admiration so deep the only thing she could do was dive in. "I would most willingly become your wife this night." She hooked her thumbs over the fabric of the kirtle and with a gentle tug, the linen pooled at her feet.

The rough calluses of his palms teased a tingle from her skin as his hands traced every inch of her torso. His caress found its way to her inner thigh. He looked up. "Beautiful. You are beautiful, my wife."

His lips folded over the little point at the top of her mound, and her nails raked trails across his bronzed shoulders as small flicks of his warm, moist tongue teased swells of pleasure from her body.

"Come, bridegroom." She barely recognized the husky voice that rolled from her throat. "Lay with your bride."

He rose and swept her into his arms. "You give me a most precious gift. I swear to you I will never do *anything* to lose such a treasure," he said as he laid her on the bed. "I swear to you, I will love you faithfully, above all else." His hand caressed her face. He stood and stripped off the rest of his clothes.

Sela was overcome by his naked strength and beauty. Overcome by the realization that he belonged to her.

"As long as I live, you need never fear. I swear to you I will protect you from every adversary." He spread himself gently around her like a warm cloak.

"Come," he whispered. "Be now my only food, my only drink, my only air, my only life." The fire in his voice burned through her, branding his mark on her, granting him access to the one thing she had carefully guarded. Not her body, but her heart.

"I shall be your only food, your only drink, your only air, your only life, as you shall be mine," she replied.

The clandestine vows were sealed by a kiss of such passion that Sela did not even feel him push open the door so long closed, but the moment he entered her, she knew she was where she belonged.

"My lord—Jamie." His name came from her lips as a breathless whisper. She closed her eyes, readied herself for the pain she had experienced in her father's brothel. To be with Jamie was worth any pain.

"Ease your thoughts, my lady." He brushed soft lips against her eyelids. "I swear to you, I will never hurt you."

She was with Jamie. She knew beyond all doubt that he would not hurt her, but the memory of her former ordeal held her body a tense captive. She gave a small nod and her fingers wove through the locks at his nape.

Hands braced outside her shoulders, he thrust forward gently, carefully easing further into her. She thought she would burst from the pleasure that seared through her as his shaft slowly sliced through her. The walls of her chamber rippled around him as he rested a moment, warm and hard inside her.

A moan seeped from his throat. "God in heaven, you feel so good," he whispered, his voice rough with desire. He fell into a rhythm of long slow strokes, stretching her further each time. Filling her fuller than she ever thought possible.

Her breath came in rhythm with his thrusts. Heat rose through her as her inner body stretched to take all of him. She wrapped her legs around his hips seeking to keep him deep inside her. Wanting him to be a part of her forever.

A sheen of sweat dampened his chest. His thrusts increased in speed. A low hum rolled from his chest, getting louder each time he plunged himself into her. She bit her lip to stop the scream that might end this bliss, but a high-pitched wail joined his rumble. She realized the sound came from her own throat, but she could not stop. The rumble became a roar, and suddenly she felt the warmth of his seed shooting into her.

Her hips pressed up against him as if not wanting to waste a single drop of his offering. Sela could barely breathe as the rapture washed over her. Her hands clasped his buttocks, pressing him deeper, until, his passion finally spent, he wrapped himself over her, his head nestled against her shoulder. The heaviness of him against her felt good. A tear ran down her cheek and onto the pillow. Then another.

"I meant not to hurt you," he whispered and kissed the tears away. "I will be more gentle next time."

"You did not hurt me," she whispered.

"Then why the tears?"

"Tears of—joy, my love. Tears of joy." For the first time she felt truly and rightly loved by a man.

"I could not ask more than that such sweetness should await for the rest of my life." His words echoed her thought.

"I love you, Jamie," she whispered. "I have loved you all these years. Even when you thought me just a serving girl, I loved you."

His chest shook, and she looked up into laughing eyes.

"I did not ever think you *just* a serving girl. Could you not tell how much I cared for you?"

Over the last weeks, she had come to remember how much he cared. She turned her face into his chest and drew a deep breath, savoring the scent of her only love. Had she known such bliss could exist, she would never have said no.

****

The candle Sela held softly lit the face of the man who now owned her heart.

"Will you not stay with me a moment longer?" He gently kissed her lips. The longing on his face made her feel like a coveted treasure.

"Nay." She pressed her hand against his cheek. "It would not do to have rumor spread around the keep."

"Would you but let me, I would quell all rumor with the truth. That I have taken to wife the most beautiful woman in all of Wales." His lips, nuzzled against the curve of her neck, tempted her to stay a bit longer, but the moon had set and she had to return to her room before Marie woke.

"Soon enough, they will know the man who is my lord." She kissed him one last time and opened the door.

Wind swirled up the staircase, and she sheltered the candle's small flame with her hand. Someone must have left the tower door ajar.

"We are but hours from meeting again," he whispered as she turned to go up the stairs. "Rest well."

As Sela climbed the stairs, she knew if she died

this instant, her only regret would be that she had wasted precious days and nights she could have spent with him.

The hinges squeaked softly as she opened the door. She slipped into her room and tossed her cloak on the bed before going to check on Marie. When Sela lifted the candle, her heart stopped.

The bed was empty.

She turned around the room and her breath released when she found the child with her head down on the writing table, next to the parchment and quill.

Sela smiled. Stubborn imp must have gotten up to finish her "hundred lines" and fallen asleep.

"Marie." She gently rubbed the child's back to awaken her. "Marie. Go back to bed."

Marie made not a sound, not even a sleepy groan.

A chill stiffened Sela's spine, but was too late to warn her of the movement behind her. Before she could turn, a hand clamped over her mouth and the point of a knife pricked the side of her neck.

"Should you scream, I will slit your throat and hers too," a voice whispered. "Do you understand?"

Sela nodded and the hand released from her mouth. She turned and Llwyd, the enemy she spied on, the devil who threatened to finish her later, grinned back at her.

A bead of moisture tickled her skin as it rolled down her neck. She reached up to wipe it away, and her fingers came back stained red. Fear gripped her gut, and she leaned onto the table to check Marie. "Is she all right?" Sela whispered.

"She is of no use to me dead." He captured both of Sela's wrists in his large hand then pushed her down on a stool. "'Tis just a dram of poppy to make this easier."

He cut the braided cloth belt from her waist and

used it to bind her hands. "I have not forgot what you did, whore."

She'd known when she'd agreed to the plan that it would be dangerous, but she did not regret for a moment what she had done.

He ran the flat of his dagger up her leg past her knee, lifting her kirtle in the process. "Or what you owe me."

Please, God, no. She was not ready for her time of reckoning. She closed her eyes and Jamie's face filled her mind. At least she would die having her one desire fulfilled. She held the love of Jamie Barnard. She fought back tears, refusing to give her captor the pleasure of seeing her fear.

"Sit quiet and nothing will happen to you." He turned the knife and sliced the hem of her kirtle. He tore off a strip, cut it in two and used half to bind her feet. He reached to stuff the other piece into her mouth, and Sela did the only thing she could think of to help Marie.

"At least take me with you," she pleaded. "Will you not need someone to care for her?" Sela nodded toward the motionless Marie. "If anything should happen to his daughter—"

Llwyd pushed the cloth far into Sela's mouth, nearly blocking her throat. He picked up Marie's limp body and tossed it over his shoulder. He stepped from the small circle of light won from the darkness by the candle, and his shadow spirited Marie toward the door. He reached to open the door, then turned. He stood there for what felt like a fortnight.

The candle seemed to be losing its battle. Sela began to feel a darkness creep toward her. Suddenly she realized what was happening. With life giving air so cut off, she would soon grow too weak even to draw breath. She kept her gaze on Llwyd, willing herself to just draw one more tiny breath past the gag in her mouth.

As the light began to dim, he returned and set Marie on the bed. He came and pulled the rag from her mouth.

Her chest heaved as her body forced her to gulp down large breaths of air. He lifted her chin with the tip of his blade. The candle lit the crude smile curved beneath his black moustache.

Her neck arched back as he slid the sharp point toward her ear.

"If you give me one wit of trouble, whore, I *will* kill you."

Her body went limp, but she managed a weak nod and he cut her free. Her mind quickly turned to finding some way to get word to Lady Amye. Perhaps...

"May I get a few things to take with us?" she asked.

He pointed the knife toward her. "Be quick or be dead."

She hurried to the chest and found Marie's winter cloak. Before she pulled it out, she removed the clasp. She laid the cloak on the bed the clasp hidden beneath. "May I get my cloak?" she asked.

Llwyd grunted his assent, but followed after her and stood by the door as she grabbed the cloak from the bed. The darkness hid her fingers as she slipped the silver fastening, a larger version Marie's, into her sleeve. Perhaps if she could leave the two clasps behind, Lady Amye would at least know her daughter was not alone. Sela carefully folded the heavy wool over her arm and returned to Marie's bed.

"I would not want her to take ill from the cool night air. Would you please lift her so I can put her cloak on?"

Llwyd slid his hands under Marie's armpits and raised her in front of him. The child dangled before him, blocking his view for a moment.

Sela slid the clasps beneath a pillow, then swept up the cloak and wrapped it around Marie.

Llwyd hefted the child over his shoulder. Marie's toes hung down against his chest.

Sela picked up the slippers from the foot of the bed and slid them on the bare feet. "May I get one thing more?"

"Enough." Llwyd sneered. "I have already been here too long."

She wrapped her cloak around her shoulders and pulled the hood over her head. She looked at Llwyd, waiting for his next command. She had no idea how he planned to escape, but if he was successful at least she would be there to protect Marie. Her only hope was that someone would find the clue she left.

Chapter Eighteen

The sun was barely up when Jamie hurried down the stairs of the tower and through the back portal of the great hall. Sleep did not find him once Sela left, and he was anxious to see her again. She was not in the hall so he went to the kitchen. "Have you seen Mistress Sela?" he asked the baker at the ovens.

"No, m'lord. Perhaps she went out with the group that left to take the bread."

"Perhaps." Jamie was quickly on his way to the field. He passed by the cooper's house where the wife was busy trying to control a group of children too small for the day's work. He reined Abelard to a stop and signaled the big warhorse to stand at ease as the little ones gathered around to gape. "*Gwraig* Cooper, did you see Mistress Sela go through?"

"No, m'lord," Bridget answered as she wiped her brow and hitched a cherub higher on her hip. "Though it would be like her to get out to the field early. Here now, you lot." She shooed the brood away from Abelard's legs. "Get back. Let his lordship pass."

Jamie nodded as he rode away.

He stopped at Rhiana's house, hoping Sela might be there, but the coals in the hearth were banked and the house was empty. He hurried on to the field. Many were there by the time he arrived. Wil was already giving orders to groups of workers.

"Where is Mistress Sela?" Jamie asked as he dismounted.

"I have not seen her," Wil said. "Though I

expected her to come out with the first group." He turned toward villagers just arriving and began to split them into work teams.

Jamie went from one end of the camp to the other searching for her, but she had caught no one's eye this morning. He poked his head into the kitchen tent. "Genevieve. Have you seen Sela?"

"No, my boy. When she was not here, I thought she might be coming with you."

Where could she be? His mouth suddenly went dry. "Most everyone is here. She should not travel out alone. I am going back for her."

****

"Lock him up!" Mother's normally calm voice shrieked as Jamie entered the hall. "He must know something."

A guard dragged away an old man and members of the court stood about, whispering to each other. Only once had he seen his mother shout at anyone and that was only because as a child he had spied outside the door to his parents' solar during an argument. What could cause such extraordinary behavior?

His mother slumped onto a bench by the hearth. She looked...small.

He had never seen her look small. Jamie hurried to her side. "What is it, Mother?"

She did not answer, but when she looked up the pallor of her skin told him all was not right.

His only thought was that something had happened to Sela.

His mother handed him a letter.

Cilgerran,

We have your daughter. If you wish to have her back, bring the deed for Cilgerran Castle and the attached lands to the alehouse at Tewder's Crossing. If you and your English thieves leave this land, she will be returned sound and whole. You have a fortnight to comply.

Jamie took his mother's hand, and they ran to the tower. In Marie's room, Lord Cilgerran stood silent. Jamie squeezed his mother's hand as they hurried to the table. The parchment there was half-covered with the carefully formed letters of a beginner's writing, and on the side, two smears of blood.

God in heaven, was there no end to the torture? Mother could not stand another death and the thought of losing a sibling as beloved to him as Marie was... inconceivable.

Cilgerran's face flushed with anger. He turned toward the door.

"Husband, wait." Mother stopped him. "What will you do?"

"I cannot let this pass." He crumpled the bloodstained parchment and hurled it to the floor. "I must go after her."

"My lord, you have just begun to recover your strength," she pleaded. "You are not yet well enough for this task."

"I must go. 'Twould be an intolerable sign of weakness to do nothing and even worse to give what they want without trying to get her back." Cilgerran pounded his good fist on the table. "I can accept no less than Gladus' head."

"Husband, what good will come of it if you die in this pursuit? You are the lord of these lands. Your life is the life of your people. If they kill you they succeed just as if we give them the deed."

"Mother is right."

Both turned to Jamie.

"I will go. I will bring her back."

"No," Cilgerran protested. "I am her father. 'Tis my duty to protect her. Keep her safe..."

He slumped onto a bench. "I have failed at that, have I not?" His head fell into his hand and a quiet, desperate sob twisted free from his throat.

Mother knelt at her husband's side. "Had you your full strength, I would not hesitate for you to go after her, but you are not well, my lord. Let Jamie go. Of all here, he is the best choice."

Cilgerran sat up, his tear-streaked face set in a stern mask. He spoke no word, but nodded consent.

Jamie started toward the door.

Cilgerran grabbed his arm as he passed.

Jamie looked into eyes filled with anguish. Though he had known Marie for little more than a month, he loved her with all his heart. He could not imagine what pain it must be to lose one's only child.

"You bring her back to me," Cilgerran said.

"Find Sela," Mother interjected. "She will know the most likely hiding places of these cowards."

Jamie suddenly remembered what brought him to the hall. "Sela did not come to the field. I thought she had gone ahead when I could not find her this morning, but no one has seen her. I could not imagine a good reason for her not being there. When was the last time you saw her?"

"Last evening when she went to put Marie to bed." Mother sat at the table next to a tired looking Lord Cilgerran. "I told her I would not need her last night, so I did not expect her later."

Jamie's heart thudded against his chest like a war drum. Sela had been on her way to Marie's room when they parted.

"Perhaps she was needed in the household," Lady Amye said, though her worried tone did nothing to lessen Jamie's anxiety. "Or mayhap she is somewhere in the village."

"No. I have looked for her everywhere. I cannot find her."

"She would have come to us this morning if Marie was gone. Could she have—"

Jamie's heart leapt into his throat as his mother

started to voice the thing he feared most. He frantically searched the room, hoping for any sign Sela had been there. "Mother, can you see anything missing or out of place?"

She walked around the room carefully looking at everything. She opened the chest and looked through the clothes.

"Marie's wool cloak is gone. But everything else is here. Even the clothes she wore yesterday."

Pale and sweating, Cilgerran clutched the table and pulled himself up. "Mayhap she was sleeping when they took her."

"Auch, husband. Sit before you do yourself more harm." She started to come to him, but Jamie helped the lord to sit, so she turned back to her search. When she reached the bed, she pulled back the covers and threw off the pillows.

He barely heard the small clink, but Jamie's attention snapped as tight as an archer's bowstring.

His mother reached out to pick up something.

"What is it?" he asked.

"The clasps from their cloaks." She held out two metal pieces, each crafted into the shape of a double falcon's head.

"I gave them the pair when we first moved here." She put the fasteners in Jamie's hand as she passed him on her way to a side room.

He followed her.

She dug through a trunk, spilling the clothes inside around it. "Sela's cloak is gone as well."

Sela was wearing the cloak last night. Jamie recalled her unfastening the unusual clasp when she dropped her cloak on his bedroom floor.

"What have you found?" Cilgerran called out from the other room.

They returned and his mother shared the unhappy discovery. "Sela must have left the clasps. She must be with Marie."

167

Her words wrapped a chill around Jamie's heart, but urgency pumped his legs as he paced the length between the hearth and the table. "We have no clue where these dogs might be by now. We will have to meet them on their own terms. I will go to this Tewder Crossing." A wave of anxiety churned his gut. "Somehow I shall get them back. I know we are short of men, but I could use five."

Cilgerran spoke. "Take however many you need."

Jamie turned and clasped Cilgerran's good shoulder. "I swear I will find them and bring them safely home."

****

News of the bold kidnapping had seeped through the castle and into the village by the time the rescue effort was ready to depart. Bleddyn, for the first time wearing his armor, stood holding Abelard's halter. The smith's sons would not be denied a place, and all three of their faces were frozen in the same menacing frown as they waited in the yard. Jamie rounded out the party with the two best trackers from the garrison.

Mother and her husband approached as they began to mount.

"Take this, my son." She handed him a small ribbon of yellow linen. At one end, stitched in silk thread, was a crude red lion. "'Twas the very last thing your father gave me before he left."

"Thank you, Mother." He tucked the favor into his gauntlet, and kissed her cheek, then turned to her husband. "Lord Cilgerran, I will not fail you in this mission."

Cilgerran extended his good arm. "I trust you in this." The two men clasped arms.

The sun was barely past its zenith when they rode over the bridge, through the narrow streets of the village and toward the western field. Jamie had sent word for work to continue, but the people lined up for a mid-day meal all turned when the group stopped.

All eyes were fixed on him. Expectant faces hungered to know of the happenings at the keep.

He stood in his stirrups and looked out over the solemn gathering. "You have heard that our enemies have violated the sanctity of our family."

A murmur snaked through the crowd. "We'll bring you back the pieces of 'em, m'lord," a man shouted. The murmur grew to a rushing river of voices.

Jamie shared their anger. He wanted to rip Gladus' chest open. He wanted to tear out the traitor's black heart with his own two hands. But in the eyes of these people, he was their lord just as surely as if he held the title. He must act the part.

"Nay." He waved his hand to quiet the mob. "You must finish your work here. 'Tis of as much import as bringing Lady Marie home. We cannot let these traitors think they have destroyed our will. Finish your meal and finish this field. We shall return our young lady home or die in the trying."

Every man, woman and child who stood there seemed to shout all at once. "Aye, lord!"

For the first time, Jamie felt what Wil meant when he said the people of Cilgerran were family. He felt the kinship. A kinship that now belonged to him. He belonged to them.

As the crowd turned back to the food tables, Wil came forward. "Would that I could go with you."

Jamie looked down from atop his horse. "I need you here to keep things going and to protect the castle until we return."

Wil nodded. "I promise you, that I shall do."

"Aside from which," Jamie said as he offered his arm to his friend, "you have a new son to take care of."

Wil clasped his arm. "God's speed."

The riders turned toward the woods. Once outside the village boundary, Jamie gave careful attention to the road as they passed. An ambush so soon after a ransom request would be unusual, but care was called for when dealing with an unfamiliar enemy. "Daed," he called to one of the young trackers.

"Aye, sir?"

"Take Justin and scout ahead." He disliked being dependent on his men, but faces that once seemed foreign and menacing to him, now held the bond of family and friendship. The people of Cilgerran took their English lord as one of their own and Lord Cilgerran had fought bravely to defend his people. It seemed Mother had chosen her second husband as wisely as she had chosen her first. The man was more like Father than Jamie expected.

By the time Daed returned, they had reached the bend in the road. The place where he had met *Alice.* The place where he had found his heart.

"All clear ahead, m'lord. Justin waits further on."

Jamie turned to the others. "Make haste. I want to be there on the morrow."

Chapter Nineteen

Marie woke in tears.

"'Tis all right, my darling." Sela wrapped her arms around the child and began to gently rock. "Please do not cry."

"But my head hurts so much." Marie had hardly been sick a day in her entire life. Llwyd's potion must be the cause.

Sela rested her cheek against the crown of soft, dark hair. "The pain will soon be gone." She stroked the creased forehead until the tears ceased and Marie sat up.

"This is not home." Curiosity steered wide young eyes all around the room. "Where are we?"

How could their situation be explained without creating a further upset? "We are *guests* in the keep of Sir Gladus," Sela finally said.

"But where are Mama and Papa?"

"They are not here just now."

"I want to see Mama and Papa." Marie began to cry again.

"Please, darling. Remember how your mother taught you to behave as a guest. Be brave. You will see them very soon. I am sure." Sela was not sure of any such thing. She *was* sure some attempt would be made to rescue them.

Failing that, a ransom would be paid. How long that would take, she had no idea. Stories were told of nobles held captive for years, but Lord Cilgerran would not stand for such. The only person he cared for as much as his beloved wife was his daughter. There would be no other heir. Lady Amye was past child-bearing years, and he would never betray her by being unfaithful.

Marie stopped sobbing and sat up. She sniffed and wiped her face with the sleeve of her chemise and nodded her head. The corners of her mouth turned up slightly.

"There, now." Sela smiled back. "T'was not so hard. Come, let us get you dressed."

Thankfully, while Marie slept, a maid had brought a few clothes. They were meant for an older child, but at least Marie would not have to spend her captivity in her chemise.

Sela brought the basin of water and a towel from the washstand.

Marie jumped down from the high bed. She splashed some water on her face and patted it dry.

After re-braiding Marie's hair into two neat plaits, Sela laid out the two kirtles the maid had brought. "Which would you like to wear today?"

"That one." Marie pointed to the green shift, then lifted her arms above her head.

Sela slid the dress on, then tightened the laces as much as possible. Still a bit large, but Marie was tall enough so the hem did not drag the floor too much as she walked around the room looking at the fine appointments.

Compared to Cilgerran, Gladus' keep was a palace. Marie stopped before a scene of a hunting party chasing down a stag. She reached out and touched the flank of a palfrey, carefully drawn on the wall in sable colored paint. "I hope someone remembers to feed Falconer."

Sela's relief leaked out in a smile. Thoughts of the commonplace still presided in Marie's mind. No need yet to worry her with their dangerous situation. But how long would that last? A smart child like Marie would surely figure out something was wrong when her doting parents did not come to see her after a day or two.

A knock at the door was followed by the scrape of the bolt that kept them locked inside. Without waiting for even an answer, the door swung open. Sela's breath stopped behind the hand she raised to her mouth. The ice blue eyes of the stranger from the market stared back at her.

"My lord, Gladus, wishes to see the girl," the tall, red-haired man said as he entered. "Come with me." He reached to take Marie.

Sela moved between them and pushed Marie behind her.

Marie clung to Sela's skirts, but peeked out to see what was happening.

"Come, now," the young man said as he moved toward them.

"I am her caretaker." Sela kept herself between Marie and the stranger. "Can I not go with her?"

"Your pardon, mistress, but my lord bade me bring him the child. Alone." He moved Sela aside and took Marie's arm.

Marie began to scream and squeezed Sela's hand tightly, but he pulled at the girl until their grip on each other was broken.

Marie turned and kicked him.

He cursed, picked her up, and tossed her over his shoulder like a sack of flour.

"Stop!" Sela shouted.

Marie instantly quieted.

The stranger stopped as well.

"Sir, are you not a knight of this realm?" Sela asked.

"Aye, mistress. I am," he answered in a measured tone, but did not turn to face her.

Two last tears glistened in Marie's large round eyes, but they did not fall.

"My lady," Sela calmed her voice, hoping in turn to calm Marie, "you must remember you are a guest here and the lord of the house wishes to see you. 'Tis nothing wrong in that. Remember what your mother taught you?"

The two braids on each side of Marie's head bobbed forward as she nodded.

"Good Sir," Marie spoke to the knight. "Would you be kind enough to release me...please?"

He set Marie down.

Sela walked to them and wiped away Marie's tears. She smoothed the child's hair and patted her cheek.

"This man is a knight in this castle. He will see no harm comes to you while you and I are parted." Sela looked up at the tall nobleman. "Will you not, sir?"

"My lord bade me escort this lady to him. No ill shall befall her whilst she is in my care." He extended his arm at a level Marie could reach.

The child looked at Sela and she nodded.

Marie placed her hand on the red knight's arm, and the two started toward the door. If not for their pitiable situation, the scene would have been humorous; the tall knight hunched over so the little girl might take his arm. Marie turned to look back.

Sela stood up straight and tall.

Marie followed the example and stretched the length of her small frame.

The knight looked back, too and nodded his thanks.

The door shut behind them, and the bolt scraped into place. She could only hope the knight would keep his word. He did not look a bad sort, and he had treated Marie with respect once she calmed down.

However, Sela was not as certain of Marie's safety once the child was with Gladus. Llwyd must surely know the consequences of harming Marie. She hoped he passed the concerns on to Gladus.

She scanned the room more closely.

From the small window she could see they were at the top of a wooden tower. Two other towers stood across the courtyard. Unlike Cilgerran Castle, no one was busy at daily tasks. No one, save the few yeomen walking their posts on the palisade.

The opposite window showed a fourth tower in the center of the yard. She could see Marie walking next to the red knight. Lady Cilgerran would have been proud of her daughter as she climbed the steps to the great hall.

****

Marie squinted as they went from the warm, bright sun of the courtyard to the cool darkness of the hall. As her eyes became used to the dim candle light, she could see Sir Gladus sitting at the far end of the room, surrounded by two men she had never met before.

Her red knight walked beside her, and she suddenly felt the need to grasp his hand, rather than let her fingers rest on his arm as Mother had taught her. She looked up at him. He had promised to be her protector. Sela said he was a knight. Jamie was a knight and Marie trusted *him*. She would try very hard to trust this knight, too.

"My lord." The red knight bowed before Sir Gladus like Sir Gladus bowed before her father.

Marie was unsure if she should, but curtsied, just in case it was the polite thing to do. She waited patiently to be introduced, but no further word was spoken.

Mayhap he did not know her name. She did not remember telling it to him. She tugged at his sleeve and he looked down at her. She crooked her finger to signal him to draw near and whispered in his ear.

He smiled and straightened. "My lord?"

"What is it, Cynan?" Sir Gladus turned to them but his sour tone worried Marie.

"This lady bade me introduce her to you."

"I know who she is."

Marie tugged at his sleeve and he bent to her again.

"The lady says the others know naught of her and 'tis only proper she should be introduced."

The three men at the table chuckled.

"Then most certainly she must be introduced," Gladus said when he stopped laughing.

"My lord, Gladus ap Giffri, I introduce Lady Marie Johanna Eleanor Nasrin merch Alun of Cilgerran."

Marie had ever heard her full name used this way before. The red knight—Cynan said it with such flair. Swirled in excitement, Marie curtsied again.

Gladus nodded and waved a hand. "Get on with it."

Cynan turned to the man on the right. "Sir Cadwallon ap Hywell, I introduce Lady Marie Johanna Eleanor Nasrin merch Alun of Cilgerran Castle."

"Sir Llwyd ap Gladus, I introduce...

Sir Llwyd.

So, this was the son of Sir Gladus. She knew of him, but he had never been to Cilgerran. The smile on Sir Llwyd's face made Marie uneasy, but unlike the others, he stood and bowed to her. She curtsied in return.

He turned to Sir Gladus. "If you have no further need of me, Father, I have duties to attend to before my departure."

Gladus waived a hand, and Sir Llwyd came down from the platform. As he passed by, he stopped and lifted her chin.

"Pretty child." His words seemed casual, but she shivered at his touch. She moved closer to her knight and tried not to draw more notice to herself.

Llwyd continued on his way. Marie turned her

head and watched until he was gone. She looked up at her protector.

He smiled a gentle smile and nodded his head.

She felt a bit better and released the tight grip she held on his hand before she turned back to face Sir Gladus.

Chapter Twenty

Why would Gladus want to see Marie alone? Sela wondered as she searched the room for a means of escape. None seemed forthcoming.

The child knew nothing of the intrigue swirling around her. Nor could she tell him anything about Cilgerran he did not already know.

Sela put her eye to the space between a large cupboard and the wall. Perhaps this place held secret passages just as Edensmouth had. What she spied there lifted her hopes. A small gap in the wall. A nook? Or perhaps, a hidden exit?

She tried to slide her hand toward the gap, but the cupboard was too tight against the wall. She threw open the cabinet doors and ran her hands along the inside edges, both front and rear, but her fingers tripped no secret latch. She pushed against the back with all her weight but the panel held firm.

She pushed the cabinet with all her strength, but the heavy piece moved barely a few inches. She tried again to reach the gap. Her hand fit, but she could not reach far enough to feel the opening.

"You shall not escape."

Sela jumped and drew back her hand. Her heart filled her ears with loud thuds as she recognized the voice. She turned to face her worst nightmare. "Llwyd."

Alone.

On the road to Cilgerran, he'd promised revenge for her betrayal. The look in his eye raised a bucket of fear from the well of her belly.

"Well, mistress Ales." An evil grin turned up the

corners of his mouth. "No knight to protect you this time?"

Sela pressed against the wall as he stepped closer. She knew what revenge he wanted. She edged toward the window, but he surged forward and forced his knee between her legs.

"Nay. You shall not be escaping me this time."

Pressed between the wall and the cupboard, she bowed her head, hoping not to stir his anger further.

He jerked her chin up and violently kissed her.

A kiss that brought back the memory of her father's house. Sela sought to scream, but the sound was swallowed as his mouth pressed her lips painfully against her teeth.

He stuck his tongue in her mouth and she bit it. He jerked away.

"Wretched drab." He drew back his hand to strike her.

Sela ducked under the blow, but he caught her hair and pulled her upright.

His backhand made her head ring and the salty taste of blood trickled over her tongue. "You tried that trick once before and caught me off guard." He twisted her to the floor by the handful of hair he held. "Not this time."

****

"You did well, my lady." Cynan gently squeezed the little fingers resting in his hand as they walked back to the tower.

Lady Marie smiled up at him. "Thank you."

In the short time they had spent together, Cynan had become attached to the little girl. Once she had calmed herself, she'd acted like the perfect lady. She answered Gladus' questions not like a child of five or six, but as if she was a grown woman. She had even thought to ask about her parents and her status in the castle.

Cynan smiled. The girl had not cowered as

Gladus had expected her to, but she stood tall and spoke directly. Her questions had put Gladus on the spot. As a result, Cynan had ended up being appointed to attend her while she was here. Though he had spent little time with children, he did not mind the duty.

She lifted her hem as they climbed the stairs.

He slowed his pace so she would not have to rush on the tall steps.

"Sir Gladus did not say when my mother and father are coming." The high pitch of a child's voice was an unaccustomed sound. It had been a long time since there were children in the castle.

They reached the top of the landing and Cynan looked down at the inquiring face. "I do not think he knows for certain, but it should not be too long."

The lie could do no harm. Most likely, she would be here for some time. Surely Cilgerran would not pay the ransom asked. "I am sure your mother and father miss you every day you are apart from them." That at least was the truth. Surely they must miss such a bright child.

She smiled at him, though she looked a bit sad. "I miss them, too," she said softly.

He took her hand and started toward her room. When they reached the door, she looked up at him. "When I return to Cilgerran, would you come and visit me?"

A pang of guilt knotted in Cynan's chest. His lord held her hostage in order to force Cilgerran Castle away from her English father. Yet, in her innocence, she considered Cynan her friend. "Perhaps."

He turned to slide back the bolt, but it was already undone. Something told him not to take the child into that room. He led her to a small storeroom down the hall. "Wait here until I come for you," he whispered. "Do not come out no matter what you hear."

Her eyes widened, but she nodded.

He shut the door, then quietly tiptoed toward the bedroom. He stared for a few moments at the open bolt, before his hand touched the wood. The alarm in his head did not prepare him for what he saw when he opened the door.

In the center of the floor, Llwyd was hunched over Lady Marie's companion.

Cynan hastened toward the bodies sprawled on the floor. "Llwyd! Brother, what are you doing?" He tugged at his brother's shoulder. "Get off her. A hostage must be treated properly."

Llwyd looked up and smiled. "Your father must have been English. You are too weak to be a Welshman. I told my father your mother was a—"

Cynan kicked his brother off the woman.

Her eyes were puffed from crying and a purple bruise had begun to spread beneath her eye. She curled into a tight ball and rolled to face away from them.

"This was the duty you had to attend to? Attacking a guest of our Father's house?"

Llwyd stood. "I merely take what I am owed." Not bothering to tighten the lace on his braes, he pulled his tunic down. "Father could care less about her. This is the strumpet who betrayed our first plan."

Anger knotted Cynan's gut. "Our plan was betrayed because you let your cock control your brain."

Llwyd reared back to punch him, but Cynan struck first. A fist just above the groin doubled the bigger man over. Cynan jerked his knee up against his brother's chin.

Llwyd's head snapped back, and he fell to the floor.

Cynan rushed forward ready to strike again. He

had been beaten bloody by his brother more than once, but it was not going to happen this time.

Llwyd merely sat up and laughed. "It matters not, little brother." He stood and moved to within a breath of Cynan's face. "I have taken what I wanted." Llwyd pushed Cynan aside. "Father will hear of this." Llwyd stomped toward the door.

"Aye, he will," Cynan snapped back before his brother slammed the door behind him.

As the echo faded away, the quiet sobs of the woman fell on Cynan's ears. He touched her back, but she cringed and he drew his hand away.

"He is gone," Cynan offered as some sort of solace, but the words seemed small comfort, even to him. He started to ask if she was all right, but he knew she could not be. "I am much aggrieved by what he did to you."

He could not leave her like this. "Come, mistress. I must bring the child back. Surely you do not want her to see what has happened here."

She turned to face him, one cheek pressed against the floor. The shoulder of her dress had ripped and the bruise on her cheek had begun to spread. She tried to push herself up, but her arms shook so much she could not hold herself.

Cynan hated his brother more than ever. To brutalize a woman so.

"Let me help you." He reached toward her, but she jerked away. "I swear I will not hurt you."

Finally she reached her hand toward him and he helped her into a sitting position.

A loud sob racked his body as she leaned against him, clutching her hands together over her chest.

He picked her up and carried her to the bed then went to the cupboard, where he found a clean chemise. He returned to the bed, but she had gone silent.

His throat tightened. Had Llwyd injured her so

much she might be dead? Cynan reached toward the body, but feared his touch might confirm his thought. As he looked down at her, she suddenly drew a deep breath. Her eyes blinked open, but she stared blankly at the ceiling.

"Mistress?" He called to her. "Mistress, come back."

After a moment, her eyes focused, and her brow drew into a worried frown. "Where is Lady Marie?" She barely croaked out.

"She is safe." Cynan assured her. "But I must bring her back to this room. Think ye you are able to carry on?"

She nodded.

He laid the shift on the bed beside her. "Put this on and give me your dress. I shall dispose of it. I will tell Lady Marie you were taken ill while we were gone, so you need not leave the bed until you are able."

Cynan turned to straighten the mess Llwyd had made of the room. He had spent much time here as a child. The room had belonged to his mother. He picked up a small bronze statue and set it back on its shelf, then straightened the floor coverings that had been thrown askew. It pained him that Llwyd's barbarous act now tainted the good memories of this place.

"I am ready." Her voice sounded a bit stronger now.

He returned to the bed where she sat on the edge. Her legs dangled over the side, her feet still in her shoes. The color of the bruise on her cheek stood out against her pale skin. He had no idea how to explain it to the child, but there was no hiding it. He knelt and slipped the shoes from her feet.

"Lie down. I shall send a healer to tend you and a woman to help Lady Marie."

She swung her legs onto the bed, and he covered

her.

"Thank you." Her eyes no longer showed her fear, though he knew it must still be there.

He reached out and touched her hand. "I pledge on my life, no further harm will come to you, and Lady Marie will be safe as long as she is in this house."

He also made a promise to himself. His brother would pay for this act, even if it cost every last drop of Cynan's own blood.

Chapter Twenty-One

Jamie sat watching the front door of the single room that was the *Tafarn ty Tewder*.

Watching men come in, wet from the drenching rain that had begun to fall.

Watching men drink the same watered-down ale the brewer had forced on him in order to keep the table.

Watching for a sign the man he waited for might be here.

He slowly sipped his drink. Though the weak brew was unlikely to have much effect, he did not like having the dullness of drink upon him when he dealt with his enemies. The others were scattered around the room, waiting for his signal.

"Well, well. 'Tis the chivalrous knight."

Jamie's jaw clenched tight. "Llwyd." Fury roughened his voice. "I should have known you would be in this somehow."

The oaf grinned while he took his time removing his rain-soaked cloak. "*Grwaig! Cwrw!*" he bellowed an order for ale at the brewer before he plopped onto the bench across the table. "My father would trust no one else with such a task. You have what we asked for?"

Of course not. The deed was locked safe, beneath the floor of Mother's room.

The son of Gladus? Llwyd showed himself as an arrogant fool for giving such information away. In the hostage game, many gambits could be played. Gladus must certainly expect something other than surrender. To send his own son into such a situation.

A nervous-looking young woman set the ordered ale on the table and tried to hurry away, but Llwyd managed to pull her onto his lap before she could manage to escape. He whispered something in her ear and terror flashed across her face.

Jamie pulled a sealed packet from his tunic and laid it on the table.

Llwyd released the girl, and she scurried away. He reached out to take the packet, but just as his fingers touched the prize, Jamie slammed his own hand onto the parchment. He carefully phrased his next words. "How do I know you even have *them*?"

Llwyd reached in his pouch then dropped a small ring on the table.

Jamie knew instantly. The falcons engraved into the gold matched those on the rings his mother and her husband wore. Anger roiled inside him, and he leaned forward with a snort that made Llwyd sit back. "How do I know she is safe?"

"Ah, on that you must trust me." Llwyd lowered his eyes, avoiding Jamie's menacing glare. "She would be no good to us dead. Aside from which, Cilgerran would hunt us down if she was returned...damaged."

Jamie leaned back against the wall. The traitors knew what they risked with Marie, but he still had no response about Sela. "What of the maid?"

Llwyd's lips parted, then formed an "O". "A day ago she was fine indeed." A row of crooked yellow teeth appeared below his black moustache. "Your little strumpet made a fine—"

Fury welled in Jamie's gut. If this lout dared touch Sela! He sprang to his feet, knocking his bench to the floor. Men at the neighboring tables scattered in

all directions as he overturned the table atop Llwyd.

He threw the table aside and lifted Llwyd by the

front of his chain mail. "If a single hair on either of their heads is out of place, I will break your neck with my own hands."

Llwyd reached up to wipe a trail of blood from the side of his mouth. His eyes held a challenge and an assured smile spread across his face. "You will never get to them...without me."

Jamie unclenched his fist. He felt a small satisfaction when Llwyd's head hit the floor with a loud thump.

The men of the Cilgerran contingent formed a half-circle around them, blades drawn. He pushed past them, but stopped cold as he surveyed the scene. Three unknown men lay on the floor.

Jamie looked to Bleddyn. Blood stained the squire's blade and those of Huw and Owain as well.

Perhaps Llwyd was not so much an idiot. If they *were* Llwyd's men, they would not be going anywhere soon.

Jamie searched the silent room until he spotted the innkeeper. "Take care of them." He nodded toward the three men bleeding on the floor.

The paunchy man started to reply, but his mouth snapped shut as Jamie moved toward him.

Jamie loomed over him and squinted an eye.

A wide-eyed nod was all the man could manage.

Jamie pressed three silver coins into his hand. "For your trouble."

Wide-eyes started to breathe again. "Thank you, sir." The man was so happy, or so scared, he bowed three times. "I shall clear up this mess right away."

Jamie turned to his men. They held Llwyd with both arms bent at a painful-looking angle behind his back.

"Bring him."

****

The reflection in the polished round of metal looked dreadful. Sela touched the wine colored

187

bruise just below her eye. At least it did not throb like it had for the past few days. The swelling had gone down some, but the spot was still tender. When the healer explained it away as part of "the illness," Marie had frowned, but she had not questioned further.

Yesterday, Cynan had been kind enough to show them the quills and ink powder hidden away in a secret drawer beneath the writing table. He brought a few sheets of parchment and Sela had been able to occupy Marie's time with writing her name for most of the day.

On further examination, the desk had also yielded a secret prize. A penknife used to sharpen the quills. It was small, but might still prove useful. She was careful to put the knife back in the same place. Perhaps Cynan had forgotten about the knife, but he might also be testing her intent.

Today he had brought a few more sheets and some verses for Marie to copy. She sat on two pillows in order to reach the height of the writing desk.

"When will Mama and Papa come?" Marie asked without looking up from her work.

"Soon, sweetheart. They will come soon." Sela could only hope so. Llwyd had not returned, but she could not feel safe knowing he would surely find a way to finish what Cynan had interrupted. "How is the writing coming along?"

"I think it is good. What think you?" Marie held the parchment out and Sela walked over to look at the work. Two stanzas of the first poem were neatly scribed in straight even lines.

"Very good. Very nice work, in—." A soft knock on the door interrupted her praise. She laid the sheet on the desk and went to answer. "Yes?"

"Mistress Sela, might I enter?"

"You are certainly welcome here, sir."

The metal scraped against wood as Cynan

pulled the bolt back and Sela opened the door.

He carried a tray with two bowls of stewed meat and vegetables, thick slices of coarse bread, and a small bowl of sweets.

"I hope this will do." A frown marred his usually jovial face. "My father's treatment of you is shameful. Please forgive his rude manner."

Sela smiled. The tall, red-haired knight apologized each time he came. First for his brother's savagery, then for the fact his father did nothing about it, then because they were kept locked in their room, now for the quality of the food.

"'Tis plentiful and smells delicious," she said, hoping to set him at ease. She took the tray and set it on the table.

He shut the door and followed her into the room.

"My lady," Sela said, "Sir Cynan has brought us our dinner."

"Lady Marie." He bowed.

Marie hopped down from the stool. She looked up at the knight and said, "Will you join us, sir?"

"Nay, lady. I have already dined with my father. I apologize that you were not invited to his table, but there was much business to discuss. 'Twas very dull. You would not have been entertained."

He pulled out the chair and waited while Marie smoothed her skirts then sat. He did the same for Sela and she nodded her thanks. While they ate, he stood at the window, staring down at the courtyard. Something was bothering him.

Sela approached. "I thank you for the care you have given us."

"I only wish 'twere more..." He continued to stare down at the yard. "Llwyd has left the castle," he whispered.

Thank God. A reprieve from the threat Llwyd imposed. The tension she felt melted away, but then his long silence gathered her concerns.

"He is on his way to see if the ransom will be paid. It should not be long now until we have an answer."

"Thank you for such good news." Now, she had something to tell Marie. "Might I ask what the ransom is?" She could not think of any sum Lord Cilgerran would not pay to get his daughter back.

"My father wants Cilgerran. To take the castle from the English would consolidate his power over the area."

"Oh." Though it would pain the lord surely even *that* was not too high a price. "Then, hopefully, we should be shortly away," she said, though she knew they could be there for months, even if the ransom was paid.

The knight looked at her. "Hopefully," he said, but his face did not appear very hopeful.

He turned back to the window and Sela returned to the table. She picked at the bowl of stew, not feeling much like eating.

Lord Cilgerran would not pay the ransom unless he could be assured of getting Marie back. Or perhaps a rescue attempt was being mounted even now. Surely Jamie would not let them be kept without trying to get them back. They had to be ready to escape in a trice. She had to be ready to travel. She sat up straight and spooned a bite of nearly cold meat into her mouth. She had to rebuild her strength. She had swallowed nearly all of the stew by the time Marie spoke.

"I wish to return to my writing."

Sela looked at Marie's half-empty bowl and the slice of bread from which one small corner had been torn. "Are you certain you could not eat a little more?"

"Nay, I have had enough."

"Very good, my lady. I shall check your lesson in a bit."

Marie tried to push herself away from the table.

Cynan suddenly appeared to pull back the chair for her.

"Thank you, sir." She curtsied before she hurried over to the writing table.

Cynan started to go after her, but Sela shook her head. "She likes to do things for herself," she whispered.

Cynan nodded. He smiled as he watched Marie climb onto the chair and settle herself on the pillows.

"Sir?" Sela spoke softly.

"Yes, mistress?"

"Might it be possible for my lady and me to have a walk around the courtyard? My injuries have begun to heal, but my legs are a little bit stiff. 'Twould be a great boon if I could walk about, even for just a short time."

"I shall ask my father if 'twould be allowable. Have you done with your dinner?"

"Yes, thank you." Sela stood and gathered up the bowls and spoons.

Cynan picked up the tray and stepped out the door Sela held open. Before she shut it, he turned.

"Perhaps you might be ready to walk just before supper?"

Chapter Twenty-Two

The wagon, taken from a local farmer, bumped along the approach to Penwydd Castle. Jamie had forced Llwyd to convince the farmer that Lord Gladus needed a load of hay delivered immediately and these men were to take it to the castle. Jamie had paid the man handsomely to silence his complaints about the return of his wagon. They left Bleddyn and the two scouts with the horses in a well-hidden grove nearly an hour away.

"We are nigh on to the bridge," Huw whispered from the driver's seat.

The hay piled on top of Jamie poked at his skin as he lay in the back of the cart. He wanted to scratch, but dared not move. He laid his dagger against Llwyd's throat.

The wagon rolled to a stop and Huw chatted with the guard.

Jamie wished he had taken the time to learn something more of the language in the weeks he had been here. His Welsh was nowhere near good enough to understand what they said, but he caught the words "Gladus" and *gwair*, the word for hay. The conversation heated and Huw jumped from the wagon.

Jamie held his breath and tightened his blade against Llwyd's neck.

Angry words flew between Huw and the guard.

Beads of sweat rolled down Jamie's forehead. The game was up. His first thought was to slice Llwyd's throat. If anyone was going to die the evil bastard should be the first to go.

The row suddenly stopped. A long silence passed before the guard said, *"Basio"*

Move on.

The cart rocked as Huw climbed aboard, and they rolled across the wooden bridge and onto a stone path.

Once they moved further past the gate, Jamie chanced a few words. "What happened?"

"The man was just trying to be difficult," Huw answered. "I told him there would be hell to pay for both of us if Lord Gladus did not get his hay and my master did not get his payment. He finally saw reason. Where do we go from here?"

Jamie pulled out the rag they had stuffed in Llwyd's mouth. "You had best have a place for us to hide until we fetch them. Your life depends on it. I swear you will be the first to die should we be discovered."

"Stay on the main path." Llwyd whispered. "Go to the barn behind the farthest tower. 'Tis close to where they are being kept. 'Tis hardly ever used."

Though he could not see, Jamie mapped out the castle in his head as they rode. The clop of the horse's hooves echoed against far-off stone walls. He counted the paces until the wagon stopped. The keep was large and fortified. They would have a long way to go if they ended up having to run, but they only crossed one bridge to enter. An easier escape if they made it to the gate.

"Open it," Huw ordered.

Quiet footsteps were followed by the creak of a door. The wagon moved forward a few yards, then came to a halt. Jamie lay perfectly still until the smelly hay was lifted from his head.

"Tis safe," Madog said.

Jamie pushed the rest of the hay aside and stood. His legs stung like a thousand ant bites. He stretched until the sensations subsided.

193

"You best get me up as well." Llwyd called from the wagon. "I cannot take you to them if I cannot walk."

Llwyd's sneer irked Jamie. The traitor deserved to lie there until he rotted, but he was right—they needed him. Jamie nodded.

Owain and Huw pulled Llwyd from the wagon and dropped him on the ground like a last bale of hay. Huw cut the ropes binding his feet and yanked him to a standing position.

Jamie stood face to face with his nemesis. "Where are they?"

"You will have to give me a minute." Llwyd lowered his head and rubbed art his temple with his bound hands. "I must have hit my head with such rough handling." One side of his mouth turned up into a nasty grin. "I seem to have forgotten."

Jamie grabbed the front of Llwyd's tunic and yanked him even closer. "Try not my patience, vermin," he said through clenched teeth. "I have little left to give you."

Llwyd's grim smile disappeared. "They are in the West Tower."

"One of us should go with you," Huw said.

"Nay. 'Twill draw too much attention. The three of you get the hay unloaded and the cart turned about. I can handle this sack of offal. If we are successful, I will return with a pass phrase. If I do not return or if I say not the phrase, you will know we are betrayed. Get yourselves out. Make sure Cilgerran knows what happened." Jamie leaned to whisper in Huw's ear.

Huw nodded and went to help his brothers.

Jamie cut the rope binding Llwyd's hands. He wrapped his arm around Llwyd's neck and squeezed hard. "One false step and I shall happily end your miserable existence. Understood?"

Llwyd nodded and Jamie loosened the pressure

that had cut off most of the bastard's air. Leaning on him like a drunken man using a friend for support, the other hand, pressed a dagger against Llwyd's side. "Lead on."

****

Jamie flattened against the wall as they climbed the tower steps. The single candle at the top of the stairwell flickered and sputtered, fighting to give off barely enough light to see.

The arm twisted behind Llwyd's back kept the black knight in check, still Jamie did not trust the knave to not have some trick in mind. He poked the dagger into Llwyd's side. "Which room?"

"The second one there," Llwyd turned his head to answer and his sour breath churned Jamie's stomach.

"Get the candle," he said when Llwyd started toward the door.

"If I remove the light, the guards on watch below will know something is amiss," Llwyd said, too calm for Jamie's pleasure.

What he said made sense. The sconce sat just to the right of a small window. Still, the viper could be up to something.

"Go on then," Jamie pushed Llwyd forward, keeping the arm twisted tight.

Llwyd pulled back the bolt, but before he could open the door, Jamie stopped him.

"Guards?" Jamie whispered. There were none outside the door. He suspected he may be walking into a trap.

"None, I know of," Llwyd said. "Why waste more men on a woman and a child?"

Llwyd had apparently forgotten Sela's prior escape.

"Open it," Jamie said.

****

The bolt screeched like a small bird against the

wood of the door, and Sela's eyes snapped open. Such a small sound, but since Llwyd's attack, her sleep had been so little and so light she never felt rested. Cynan would have knocked. This time it might be Llwyd on the other side of the door.

Unlike Sela, Marie had been sleeping like a bear in winter. She shook the little girl awake.

"What is it?" the little voice asked with a drowsy yawn.

"Come, my darling. You must hide."

All signs of sleepiness disappeared and Marie jumped from the bed. They had discussed the possibility of impending danger and Marie understood the importance.

"Quickly." Sela rushed to the armoire. "Into the cupboard," she whispered. "Remember, no matter what you hear—"

"—do not come out," Marie finished the instruction as she climbed inside.

Sela nodded and quietly shut the door. She hurried to the writing desk and removed the penknife from its hiding place. It was not much of a weapon, but it was the only one she had. She crouched in the shadows at the foot of the bed.

The door creaked open, and not one but two men entered. Fear flamed up from her core, clouding her vision. Had Llwyd brought someone to hold her down while he finished what he started? Did the bastard just want to humiliate her further by having his friend watch or had her worst nightmare finally come true?

More willing to beg or steal rather than fulfill her father's promise that two men could have her at the same time, she'd run from home. The thought of being crushed between two rutting boars chilled her fears to an icy stillness. The shaking inside her ceased.

She could not defend against two men, but

perhaps if she could stab at the right place, she might be able to stop one of them. That might keep the other at bay. She had to try. For Marie and for herself.

The two forms moved slowly and quietly toward the bed.

She steadied herself and raised the small knife, ready to strike.

"Sela?"

The voice was not Llwyd's, but—

"Jamie?" Her heart leapt into her throat as she spoke his name. "Oh, Jamie." She ran to wrap her arms around him. "I am so glad—"

Fetid breath assaulted her nose.

Llwyd wrapped his arm around her. "I am happy to see you, too."

Sela tried to scream, but panic filled her lungs, drowned her voice. She stabbed the knife into his arm, but instead of releasing her, his hold tightened. She struggled to break free.

"Let her go, you bastard." Jamie's voice pierced the darkness.

Llwyd flinched, then his arm opened.

She stumbled away.

"Are you all right?" Jamie's voice slowed the drumming of her heart.

"I am now," she whispered.

"The smith's sons wait in one of the barns," Jamie's voice calmed her breath.

"And I made this scum bring me—"

Llwyd's elbow crashed into Jamie's side.

Too late Sela realized her mistake. "Look out," she shouted. "He has my knife!"

Jamie spun to stop Llwyd's slash, but Sela could not get out of the path. The small sharp knife sliced her shoulder. The force of the blow knocked her to the floor.

The black knight slashed again. Jamie's dagger

clattered against the hearth stones. The orange glow
of the coals glinted off the blade. Sela crawled over
and snatched it up. Her heart pounded as she
watched the two men struggle.

Jamie caught Llwyd's knife hand.

Llwyd punched Jamie in the side again and
again, but Jamie held tight. They twisted around
and Sela could no longer tell which man was Jamie.

She followed the scuffle across the room. They
twisted about again and Jamie's face was lit by a
single beam of moonlight. Her hand touched his as
she laid the dagger in his palm.

He forced Llwyd's arm upward, and thrust the
blade into the right side of the chest.

Llwyd, crumpled to the floor.

Sela let out the breath she held and ran to
Jamie. "You are hurt."

He shook his head. "'Tis nothing. Just a scratch.
We must go quickly," he whispered. "Where is
Marie?"

Her shoulder still stung, but she hurried to the
armoire and threw open the door. "Jamie has come
to take us home."

Marie darted to her brother and threw her arms
around him. "Thank goodness and light."

"Hurry. Dress yourselves." He ripped a strip
from the bottom of his tunic and wrapped it around
his hand. "We must go."

The pain of cloth rubbing against her shoulder
forced Sela to move slower than she wanted, but she
pulled on a kirtle, then helped Marie tighten her
laces.

"We're ready." She whispered.

Jamie picked up Marie, but when they turned to
the door, they came face to face with Cynan.

Chapter Twenty-Three

The tall red-haired man stood in the door, holding a candle high. Jamie readied his dagger, but Sela grasped his arm.

"He has helped us," she whispered.

The man entered the room and quietly closed the door behind him. "You have killed him?" He nodded toward Llwyd's limp body.

"Aye." Jamie whispered. "Though I hated the man, I did not wish more blood to be shed. He forced my hand."

"'Twas supposed to be my duty to kill him," the stranger said. "For what he did to this woman."

Jamie put Marie down and turned to Sela.

"What did he do to you?" Rage so tightened his jaw, he had to force the words from his mouth.

"Nothing that will not mend," she stroked his arm. "He tried to break me first with his words, then with his fist. He would have violated my body as well, had not Sir Cynan prevented it."

"My father will not be happy about Llwyd's death," Cynan whispered. "If there is hope of escape, you must be gone. Now."

Jamie pointed the dagger at Gladus' son. "How do I know you can be trusted?"

Marie tugged at Jamie's tunic. "Because Cynan is sworn to protect me."

"'Tis true," Sela added. "He protected both of us at his own risk."

Apparently he owed much to *this* son of Gladus. He slid his dagger into his boot. "I am Sir James Barnard. Son of Lady Cilgerran."

"And I am Cynan ap Gladus." He extended an open hand.

Jamie grasped Cynan's arm and gave it a hearty squeeze. "You have my gratitude for helping my wife and sister."

"Llwyd's return is expected on the morrow," Cynan said showing no grief over his brother's death. "My father has already doubled the guard and I volunteered to watch over our guests. Once the body is discovered, the ward will be locked tight. There will be no escape."

"My men are hidden in a barn to the west. Is there a way to get to them?"

"Too many walk post now, but we shall have to take...perhaps..." Cynan hurried to the cupboard. He handed his candle to Sela, then leaned his back against the huge wooden piece. "Come. Help me here."

Jamie added his weight to the effort. The heavy piece slid away from the wall, revealing a portico barely as tall as Marie.

"The room was my mother's," Cynan said as he knelt and looked into the opening. "Though I have never seen it, she told me of the passageway. My grandfather built it in case there was need for an urgent escape. The stairs go down to the river, but any escape vessel is most likely long ago rotted away. However, there is another exit about half-way down. It should bring you out by the western wall. Near your men."

Cynan crept to the far side of the room and felt along the edge of the table. Jamie squatted and looked into the blackness beyond. Dank, fetid air assaulted his face.

He looked up when he heard the release of a catch, and Cynan returned with two short candles. He lit one of them from the one Sela held. "I will meet you at the other end. If you arrive before I do, stay hidden inside until I come. I will alert your men."

"You must give them the watchword. Tell them *Je suis deulu*. Only those exact three words will gain their trust."

"*Je suis deulu*," Cynan repeated the code. He handed Jamie a candle. "Go quickly, but carefully. I do not think a foot has touched the stairs for many years. They may be treacherous. Do not let the light falter. I fear you shall have need to see where you go in order to pass safely."

Jamie handed the candle to Sela and knelt down to crawl through the low opening. Blackness shrouded him like a traveler's cloak, but he could hear the river splashing by below. He slowly extended his arm in front of him. Damp wood met his hand as far as he could reach. "Give me the light." His words echoed back to him.

Like a ghost on hallows eve, Sela's hand floated through the opening.

When he lifted the candle, Jamie could see he was on a wide ledge of planks. The space above him was just tall enough to stand. Carefully testing each plank, he made his way to the edge and peered down.

Cynan's concern about the need to see was well founded. Narrow wooden steps disappeared into the darkness. Even from here Jamie could see cracks in several of the treads and one was missing. He returned to the portal. "Send Marie through."

A few moments passed, but then a cloak-wrapped Marie ducked through the hole.

"Stay still." He handed her the candle. "Do not move a hair without me."

Marie nodded and Jamie stuck his head back inside the room. Sela stood beside Cynan. "Come, my darling." Jamie whispered. "We must be away."

"You will come to a stone ledge on the staircase,"

Cynan said, as he nervously watched the door. "A shallow cave on the right will take you to a dead end. Above the passageway is a small exit. Wait for me below. I will come and lead you to your men."

Sela handed Jamie her cloak, then she turned back and squeezed Cynan's arm. "Thank you. We shall see you at the other end."

****

Sela held her cloak closed with one hand and held her candle up with the other as they made their way down the perilous stairs.

The wooden steps were slick with moisture drawn from the mists of the river. Many had rotted through and Jamie had to lift Marie over the places where the gap was too wide for her to cross on her own.

The damp cold made Sela's shoulder hurt, but there was nothing to be done about it now. They must be near the stone landing by now. She had to keep going. A draft from below swirled the musty air about her. A small tickle fluttered in her throat and she coughed.

Jamie looked back.

"I am all right," Sela whispered, afraid to give away their location to anyone who might be above.

He turned and continued through the darkness.

Sela tried to focus on carefully placing her feet, but pain clouded her mind and her thoughts drifted back to the room. Back to the words Jamie had said. "...for helping my wife." He had called her his wife. She had a chance to be with him. To bear his children. To build a life together.

She put her foot on the next step. With a loud crack, it gave way and she lost her candle as she flailed at empty air. The cloak slid from her shoulders and slowly floated into the darkness. Hope changed to doubt as she began to fall. *The king would never approve. Jamie would find another if I*

202

were no longer here.

Marie's scream echoed through her head as the thought of Jamie's lips against hers flashed in her mind. Resigned to her fate, Sela closed her eyes and began to fall.

Then his hand clamped tight around her wrist.

"Oh Jamie, let me go," Sela cried as her feet dangled above the blackness.

But he gave a hard yank and pulled her up on the landing beside him.

"You think me not strong enough to hold you safe?" He shivered and clutched her to his side.

"Nay," She leaned against him, her heart still racing. "I know you are." Her breath began to return as they sat on the narrow stone ledge. "'Tis just—I could not stand the thought I might drag you over with me."

"What kind of a man would I be to not raise you back up when you needed me?" He let out a long breath and kissed her temple. "Come. We must go." He stood, then helped her up. "Take care. I promised to bring you *both* safely home. I would not lose you when we are so close."

Jamie was right. It would not matter if Lady Amye approved or whether the King would allow the marriage, if they failed to escape.

****

It seemed to Jamie they had been waiting a good while, but Cynan had yet to arrive. He worried that someone might have heard Marie's scream when Sela fell. Even now, the castle might be astir with men searching for them.

Sela sat on the stone floor, holding the remains of their candle. After the misstep on the stairs, she had been withdrawn and quiet.

Marie rested her head against Sela's shoulder. Once they had sat down, the child had whispered unceasingly until she fell asleep.

The thought that the son of Gladus might not be coming drove Jamie to see where Cynan had led them. The door scraped as he pushed it open, and Marie awoke. Hopefully the sound had not been as loud outside. A covering of vines blocked his view, but all was quiet. He lowered the door and sat beside Sela.

"No sign of him yet," he whispered as he rested his head against the wall. He reached out and took her hand. Her skin seemed clammy and she barely closed her fingers around his. "Worry not, my sweet. We will escape if Cynan does not betray us."

"He will come," Marie whispered with a certainty. "He promised to protect me and he will."

Jamie sighed. He wished he had her innocence. She had yet to learn not all men were true to their word.

A quiet scratching from above brought Jamie to his feet. "Go back to the stairs," he whispered to Sela. "If there is trouble go back as far as you can and wait."

She shook her head and clutched his arm. "I will not leave you," she whispered frantically.

"Without Marie they have no hold over Cilgerran. You must try again if—"

The door lifted and Jamie pressed them against the wall, not even daring to breathe.

A head appeared through the hole. "Come. Make haste," Cynan whispered.

Jamie lifted Marie up and Cynan pulled her through. Sela followed next. As he wrapped his hands around her waist, her clothing seemed damp. Her ribcage expanded sharply when he lifted her up, and he thought he heard a stifled cry as she disappeared through the hole. Jamie jumped up to grasp the sides of the opening. Cynan grabbed his arm and helped him pull his legs through.

Neatly trimmed hedges and vines full of scented

flowers surrounded them. A garden.

Cynan signaled for them to keep silent. Jamie helped him slide the cover back over the opening and pull the vines back into place. Cynan led the way and Jamie took up the rear as the group exited the garden. They made their way around the edge of the list, keeping to the shadows rather than taking the risk of cutting across. The barn came into view. Until now they had been able to use the darkness to hide, but Jamie could see that from this direction, they would have to cross a small open space to get inside.

Cynan wrapped his cloak around Marie and pulled the hood over her head. He hefted her over his shoulder.

A moonbeam filtered through the planks of the palisade and Jamie could see the sparkle in her eyes. She seemed to be enjoying herself. He had to smile at his sister's sense of adventure.

Cynan started to step from the shadows.

The hair on the back of Jamie's neck crackled like the embers of a fire. He reached out and pulled Cynan back. The sound of footsteps echoed above. Slow measured steps.

The guard stopped on the parapet just above them.

Jamie put a finger to his lips.

Marie squeezed her eyes shut and held perfectly still.

The guard began to walk. The sound of his footsteps retreated into the distance, but Cynan waited a few moments more before he broke from the darkness and raced across the yard. He disappeared through a small door in the side of the stable.

Jamie grabbed Sela's hand and started across. As they reached the middle, the sound of footsteps jolted into his awareness. Faster. They must run faster.

Sela stumbled, but knowing their lives depended on making it through the door unseen, he held her hand tight, keeping her up, pulling her along. The opening suddenly loomed before him. He pushed her inside, then launched himself in after her.

"Please come with us." Though Marie's face was shadowed in the dim light her voice pleaded as they approached the cart.

Cynan picked her up, and she wrapped her arms around his neck.

"You promised to come see me at Cilgerran," she said as he set her in the cart.

"Given the way you have helped us, I am sure you would be welcome at Cilgerran," Jamie offered. "Your betrayal of Gladus could not bode well for you should you stay."

"You are most probably right. But with Llwyd dead, I am my father's only lawful heir." His face suddenly turned sad, but he drew a deep breath and continued. "I shall do my best to get you through the gate and safely off my father's lands. Beyond that, I cannot promise more. Since there can be no hay going out, we must disguise you another way. Which men walked as you came in?"

"Madog and Owain." Jamie pointed to the two brothers.

"You must now ride," Cynan said. "Ladies I much regret that whilst we pass through the gates these heavy brutes must sit atop you, but 'twill pose a more convincing scene for the guards."

Jamie jumped up into the wagon bed. "I will lie to one side. They can put most of their weight on me and rest only their legs over the women."

Cynan nodded and they took their places in the wagon, Jamie to one side, Sela to the other, and Marie in the center.

"I will make all efforts to get the guards to open

the gate without trouble." Cynan said. "Should anything go awry, I will leave you and open it myself. I will try to stay with you, but should I fall away at any point, you must make it across the river to the south. 'Tis there my father's lands end and Cattwg's begin. Cattwg is allied to Cilgerran. He will protect you."

Jamie nodded, and Cynan helped Huw pull a heavy cover over them.

Madog and Owain sat on him, no small weight between the two of them.

"Are you two comfortable?" Jamie quipped, barely able to breathe.

"Hardly." Owain snapped back. "You?"

"Lift yourselves. Let me turn over."

They removed their weight and Jamie twisted onto his belly. "Try now."

They sat again.

Better. At least he could breathe a bit.

The cart shifted as Huw climbed aboard.

Cynan spoke. "Once the gate is open drive straight through. Do not stop for anything."

The door creaked open. The wagon rolled forward and stopped. A second creak followed, then the clop of horses hooves sounded off the distant stone walls as the wagon rolled all too slowly toward the gate.

Chapter Twenty-Four

The wagon came to a halt, and Jamie could hear Cynan talking to the guard.

Sela lay across the wagon. His arm rested around her waist with Marie tucked between them. As the cover had been drawn over them, he had looked closely at her. This woman he loved so much. A bruise marred her beautiful face, and Jamie wished he could kill Llwyd again for what he had done to her.

Her fingers gently stroked his forearm, and her hand was warm against his skin. He could not see her through the darkness, but her scent so close to him was a comfort. Even though it must be tainted with fear, the scent of lavender clung faintly to her. It reminded him of his youth, running through the fields at Edensmouth. He did not know how he knew it was her scent, but in his soul he was certain. He gently rubbed the small of her back, glad to have her back again.

The creak of the portcullis rising brought him back to their current situation. The hollow sound of the wagon wheels rolling across the bridge reached Jamie's ears and he let out a breath he did not realize he had been holding.

He was unsure if Cynan was still with them, but he hoped so. A huge debt was owed the man. Without the knight's help, escape would have been a near impossible task, and the man had gone against his own family to protect Sela and Marie.

The wagon moved slowly along the bumpy road. After a while, Jamie began to wonder if Madog and

Owain were ever going to get off him. "What goes out there?" He chanced the words in a low voice.

"We passed a few men a way back," Owain answered. "'Tis best you stay put 'til we get back to the grove. If you can move over a bit, we wouldna' need to be so heavily on ya."

Before Jamie could even think, Sela slid her arm around his waist and pulled him closer. With Marie safe between them, Jamie thought how perfect it would be to have their own child resting thus.

Jamie had never been happier than when the wagon came to a halt. Madog and Owain rolled off him. His chest and back ached, but he drew a deep breath of air into his lungs as the cover was drawn away.

"Where is my knight?" Marie asked as she sat up.

Jamie wondered the same. He looked to Huw.

The big Welshman ran his fingers through his dark hair, but did not meet Jamie's eyes. "He waved us through, but did not follow after us. I kept watch for him the whole way here, but..."

"We could go back and search for him," Owain offered.

"Please, Jamie," Marie pleaded. "You must go back for him."

Jamie understood her plea, but knew they could not turn back.

"Nay, little one." He picked up his sister and hugged her. "Our first duty is to get you and Mistress Sela to safe ground. Any sacrifice Sir Cynan has made would be wasted should we fail. Do you understand?"

Marie looked at him sadly, but she nodded. A tear rolled down her face and she laid her cheek against his shoulder.

"We best be goin'," Justin said as Bleddyn brought Abelard to Jamie.

"Head for the river," Jamie directed. "Once we crossed to the southern shore, we will be on Cattwg's land. Gladus would not risk breaking the truce between them by following us."

"'Tis a fair ride to get there," Daed said. He was already mounted. "Nigh on half the morning."

Jamie glanced at Sela sitting on the edge of the wagon. Her skin was sallow above the dark green of her kirtle. The bruise beneath her eye stood out even more against the pallor of her skin. This did not bode well. "Can you ride, my love?" He asked as he reached the wagon.

Sela took a deep breath and stood. Her head began to spin. "Yes, I can."

She swayed a bit, but felt a little stronger when Jamie's touch steadied her.

"I think 'tis best you ride with me," he said.

"Nay, Marie should ride with you," Sela whispered back.

"Marie can ride with one of the others. I cannot concentrate lest I know *you* are all right. The best way is for you to ride with me."

Sela did not have the strength to argue with him. She gave a sigh. "As you wish, my lord."

She gazed around the group. Bleddyn stood holding the reins of Jamie's horse. Two young men she recognized from the village were already mounted. Owain sat on a stone chatting with Marie. A good match, Sela said to herself. Those two could talk from Sun to Sun and never run out of things to say. Madog leaned against a tree, holding the reins of his horse. Huw simply smiled at her.

Though she felt a bit unsteady, Sela dropped into a deep curtsey. "Our thanks to you all for securing our freedom."

"'Tis only acquired and not yet secure," Jamie said.

She was relieved when he took her hand and

helped her stand.

"Bleddyn, Lady Marie will ride with you. Mistress Sela will ride with me."

"We would move faster if she rode the extra horse," Huw interjected.

"Aye, but Mistress Sela was taken ill while in Gladus' *care* and is not yet recovered enough to ride alone."

"What would you have me do with the extra horse?" Huw said.

"Tis a pity to leave behind such a fine animal," Jamie said as he patted the black stallion's neck, "but turn him loose. He will only slow us down."

Huw took the horse to the edge of the glade. A sharp pat on the rump sent the animal galloping into the wood.

Sela took a deep breath as Jamie lifted her onto the tall white destrier's back.

He climbed on behind her and she leaned forward to gather up the reins. Her head began to spin again, and she took another deep breath hoping to stop the whirling.

Jamie's arms suddenly surrounded her, and he took the leather from her hands.

She leaned against his chest, and his body felt solid against her back. Strong and secure.

"Worry not, my sweet," he whispered into her hair as the group cantered out of the grove. "I swear I shall keep you from harm."

Sela felt sure he would keep that promise. For the first time in many days she felt...safe. Safe in the arms of the man she loved. She struggled to keep her eyes open, but the gentle sway of the horse's gait eased her into slumber.

****

Jamie called a halt to give the horses a rest. They had ridden for nearly two hours before reaching the river. Now they only had to make it to

211

the shallow place near the castle where Cynan had said they could cross to safety.

Sela had not woken the entire time. She burned with fever as she slept in his arms.

He handed her down to Huw, and they carried her to rest under a tree by the water.

"She is so sick," Huw whispered. "I wish we had some herb to bring her fever down, but she is the only one who would know which leaf would help and which would be poison."

Jamie slipped off his boots then knelt beside her.

"We have no plant," he said, "but we do have the river. Help me get this dress off her."

Two apple-red rounds colored Huw's cheeks. "But, Jamie—"

"Huw! If we cannot bring her fever down, she is likely to die. She will need something dry to wear to keep the ague at bay. Now help me get her out of the dress."

Jamie held Sela against himself, while Huw undid the laces. When the kirtle slid from her shoulder, Jamie's heart nearly stopped. An angry, red cut marked her skin.

She had not said a word about the injury. He had thought her weakness an effect of Llwyd's beating. The redness had spread along her arm disappearing beneath the sleeve of the kirtle. No longer concerned with modesty he stripped the linen from her and it fell to the ground when he gathered her into his arms.

He carried her into the river until he stood chest deep in the cold, rushing water. The strong current tried to tear her from his arms, but he stood firm and held her tightly.

"Come, dear wife. We are so close. Do not leave me now."

Sela laughed as Jamie whirled her about the

field of flowers. She had never been so happy. They danced until she was out of breath, then he swept her into his arms and kissed her. They walked in a green wood, holding hands. She looked up into Jamie's eyes, but it was Llwyd's face she saw.

He laughed his wretched laugh and Sela yanked her hand away. She ran as fast as she could, but the laughter followed her no matter how far she ran.

She ran into a castle and up the stairs of a tower. At the top, a locked brace of iron bars blocked her way. But just beyond, Jamie slept on the incline of a round turret.

"Jamie!" she shouted.

He did not answer.

The torturous laughter became louder.

"Jamie, help me," she shouted again.

Still, he did not wake.

The gate was chained shut.

She shook the bars in frustration.

Fire began to lick at the sides of the turret, but something was different about this fire. The flames were not red, but black.

"Jamie!" She cried. "Jamie, wake up."

But he did not move.

She frantically tried every key on the ring at her belt, but none worked.

The hot metal scorched her skin as she tried to break open the heavy lock with her hands.

She reached through the bars to touch him, but the black flames rose up, blocking him from her sight.

A drop of water plopped on her head. Sela looked up.

"Rain? Yes. Thank God. Rain will quench the fire."

The rain poured down.

The flames disappeared, but Jamie still did not wake.

Soon she stood ankle-deep in water and the flow began to cover the floor of the turret.

"Oh Jamie, please get up!" she sobbed.

She pressed against the bars.

"If only I could touch him, he might revive." But try as she might, he was just out of her reach.

The water rose up and covered his sleeping form.

"Jamie! Jamie!"

"...Jamie!" She screamed his name as she jerked awake.

"'Tis all right, love." He stroked her cheek as her head rested in his lap. "I am here."

Her eyes came into focus, and Sela saw a pattern of green leaves behind his head. They had stopped? She rubbed her fingers against her temple, hoping to stop the throbbing. Her throat felt as if she had been swallowing tree bark. The sound of moving water made her thirsty, and she sat up. They must have crossed the river.

Sela threw her arms around his neck. "Auch, we have made it safely," she croaked.

"Not quite, but nearly so," Jamie answered.

Sela drew back. "If we have not crossed from Gladus' lands, then why have we stopped?"

"You became so fevered, we had to stop and cool you in the river."

Sela suddenly realized her hair was wet, and Jamie's clothes were soaked as well.

"I could go no further when I was thinking you might not survive." He stroked her cheek. "You still have fever, but not near as bad.

Huw brought her a small bladder. "'Tis good to see you back with us, Mistress Sela."

Sela took the skin and tilted it upward. Cool water trickled down her throat. "Thank you. I am glad to still be here."

Huw suddenly stood and turned. After nodding

to Jamie, he ran off toward the river.

Sela felt the pounding of hooves against the earth, and heard the snap and crack of branches breaking as a rider approached.

Jamie quickly carried her to a spot at the edge of the clearing. Hidden behind a fallen tree, they watched as a horse broke through into the glade. The rider looked about for a moment then started onward. Jamie stood as the rider approached and Cynan reined his horse to a halt.

Chapter Twenty-Five

"I had hoped you would be on the other side by now." Cynan dismounted as Huw came from the direction of the river with Marie.

"Cynan!" she shouted as she ran to greet him.

"My lady." He bowed.

She curtsied, then leaped against him, wrapping her arms around him as far as she could.

He lifted her into his arms. "Make haste, my friends." He carried Marie to his horse. "We are still too far from the crossing. My father and his men are not far behind me. We shall have to take a more challenging route."

They all mounted, Marie refusing to ride with anyone but her knight. Jamie lifted Sela onto Abelard's back and mounted behind her.

Cynan took the lead, guiding them to the nearest place where they could attempt a crossing. He carefully routed his horse down the slippery brae to the river's edge. Jamie went next with Sela. One by one the others followed.

Jamie gazed out at the swift currents. "Are you certain we can cross here?"

"The other shore is nearest at this point than any other," came the answer. "We must ford here or risk capture."

Justin had just begun his descent when the zing of an arrow caught Jamie's ear. He winced when he heard the sickening thud as arrow struck flesh. The frightened horse skittered to the side and slid into the water. Justin's body rolled down the hill and splashed onto the muddy bank.

"Come!" Cynan spurred his horse into the water. "'Tis now or naught."

The others were already in the water. Bleddyn turned, waiting for Jamie to follow.

"Hold tight, love," Jamie said to Sela as Abelard splashed into the currents. He looked back and saw Gladus and his men standing at the top of the ridge. A sharp whistle from Jamie, and Abelard began to swim harder.

A rain of arrows showered around them. Jamie whistled again, followed by a tap to Abelard's neck.

The horse started to swim in a weaving pattern. It would take longer to reach the far bank, but they would be a more difficult target for the archers. An arrow zinged into the water just to their right. Then another and another.

Jamie looked over his shoulder. The archers readied to fire again. He turned back to the distant shore and urged Abelard to swim faster.

Cynan was already across. At least Marie would be safe.

Another brace of arrows splashed into the river, but they fell just short.

Thank God. They were out of range, but Jamie did not slow until Abelard stumbled up the bank on the far side.

****

At last. The tower of Castle Cattwg came into view as they rounded the bend. Jamie had never been so relieved. They had avoided capture by Gladus, but the cold river and the ride in wet clothes had not helped Sela.

"Please, my sweet," he whispered against the cold, damp skin of her neck. "We are almost there."

She shivered in his arms, barely conscious, mumbling words he could not understand. She needed a healer right now.

"Can we not go faster, Cynan?" Jamie yelled

ahead.

"No," Cynan replied.

"Why not?" A pinch of anger seasoned his tone.

From behind them, an arrow zinged into a tree and the party came to a halt.

"Is that reason enough?" Cynan answered.

"Son of Gladus," a voice shouted from above, "what would make you so bold as to tread on Cattwg land?"

Cynan looked directly at the spot from which the voice had come. "I am guide to a party from Cilgerran."

A long silence was followed by a rustling of leaves and four men dropped from the trees above.

"From Cilgerran you say?" A tall, muscular, young man blocked their path. The others aimed their arrows at the group.

Jamie held his breath. Could they not see the child sitting in front of Cynan? He rode forward, but before he could get a word out, Marie spoke.

"I am Marie Johanna Eleanor Nasrin de la Vierre, daughter of the Lord of Cilgerran," she said in stilted Welsh.

The man blocking the path looked at her a moment, then broke into laughter.

"Indeed you must be the stolen princess," he said in English. "No other child would be so...bold."

He waved his hand and the archers put down their weapons. "I am Glyndwr ap Cattwg. I welcome you to my father's demesne." He turned to Cynan. "So, you finally see the light of reason?"

"Aye, cousin. This time my father has gone too far."

Cousin? Was this a long standing family feud or a recent development?

"And Llwyd is dead as well," Cynan added.

Glyndwr stopped smiling. "A good riddance." He spat on the ground.

Sela stirred in Jamie's arms. She labored to draw a breath, and she was too hot for his comfort.

He leaned over and whispered to Cynan. "We need the healer...now."

Cynan nodded. "Cousin, Lady Marie's companion is taken ill."

Glyndwr looked over at Jamie.

"Sir James and his men are escort to these ladies," Cynan said.

Glyndwr nodded. "Ride on to the castle. They will be expecting you."

****

The face that filled Sela's view when she awoke belonged to a stranger.

"Welcome, m'lady." The woman laid a cool cloth on Sela's forehead. "I have a bit of potion here." The unfamiliar voice was calm and soothing. "I am hoping you can drink it."

Sela smelled the familiar scent of willow bark brew. She nodded and the woman smiled.

"I am Eswen, healer to Lord Cattwg." She removed the cloth from Sela's forehead.

"You were very lucky, m'lady." She propped Sela up with a few pillows. "Too much longer and I would not have been able to help you." She stood back with her hands on her hips. "There now. Ready for the potion?"

Sela nodded and the healer handed her a cup. She took a small sip. The normally bitter brew had been sweetened with honey and was soothing as the warm liquid ran down her throat. She took another few sips, then rested the cup on her lap. "Thank you," she whispered, her voice still a bit hoarse.

"Would you like to see your husband? I had to make him leave so I could tend to you, but he has barely moved from the door. Each time I go out he demands to know your progress."

Sela smiled. How very like him. "I hope he has

not been a bother to you."

Eswen smiled and shook her head. "No bother at all. I know a man in love when I see one, dearie. I think he would like very much to see you."

Sela pushed a damp, limp, strand of hair behind her ear. As much as she wanted to see Jamie, she must look terrible. "Oh, please, not like this."

"I think it would not much matter to him, but mayhap we can get you cleaned up a bit?"

****

Jamie sat outside the door to Sela's room. The healer had brought a stool when it became obvious he was not going to leave. For a man as big as himself, the small stool was not comfortable for long periods of sitting, but when he could stand no longer or was too tired to pace the length of stone outside her room, he sat. Two days he had waited outside this door. Two days and Sela was not recovered.

When Huw had brought bread and ale the first day, Jamie had not even thought about food. The only hunger he had was to hold Sela safe and well in his arms.

This morning, Cynan had come saying Marie begged to see her brother. Jamie had not wanted to go, but Cynan reminded him of his duty to see to Marie until her parents arrived. He had knocked at the door and told the healer where he would be and to send word the moment Sela was awake.

Now, again, he sat outside the door. Exhaustion overwhelmed him and he leaned back against the wall. He closed his eyes for a moment's respite, but they flew open at the whoosh of the door. Too tired to stand, Jamie looked up at the round, gray-haired woman.

She smiled at him. "If you promise not to excite her too much..."

Excitement and gratitude overruled tired muscles, and he sprang to his feet.

"...you might see your lady now."

Jamie rushed past the healer, but remembering her words, he slowed his steps once through the doorway.

Sela sat amid a mound of pillows in the middle of a large bed, wearing a white chemise. Her hands neatly folded in her lap, she smiled. "You look terrible, my lord."

Thank God in heaven. Jamie hurried to her side. He took her hand. Kissed it more times than he cared to count. He closed his eyes hoping to keep the tears back, but they fell on her fingers as he pressed them to his cheek. He looked into her eyes and stroked the long braid that fell across her shoulder. "I thought I had lost you."

"Nay. I am with you still. I promised I would be. I keep my promises." She reached forward and stroked the back of his neck.

Jamie leaned in and gently kissed her. Then he laid his head in her lap and she stroked his hair until he fell asleep.

****

"Go sleep in your own bed."

When the healer woke him, Jamie had not realized he slept.

"This lady needs to rest," she chided.

Grateful just to know his wife was alive and well, he went to his room and fell onto the bed. Exhaustion pressed sleep upon him, but he was up before the sun. He shaved himself and put on the clean clothes Cattwg had given him. He checked in with his men and broke fast with Marie. By then, the sun was long up and he could wait no longer to see Sela again.

The armful of flowers Marie had helped him pick from the garden was damp with morning dew. His wife must be surrounded by every possible luxury while she recovered. He knocked at the door and was surprised when Sela answered it herself. "You are recovered. So soon?"

The tunic she wore brought out the blue of her eyes, and the color had returned to cheeks. Her hair flowed loose around her shoulders. It shone as if it had been freshly washed and was soft against his lips as he bent to kiss her temple.

"Aye, Mistress Eswen is a most excellent healer. 'Twas a simple cure once the proper medicine was available."

Jamie shoved the flowers at her. "I thought you might like these."

She lifted them to her nose. "They smell wonderful. Thank you, my lord." The formality of her voice surprised him. "Please, enter."

"Mistress Eswen?" Sela said.

The healer sat on a stool by the hearth, working on a piece of needlework. She stood. "Aye?"

"Might there be a ewer to hold these lovely flowers?"

The old woman laid her needlework on the small table next to the hearth. "Certainly, Mistress Sela. I shall fetch you one..." The old woman looked menacingly at Jamie. "...if you like."

"Thank you," Sela said.

Eswen took the flowers. "I shall be back in a moment." She turned and left the room, but failed to close the door behind her.

Jamie shut it, then took Sela into his arms. He pressed his lips to hers, but the fire of yesterday's kiss was gone. She laid her head against his chest for a moment, then shivered. She turned away and walked back to the hearth.

He followed her. "I nearly lost you once, my darling." He turned her to face him. "I can wait no longer."

A tear rolled down her cheek as she lifted her eyes.

His fingers played against her cheek as his thumb wiped away the tear. "I will not risk such loss again. I spoke with the magistrate. We can sign the contract this day. Cynan will serve as witness."

"Jamie, I must break my vow."

"You cannot, I have already taken you to my bed. That cannot be undone."

"Jamie, I cannot marry you."

Hurt tore at his heart. "Why not?"

He took her shoulders and anger forced itself into his voice. "Answer me!"

She shook her head wresting loose more tears.

"Is it my mother? What she says matters not."

"It matters to me." She turned back to the hearth.

"Why? You are a free woman. You need no release. There is no payment to be made." Jamie knew if she would answer him this one question, he could have what he wanted. "Why does her word matter more to you than our happiness?"

Sela plopped down on the stool and began to wring her hands. "Because of what she did for me."

"What has she done that binds you to *her*, more than to *me*?"

"Jamie, what would your father say to you marrying a whore?"

"Why? What does it matter? I did not marry a whore."

"You did. You have fallen in love with a common brothel woman.

Disbelief filled his eyes, and he shook his head. "No! There was blood on our wedding sheets. That could not be if you were a whore. I know you love me. Why are you trying to drive me..."

"Jamie, listen to me. The blood could not be virgin's blood, for I was not a virgin. That gift was stolen from me long ago. 'Tis truth I speak. 'Tis how I found your mother. Or how she found me.

223

"My mother would never set foot in a whore house."

"She did, but only once. My father owned a brothel in Crecy. My sisters worked there and I served drinks until I was old enough for men to want more.

"I didn't want to lie with a man, but father forced me to do it. I could only stand it once. I ran away. The only other way I could live was to steal.

"Your mother caught me trying to steal her money in the market place. She could have turned me over to the sheriff, but instead, she bought me from my father. That is how I came to live at Edensmouth. I owe my life to your mother, for without her, I would surely have died on the streets of Crecy long ago."

Jamie closed his eyes. Her story sliced at his gut like an assassin's dagger, poisoning his heart with distrust. He could see now why no one would speak of it, but why had *she* not told him? That hurt more than anything. Did she not see that he would love her regardless?

Apparently not.

Finally. The answers he had tried so hard to find, but he did not know what to do with them. He no longer knew how he felt. He wished he could wipe her words from his mind, but the fact that she could not trust in his love enough to confide in him shrouded feelings that moments ago had been clear as a summer day with a wintry haze of gray. Without a word, he turned and marched from the room.

****

Jamie gulped down a third cup of the sourest wine he had tasted in many a month. He didn't care what it tasted like, only that it could wash away the hurt. He waved his hand, and the servant filled his cup again.

"Sir James?"

He looked up into the face of Cynan. Their savior. Savior of what? Certainly not his marriage. All the fighting he'd done to earn her heart. All done for naught. Given his heart to a strumpet, he had. Well at least Marie was all right.

"Sir James?"

"What?" Jamie snapped back.

"Lady Marie was hoping to see you, but she cannot see you like this."

Jamie didn't want to see anyone, much less Marie. "No, she cannot." He drained his cup and waved to the servant who hurried to assist him. For the first time he noticed the girl who served him.

Her red-brown hair was twisted into a braid that fell over her shoulder nearly to her waist. The curve of her hip, just at eye level as he sat, reminded him of Sela, standing before him on their wedding night. Before the girl could pour he stood, knocking the bench to the floor in his haste.

She jumped back, fear filling her face as he towered over her. "Your pardon m'lord. I thought—"

He grabbed the wine jug from her hands and hurried from the hall. There must be someplace they could not find him. Someplace he could be alone.

****

Night had settled by the time Bleddyn managed to find the hiding place on the far side of the high tower. The wine had disappeared long ago replaced by a pounding Jamie hoped would crack a hole in his skull big enough to let his brains leak out.

"Master, come down, before you fall down," Bleddyn pleaded as he stood over Jamie.

Jamie laughed. "No reason for me to come down." Forgetting his earlier consumption, he lifted the wine jug to his lips.

"More fool than knight..." He set the jug beside him, but was shocked when a moment later he heard

225

it crash on the stone floor below. He fell back against the palisade wall. "You are pledged to a fool, squire. How feel you about that?"

Bleddyn sat down beside him. "Fool or not, I can think of no other that I should want to be pledged to, my lord. You have been kind to me. Taken me on when I was far too old. You have taught me how to fight. How to lead. Shown me the meaning of hard work, honor, and valor. Surely you will not abandon me when there is so much more to learn."

The whirlpool of self-pity and hurt had blinded Jamie to the fact that there were others depending on him. Others that were important to him.

"Whatever it is that troubles you, sir, I am sure we can find an answer."

God, if that were only true. "I suppose, squire, I should find my bed."

"Yes, my lord. That might be of best service."

Bleddyn helped Jamie climb down from the tower without breaking his neck, then helped him undress and crawl into bed. As he fell into slumber, he still had hopes that his brain might seep out before morning.

Chapter Twenty-Six

Twisted faces intruded on Jamie's slumber. Familiar voices mercilessly taunted him.

"You do not deserve such a fine woman as my Sela." Huw laughed at him.

"Life with you would be nothing but boring drudgery." Owain laughed at him.

"I am the man for her." Even quiet Madoc added his voice to the taunt.

"I am a better lover than you could ever hope to be." A faceless man said in French.

Llwyd's face appeared, dead eyes shining, blood spattered mouth laughing. "I gave her better than—"

Jamie jerked awake. He sat up, his head pounding like a smith's mallet against an anvil. God in heaven, what was wrong with him?

She had finally trusted him enough to tell him her horrible secret and he had abandoned her, just as she must have thought he would.

He jumped from his bed.

Bleddyn jumped up from his pallet. "How can I serve you, my lord?"

"No need." Jamie pulled on his breeches. "You can use the bed, I shall not return tonight."

He raced across the courtyard. The summer's night air was warm against his chest, but the stones were cold as his feet slapped against them. He climbed the tower stairs and walked to the room he knew so well. He lifted the latch, but the bar had been set in place. "Sela!" He pounded his fist against the door. "For God's sake let me in, Sela." Just as he thought he would have to break the door down, he heard the bar lift and the door opened.

Eswyn peeked out from the small gap.

"I must speak with my wife," Jamie said.

"She is sleeping, m'lord."

"I care not. I must see her now."

Against Eswyn's loud protest, Jamie pushed open the door and entered the chamber.

"Get out!" He ordered the healer from the room.

"I think you would be the one who had best be going, m'lord."

Jamie picked up the old woman, set her outside the door, and slammed it shut. He dropped the bar into place as she pounded on the wood. He turned toward the bed.

Sela had risen. In the light of the fire, her white chemise stood out in the darkness.

He hurried to her. Pinned her against the wall.

She looked at him through eyes wide with fear. He didn't care. He had to know. "Is there some other man you want? I will gladly free you if you tell me you love another."

She lowered her eyes, then with a sniffle, she shook her head. "You know there is no one I could love but you."

He clutched her to him. "I too feel the same. No matter what happened in your past. You have made yourself into the woman I love. Right here. Right now. I would no more give you up than air or food or drink."

Her tears wet his skin.

"Shush shush shush, little rabbit. Do not cry. I am here. Forgive me for abandoning you. I was lost, but I have found my way again."

Jamie picked her up and looked into the darkness of her eyes. "I love you."

She laid her head against his shoulder.

"I am your husband. You can trust me with anything. Is that clear?"

Her cheek rubbed against his chest as she nodded.

He laid her on the bed, stripped off his breeches, and climbed in beside her. "No more talk of broken promises?" he said as he knelt above her.

"No. No more," came her soft answer.

"My only wish is to give you pleasure." He cupped her face gently between his hands. "Whether it be in our daily life or in our marriage bed."

She turned her soft, moist lips against his palm.

He bent and pressed a row of kisses down her neck to her collarbone. Her skin was soft and tasted sweeter than any honey made by bees.

Her chest rose, pressing her full breasts against him. He slid down beside her then tasted her lips. Explored her tongue.

The chemise rose as his foot rubbed against her toes and smoothed over the curve of her calf. He slid his hand under the linen, his fingers rediscovering the well-rounded bottom, the soft curve of her hip, the smooth indentation of her waist.

The chemise slid higher exposing the soft skin of her belly. He wrapped his legs around her, tightening her neatly against him.

His hand slid up and found one of her firm hard nipples. His thumb buffed the button, circling it until the quiver of her body between his thighs almost made him explode. He rolled onto his back, pulling her on top of him. Her legs wrapped around his waist, the warm moist lips of her opening wrapped over his hardness. The weight of her against his erection, curved beneath her, sent a wave of pleasure through him. "To make you happy—" he whispered as he slid the chemise up over her shoulders.

She pushed herself up, finished removing the garment, and tossed it to the floor.

"—is my one desire." Jamie had never said

words more true. He cupped her breasts in his hands trapping both nipples between his fingers.

She gasped, and her eyes fluttered closed. "Now, Jamie. I need you now." She moaned and leaned against his arms. Her hips lifted and he was in heaven, the head of his shaft inside her warm, moist chamber.

She took him in slow and easy, each move pulling him into her a bit deeper. Soon she slid along his entire length, each rise and fall taking him one step nearer to his own ecstasy.

"Yes, my heart." He looked at her through hooded eyes. "Can you feel me inside you?"

His hands grasped her hips, held her still as he pushed up. His thrust brought a gasp from her throat.

Yes. This was the duty he wanted to fulfill. To see such pleasure on her face. Pleasure no other man could give her. The face of her pleasure belonged only to him.

The sound that came from her as she began to quiver seemed not a laugh, not a scream, but a sound he had never heard before, but her face showed him it was the sound of her pleasure. The gift he might have if he fulfilled his duty.

Her inner chamber began to ripple around him, rousing his passion from base to head. He thrust up wanting to be even deeper inside her as he felt his hot seed begin to pump into her. He tried to hold back, make the sensation last longer, but the passion of her release dragged him with her, and his rapture leaped from him with a roar.

She fell forward against his chest. Her body was warm in contrast to the coolness of his sweat.

Breath came to him slowly, in short huffs. He wrapped his arms around her. "I could not now give you up for any award. To me there is no title, no land, no treasure more valuable than you."

He kissed her forehead and nestled her by his side. "When my mother arrives this will be settled. You are *my* wife. No other shall have you."

"Yes, my lord."

Chapter Twenty-Seven

Daed returned with a brace of men from Cilgerran. The lord and lady rode in with them. Jamie and Marie waited as they entered the courtyard.

Sela looked on from the window of her room as Lady Amye knelt down, hugged her daughter, then burst into tears. She turned away as Lord Cilgerran clutched Jamie's arm and hugged him. She should have gone to meet them as well, but her stomach splashed and twisted like a milkmaid's churn.

Jamie had sat outside her room for two days even though she'd had Eswen say she was not up to seeing him. He had sneaked past the healer's guard when she was mysteriously called away to attend someone else. He had brought a supper tray, refusing to go unless she ate. He had sat there watching until she emptied the trencher of meat and drank down a cup of weakened wine. He'd looked at her as if he would eat her up like the dish she supped on. It set her insides aflame when he looked at her that way.

The night he'd begged her forgiveness and made passionate love to her, she'd had no doubt he would not stop until they were officially wed. But she was not so sure of herself. Not so sure she could stand against Lady Amye's wishes. Against the wishes of the King. But she did know that she would stand with him no matter what the outcome. Even if it meant she would only be his mistress.

Sela lay on the bed until a soft knock drew her attention to the door and Lady Amye entered. Sela stood up as her mistress approached the bed.

"Jamie says you are not well, dear. What is it? Did they hurt you at Penwedd?"

"Nay, 'Tis just ..." Sela bowed her head and tears began to stream down her face. She did not know what to say. Lady Amye had warned her not to fall in love with Jamie. Now Sela wished she had been able to take the advice. But it was much too late.

"Oh. I see." Lady Amye pulled a cloth from her sleeve and dabbed the tears from Sela's cheeks. "Do not fret, child." She wrapped an arm around Sela's shoulder and gave her a hug. "We have enough men that you and I and Marie can leave right now. The men can come later. We will un-tie this knot once we are safe home. Will that help you feel better?"

Sela looked up. "Thank you, my lady."

"Can you ride?"

Sela nodded her head.

"Good. Then I will go and inform my lord of our plans."

****

"Is it safe for her to ride?" Jamie questioned his mother as she looked down from her palfrey.

"I will look after her." Mother patted his hand then took up the reins. "She will be more comfortable at Cilgerran."

Jamie looked over at Sela, but she merely kept her eyes lowered. Now he was truly worried about her. He should have waited. She was not well enough for such strenuous lovemaking.

"We shall see you when you return, dear boy."

Lord Cilgerran stepped forward and kissed her hand. "Safe travels, my lady."

She leaned down and kissed her husband. "And you, my lord."

"Take care, Llandon," Lord Cilgerran called out.

The sheriff nodded, and the retinue started

through the front gate.

Marie waved as she passed by and Jamie winked at her knowing she was excited to be astride a big horse again. She rode with Cynan. She would not have anyone else as *he* was her protector.

The knight nodded, and Jamie smiled at him. He would make a good addition to the Cilgerran knights, replacing his father's treachery with his own extreme honor and loyalty. He truly wanted to repair the damage his father had done.

At his mother's side rode Sela.

Jamie waved to her, and she turned to look back. A wan smile tugged at the sides of her mouth before she disappeared through the gate.

To ensure the safety of his family, Lord Cilgerran had insisted the majority of the contingent return as well. Twenty men rode with them. There should be no further trouble.

As the portcullis rattled shut behind the last rider, Jamie knew Sela loved him, but he was unsure that that was enough.

He turned to Lord Cilgerran. The man was only four years older than Jamie, but he had captured the heart of the most willful woman Jamie knew. "My lord, would you tell me how you came to know my mother?"

The lord looked at him, raised a brow, then laughed and clapped him on the shoulder.

"My first memory of your mother is of her sitting at my bedside reading her book of poetry. It was a strange sight. Not many women read or write."

"My father taught her, and together they taught all of us children."

"I could see how beautiful she was, but the fact she could read proved her intelligence. I had taken a bad fall and she nursed me back to health. She was kind and generous to everyone around her. I fell in love with her and she with me, but at the time, I thought I had nothing to offer her. So I left.

"But I could not get her out of my mind or my heart. So I came back and begged her to take me even with nothing. We were able to persuade the King to let us come here. It has been hard work but together we have built a home and a family."

He stopped and turned to Jamie. "Perhaps your lady thinks she has nothing to offer you. If you truly want her, mayhap you should find a way to convince her *you* are worth all the hard work it will take to build a life together."

Jamie smiled at Cilgerran. "Thank you, my lord. When do we return?"

"I have a bit of business with Cattwg. We need to decide what to do about Gladus. Aside from that the womenfolk could use a few days without us. 'Twill be good to let the dust settle a bit before stirring it up again."

He turned toward the Great Hall. "Let us hunt and talk a bit with our allies. We shall start back by the end of the week."

****

Jamie sat on a bench along the wall of the great hall and watched as his mother and her husband whispered between themselves. Cilgerran himself had asked Jamie to attend today's court. He had sat through at least two dozen petitioners and the hall was still full. It seemed that everyone in Cilgerran was here.

Lord Cilgerran turned and looked in his direction. "Sir James."

Jamie stood and moved toward the head table. "Lord Cilgerran?"

"You have restored to this house something more precious than gold."

Jamie bowed. "I could not have done otherwise."

"I must reward you for this service." Lord Cilgerran held out a box.

Jamie took it. "Thank you, my lord." Puzzled, he looked at his mother.

Her eyes sparkled, and she silently formed the words, "Open it."

He could not have been more surprised by the gold ring inside. It matched the ones his mother, her husband, and his sister wore.

"If you would have it, I would claim you as my successor until such time as my daughter shall be ready to marry," Cilgerran said.

An excited whisper raced around the room.

Sela stood just to the side of the two tall settles, amidst a crowd of nobles. Her face was lit by a surprised smile. Apparently she had not been privy to the event.

Jamie smiled at his mother then turned back to her husband and bowed. "I would consider it an honor, my lord."

"I would also grant you deed to a parcel not far from here. It already has a small keep built by its former owner. Though I dare say, last I saw of it, there would be some work to do before it could be occupied."

"You are too generous, my lord." Jamie bowed again.

"I shall have the magistrate record the documents if you would meet me in the solar this afternoon."

"Certainly, my lord."

"In that case, I am hungry. Let us have dinner. Will you join us at table...my son."

****

"Your father would be so proud of you." Mother said as she took Jamie aside after dinner.

"There is nothing that could bring me more pleasure than hearing you say such, Mother."

"Nothing?"

"I have land now. And I want to build a demesne

of my own, like my father did."

"Then you will need someone to help you." Mother smiled at him with a knowing glance. She grasped him by the shoulders and looked up into his eyes.

"I know from my own experience, it will not be easy. You have to fight for the things you want. For a strong fief, for the respect of your people..." She reached into her pouch, withdrew a small wooden box, and placed it in his hand. "...and for the woman you love."

Jamie removed the lid. A beautiful ruby ring sparkled in the sunlight. He looked at his mother.

"Your father gave it to me on the day he asked me to marry him. It came with the promise of a good life together."

Jamie nodded his understanding. He hugged her tightly and kissed her cheek. "Thank you, Mother."

****

Sela walked slowly down the covered path toward the kitchen, Jamie at her side. Her heart pounded in her chest as he spoke.

"Now that I have land, I want to build a demesne of my own."

"A noble task, to bring some sense of order here."

"You know I want you to share that task with me."

She stopped. Turned away from him.

He wrapped his arms around her and pressed himself against her back. She touched the hand resting on her belly and was surprised to find something there. Sela looked down.

His fingers held a ring.

Lady Amye's ruby ring.

"Oh, Jamie." She turned and looked into laughing eyes.

"Yes, my darling. Now you must keep your

237

promise."

"Are you sure this is what you want?" She searched his face, looking for a moment of doubt. "I have loved you since first we met, but you know what I am. My past could bring the house you build to disgrace."

He swept an errant lock of hair behind her ear. "You are kind and brave and beautiful. The people here respect you. I cannot think of another who would make a better match for this wild land." His thumb stroked down the line of her jaw. "...or for me."

"It will be hard..." she started to raise another objection, but he took her hand and pressed it to his heart.

"I love you. You are my only wife. To be with you is worth any hardship." His eyes said what she needed to know.

She nodded and he slipped the ring on her finger.

"It will not be too hard to convince the King of the worth of having another foothold in this country. We will build a great house here, you and I."

"You know I want that more than life, Jamie. I pray you speak true. My heart would break should you be denied."

He brought her hand to his lips and gently kissed the palm. "Then I shall not be denied."

****

Sela sat in a willow chair by the window of Marie's chamber. She turned the small tapestry piece she worked on and started a new row.

When Jamie had left, she'd known it would take time, but with each day her hope grew fainter. Over three months had passed since he departed for the court in France. At first his letters had come frequently, two or sometimes three a week. Now, nothing for almost a month. She feared he was afraid to tell her the King had denied his request or worse yet, that he had been forced to marry the Norman heiress.

She put the needlework on the table and crossed her hands over her belly. She could feel the life stirring there. At least she would have this much of him.

"Sela."

She looked up at Marie's touch.

"Please do not be sad. Have faith."

Sela held out her arms.

Marie climbed onto her lap and wrapped her arms around Sela's neck. "Jamie will return. I promise."

"Yes, he will," she quietly responded. She hoped to convince herself to believe as strongly as Marie did, but a tear rolled down her cheek.

Marie looked Sela in the eyes, and her small fingers wiped away the tear. "You shall see. He will win. Mama says he is like her. Stubborn and ten—ten-a-ci-ous."

Marie's tongue twisted a funny pronunciation around the big word and Sela suddenly felt better. "Of course he will win. You are right. We must have faith."

Marie jumped down and tugged at Sela's arm. "Come. 'Tis time to feed Falconer."

****

Sela held the pony's halter, stroking his shaggy forelock while Marie curried his coat to a high sheen.

The door to the stable opened and a tall figure entered. He stood silently in the shadow.

She could not make out who it was. "Hello? Am I needed?" she asked.

When he stepped into the golden afternoon sunlight flowing through the first row of windows, she dropped the halter. She ran into his arms and Jamie lifted her up high and whirled her around.

"God, woman. I missed you so." He set her down and kissed her soundly.

Marie reached the pair and Jamie knelt down to kiss her on the cheek.

"There now, my girls. I looked everywhere for you two. I should have known you would be taking care of your favorite gentleman."

Jamie took both their hands, and they walked back to the pony. He ran his hand over the shiny coat.

"You did a fine job here. Why do you not go and get him a pail of water?"

Marie nodded and threw her arms around Jamie's waist before she grabbed the bucket and scampered off.

Jamie pulled a neatly folded document from inside his tunic and handed it to Sela. It was addressed to Alain de la Vierre, Lord Cilgerran.

She turned it over and looked at the red seal. Her heart leapt to her throat.

The King's signet was stamped in the wax.

She looked up and the smile on his face told her what she needed to know.

"Twas not as easy as I thought it would be, but the King eventually saw the value of another fortification in the region. Plus he did not mind not having to give me a valued piece of property to maintain my allegiance. I am to be Lord of Maddywn Castle, and, should Lord Cilgerran agree, you will officially be my lady wife...If you would have me."

Never in those years as a young maiden at Edensmouth had Sela truly thought she would marry, much less marry the man of her dreams. She wrapped her arms around his waist and pressed herself against him as tightly as she could. "Oh Jamie, I could never want anything more."

Epilogue

The silk of Jamie's *robe de chamber* made a whooshing sound as he paced back and forth outside the bedroom door. When the servant pounding at the door in the small hours of the night had wakened him, he had not taken the time to dress before hurrying to the confinement room where his child would be born.

"Sit down, my boy." Lord Cilgerran said as he sat at the table sipping a cup of wine. "There is nothing we men can do now."

Sela groaned. She sounded like she was dying.

Jamie wanted to go to her, but Mother had bolted the door the last time he tried to enter.

He had hoped to have the keep at Meddwyn ready by now. Since Sela told him of the expected child, he had worked feverishly to have their new home finished before the birth. She should be in her own house for the birth of their first child.

But the progress was tediously slow, and the harsh winter had brought work to a halt. They had spent the last six months in the small guesthouse Mother had insisted be built beside the tower at Cilgerran. The happiest six months he could remember since his childhood.

"Worry not, Master Jamie." Bleddyn followed after him as he roamed back and forth in front of the door. "There is no one better to be with her than my sister."

Jamie nodded. The lad was right. According to word around the village, Rhiana had midwifed nearly every child born for the past eight years. Still, anxiety churned his stomach.

A long groan assailed his ears, but was suddenly cut off. He stopped dead in front of the door. The silence lengthened. Fear pressed his hands against the wood, but neither his will nor his arm was strong enough to free the bolt that held it shut.

Then, a wail, the first sounds of his first child, graced his ears.

Cilgerran and Bleddyn slapped his back and heartily congratulated him, but too much time passed before footsteps approached. The bolt was pulled back and the door opened.

"Well," Mother said, the warm smile in her eyes melted his anxiety. "Come in and meet your daughter."

Jamie rushed to kneel by the bed where Sela sat nursing a small bundle swaddled in linen. Her hair was plastered to her head by sweat, and her face was drawn and pale, but she had never looked more beautiful to him. Unable to take his eyes off her, he asked, "Is she all right?"

"They're both fine and healthy." Rhiana answered.

Jamie let out a small sigh and kissed his wife on the temple. "I love you, my sweet."

She looked up at him and patted the bed. He sat next to her and she put her hand in his. "Is she not beautiful, husband?"

He lightly brushed his finger over the reddish-brown curl that peeked out beneath the swaddling around the tiny head. "Equally as beautiful as her mother."

Unruffled, the baby continued to nurse.

"She has a hearty appetite," he whispered, wary of disturbing the child.

"Aye, she does." When the baby finally slept Sela looked up at him. "Would you like to hold her?"

Jamie leapt up as if the bed was on fire, his

heart pounding as if he prepared to charge into battle. He had never held a baby. Being the youngest of his mother's children, he had not even experienced a household with one. He had no idea how to even pick up the small bundle with his big hands.

"Here." Mother stepped in. "Let me help you." She lifted the baby and laid the child along his arm.

As the tiny head rested in the bend of his elbow, fatherly instinct told him to hold his daughter close to his body, and he wrapped his other arm around to protect her even more.

"There, now. 'Tis not so bad, is it, my son?"

He looked down at the little round face. "No Mother. 'Tis wonderful, indeed."

The baby seemed to smile at him and made a gurgling noise before she suddenly spit a little white blob onto his robe. He looked up and held her out toward his mother. "Something is wrong?"

The women all chuckled at him.

"No, m'lord," Rhiana answered. "She just swallowed a bit of air. Did you not my girl?" She leaned back and laid one hand at the small of her back and the other across her belly, a stance Jamie had come to recognize as one pregnant women often used.

He wondered if Rhiana had told Huw and Bleddyn that they would soon be a father and an uncle. She cooed at the baby and wiped the globule away with a piece of swaddling. She laid the long piece of linen over his shoulder and down the front of his robe. "Sit down m'lord. You will both be more comfortable."

Jamie sat on the bed and held his daughter until a yawn twisted her tiny face and her head lolled against his upper arm. Though he had hoped for a family one day, he had never thought holding one's child would be such bliss.

"What shall we name her?" He asked as Sela

laid her head against his shoulder.

She looked at the baby curled against his chest. "I was thinking perhaps Alice."

Jamie smiled down at his wife. "Alice it shall be. A-L-I-C-E."

"No, I meant A-L-E-S. The name I used when we first met on the road."

Jamie's brows drew together. Recognition slowly floated to the surface like cream on fresh milk.

A-L-E-S...S-E-L-A.

He gave his wife a wry smile, then looked lovingly at the new girl in his life.

"Ales it shall be."

A word about the author...

Hanna Rhys Barnes is one of those people with an evenly balanced right and left brain. She has a BA in English, but retired as a high school math teacher. She loves to cook and was a pastry chef in a former life.

A member of RWA's national organization and of several local chapters, she currently lives and works on Whidbey Island in beautiful Northwest Washington State. Book One in the Scorpion Moon Trilogy, *WIDOW'S PEAK*, is available from the Wild Rose Press.

Thank you for purchasing
this Wild Rose Press publication.
For other wonderful stories of romance,
please visit our on-line bookstore at
www.thewildrosepress.com.

For questions or more information
contact us at
info@thewildrosepress.com.

The Wild Rose Press
www.TheWildRosePress.com